Reflection is a way to make the abstract concrete.

~ Angelo Letizia

Also, by Angelo Letizia

Letizia, A.J. (2025). *Temporary Gods and Arbitrary Arrangements.* British Columbia: Silver Bow Press.

Letizia, A.J. (2024). *Poetic Inquiry and arts-based research for the maintenance of the Republic and what comes after: A Vision for Metamodernity.* Routledge.

Letizia, A.J. (2024). *Learning to love in Winter.* Victoria, Australia: In Case of Emergency Press.

Letizia, A.J. (2024). *There is still beauty here.* British Columbia: Silver Bow Press.

Letizia, A.J. (2022). *Toward the real: Poems for a new reality.* Victoria, Australia: In Case of Emergency Press.

Letizia, A.J. (2022). *We are the winding down.* British Columbia: Silver Bow Press.

Letizia, A.J. (2022). *Pilgrims of infinity.* British Columbia: Silver Bow Press.

Letizia, A.J. (2021). *The starry devil and other unwanted poems.* British Columbia: Silver Bow Press.

The Last Number
and
Other Stories

by

Angelo Letizia

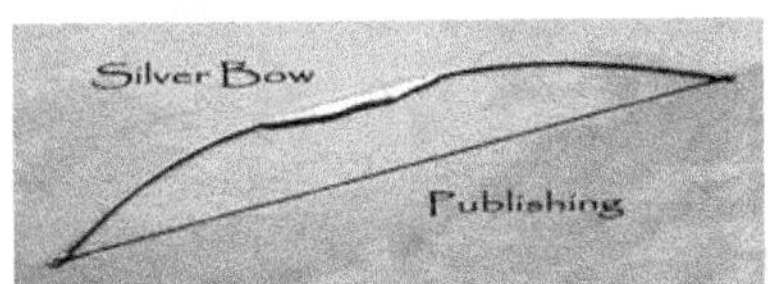

720 – Sixth Street, Unit # 5
New Westminster, BC
V3L 3C5   CANADA

Title: "The Last Number and Other Stories"
Author: Angelo Letizia
Cover Art: "Interrogatory Man" painting by Candice James
Layout and Design: Candice James
Editor: Candice James

www.silverbowpublishing.com
info@silverbowpublishing.com
© Silver Bow Publishing 2025
ISBN: 9781774033753 softcover
ISBN: 9781774033760 e book

Library and Archives Canada Cataloguing in Publication

Title: The last number, and other stories / by Angelo Letizia.
Names: Letizia, Angelo, author
Description: Contains a novel, two novellas, and some short stories.
Identifiers: Canadiana (print) 20250249537 | Canadiana (eBook) 20250249545 | ISBN 9781774033753
  (softcover) | ISBN 9781774033760 (Kindle)
Subjects: LCGFT: Novels. | LCGFT: Novellas. | LCGFT: Short stories.
Classification: LCC PS3612.E79 L37 2025 | DDC 813/.6—dc23

To Troy, Rosalie, and Cecelia, as always

To Ann and Jake, my family

Preface

This book contains a novel, two novellas and some shorter pieces. Each story deals with larger, abstract ideas, such as infinity, progress, the irrational, and loneliness to name a few. But what exactly are these abstract ideas? What is infinity, progress, the irrational and so many other abstract words we use without thinking about them? In some sense, they are just words, syllables and phonemes, arbitrary marks on a paper or computer screen, random audible sounds. But the word infinity can never actually denote what it tries to denote, not really anyway.

Perhaps the human mind can conceive of some vague notion of progress or infinity or dread or loneliness, but the human mind must feel these things, experience them on some existential level. I do not claim the stories in this book will allow the reader to do that, at least fully, but my hope is that the stories in this book do allow a reader to experience something more than an abstract word. And one of the ways to make these ideas more than abstract words is by reflection.

All the characters in these stories endure an intense period of self-reflection, where they learn things about the world and themselves. So, reflection is a way to make the abstract concrete. I hope it resonates with you in some way.

Angelo J. Letizia, PhD
May 24th, 2025
Manchester Maryland

Table of Contents

The Last Number

Prologue

Eight hundred years before Christ in what is today Acapulco Mexico. There is nothing but humid forests and mountains. A priest carves sacred figures into a stone praying for rain. Before technology, before science and the rigorous rules of logic, he understood the universe with a rock and a stick.

Roughly three hundred years later, Greek philosophers searched for the same meaning of the universe, yet they unknowingly became lost, they strayed further than the priest, into unknown realms. Pythagoras, who bordered on a mystic or cult leader, founded a secret society. This society believed in the divinity of numbers. Indeed, number was believed to be the foundation of the universe. Planets and animals and all of existence were thought to follow the neat and orderly pattern of number. The rational rules of number regulated the world and all its laws.

Yet there was a dark side, an irrational side to number. Wielded in certain, dark ways, almost like magic, number does not end. It can divide itself into eternity, not able to be understood. How could a rational universe be built? The Pythagoreans, as they came to be called, tried to hide this fact, almost pretend this irrationality didn't exist. The Greeks built their laws, indeed their entire universe, on the purely "rational" property of number. The irrational was a ghost, a figment never to be mentioned, suppressed into the deepest regions of the human psyche. Outwardly, sculpture, art, mathematics, architecture was all built on "rational" premises. The irrational was forced within.

Yet one of their own, who shall only be called H----, discovered the secret. He simply divided two rational numbers and discovered the un-ending torrent of infinity. He took this secret and wanted to spread it, but he violated the Pythagoreans sacred code; he threatened the entire universe. And for this he was to perish.

H---- sits in a dark room, he can smell his own rank sweat. But what does that matter now? He's sat in this room for days, harboring his discovery. It sits in him as a malignant sage, cross-legged, cancerous, and multiplying infinitely. A violent knock on the door interrupts his thoughts.

"Come out H----, come out and share your discovery with us."

But H------- knows it is a trap, he knows they will kill him.

"Come out H----!" the voice is more forceful.

But what if they killed him? They could pierce his flesh and stop his heart, but they couldn't stop...*the numbers*.

The thin wooden door begins to splinter. Seconds later it shatters but H——does not move, he does not startle with surprise, instead he waits. Half a dozen men forcibly seize him. The boots and clubs rain down upon him. Then the burn of a thick rope bound his feet and hands. The leader of the men stands over his bound body.

"You have violated our order." The leader did not look at H—— as he spoke. His voice was far away, as if he were talking to the Gods. "You discovered the secret that threatens us, that threatens the very universe in which we all live, you found a secret reserved for the Gods, or perhaps, more powerful than the Gods themselves."

H—— stared straight ahead, the only thing in his view, the leader's sandal. Yet H—— knew there was more.

"Your discovery threatens all of existence, and for that, you must die."

Even as his eulogy was pronounced, H—— knew the secret could not die with him, societies would be built, different worlds constructed, nice, neat, and orderly, but at the heart of it all would be '*a higher number.*'

The captors fixed a second rope around his ankles and dragged him to a lake. The leader stood above H——, praying, offering sacrifices to the Gods, trying so desperately to curb the irrational. The captors kneeled as their leader prayed for their restoration. But H—— began to scream, he began to divide the rational.

"Two divided by three! Five divided by four! Eight divided by-"

His teeth broke and a small cloud of dust rose from the leader's sandal. But it did not matter; he exposed their "rational world" for the sham it was. Even as he was heaved into the lake and his lungs burst, those division problems would continue forever.

And so, the Pythagoreans thought the secret was safe. For centuries, the idea of infinity was flirted with, but never seriously taken, never paid attention to. Instead, the world built its reality on the rational. But sometimes it becomes hard to ignore the structure when the foundation is rotten.

Part 1

I

1944. A small town
outside of Munich Germany.

Over 2000 years ago in ancient Greece, a man named H——— discovered a secret. A man who is never mentioned in the history books, never taught or learned about. Yet, his secret threatened the universe, perhaps, threatened even the Gods. And for his discovery, he was put to death. But it was a secret which was not to die in obscurity like its founder. Throughout history, from ancient Greece to Buddhist India to Renaissance Italy, the secret was always at the core of civilization and it's so-called "progress." In Nazi Germany, it was rediscovered again by another obscure source. Yet, it would flower in her brain as cancer, and even Adolf Hitler could not exterminate the bastard secret.

Maria Altendorpher twisted the bed sheet. Bluish veins rose out of her hands, but she only twisted harder, almost coaxing them to rise. Across the room her fingers appeared to knot like a misshaped pretzel.

Quietly she whispered to herself "Four hundred milligrams, twenty-one hundred hours, twenty-three kilometers..."

Her eyelids squeezed tight to shut the numbers out.

"Ten fingers, two ears, four limbs, two eyes...oh god! Stop! Stop! Please...give...me rest!" But no rest would come to Maria Altendorpher. Not as long as there were things to count.

"Aunt Maria, time to take your medicine."

Her niece-and caretaker-Bridgette Altendorpher administered Maria's medication.

"Here you go." The spoon slid off Maria's lips. Bridgette surveyed the bed. A faint but familiar smell overtook her. A smell of sweat and warmth. Even in the dark, Bridgette could see the black circles under her aunt's eyes. "Aunt Maria, you didn't sleep at all." She said with a slight frown. "Try to get some rest."

But her niece did not stand next to her, no, she stood at the bottom of a canyon, far away. Bridgette uncrumpled the blanket. When she left the room, she gave the woman who used to be her aunt one last glance. A woman who at one time took her to the park and played cards with her. A woman who used to look stunning in her Sunday dress. However, through that open door, Bridgette did not see that woman. She only saw an invalid.

II

A tea kettle whistle made Eva Barton jump. Bridgette took the kettle and sat down with her friend for their ritual tea.

"I don't know what to do." Bridgette poured sugar in her tea.

"Maybe you should think about putting her into a home."

"I know. She is getting worse. Much worse."

"How long have you been taking care of her?" asked Eva.

"A little over a year."

"How are you doing with money?"

Bridgette waited a moment to answer. She poured a glass of tea for Eva and herself. "It's hard keeping the house on my salary from the factory. But I don't care about that. Money isn't the issue. She's family." A slight hesitation crept into her voice. The money didn't matter. Everyone was struggling. Everyone had to cut corners and sacrifice during the war. Something else got to Bridgette. Some unexplainable terror seized her when she looked at her aunt.

There was a short, awkward silence before she spoke again. "She hasn't talked to me for over two months." Her voice sounded desperate. "She hardly sleeps, she cries, she talks to herself; I just don't know what to do."

"She talks to herself?" Eva asked. "What does she say?"

"She just mumbles." Bridgette said. "I'm not sure, but I could swear she's counting."

"Counting?" Eva asked.

"Yes, it's the strangest thing. When I go in there to give her medicine, sometimes I swear she is counting."

"What does she count?"

"I don't know. If I try to talk to her, she won't respond.

"I'm sorry," Eva paused, wording her request carefully on the touchy subject. "But I really think you should consider an asylum." Eva gave Bridgette a frown.

"I know," Bridgette sighed. It's the right thing but... I feel guilty. Aunt Maria and I used to be close, that's the main reason I agreed to take care of her. But now, this is horrible to say but... I don't think of her as my aunt." Bridgette looked to the floor as she said that.

"She will always be your aunt." Eva said sternly.

"In blood maybe. But the woman who took me to the park as a little girl is dead."

All the while, a faint voice echoed in the room. A triumphant whisper bellowed almost inaudibly from Bridgette's room. Both women talked unawares, but the voice trickled through the open door. It seized Maria as a pair of strangler's hands and pinched her windpipe. She didn't hear the entire broadcast. She didn't have to.

"Send your son's..."

"Oh God! Take it away!" she whispered into the pillow. But the radio did not listen to her pleas.

"We need to rid this country of its criminals..."

A few stands of grey hair twisted around her fingers, but she continued to drag her fingers across her head.

"Jews! Communists! They are everywhere!" the radio screamed.

Sweat marks streaked her face.

"Help purge this great nation! *Sieg Heil! Seig Heil!*"

The voice sounded as if it were in the room, next to her. She sank into the rumples of her bed sheets. The Fuehrer spoke over the radio, but all Maria could think of was *'bodies.'*

German's, Americans, Italians, English, their faces molded into one flesh countenance, one dead body, a hundred dead bodies with broken teeth. Dead eyes rolled back into dead skulls. And there was the great Fuehrer, standing, watching the bodies. His voice paralyzed her; it drew her into an unholy connection. Hitler made her count the dead. The endless, infinite dead, piling....

"Oh no! Aunt Maria!" Bridgette rushed in and picked her aunt off the floor.

"I left the radio on in my room!" Bridgette said to Eva. "It upsets her when they broadcast about the war. *Ich bin ein dummkopft!*

"I'll go shut it off." Eva said as she went into the other room.

Bridgette held her aunt. She gently rocked her and dried her face.

"I'm so sorry, I forgot to turn the radio off. But you're safe here. I promise."

Maria wanted to believe her niece. She wanted to play cards with her again. But all she could do was stay in her niece's arms and cry.

III

"I am three meters tall" Maria whispered the numbers to herself. "62 years old, zero money..." she pulled the covers back and quietly walked over to her dresser where she kept her prize possession-her only possession. A small porcelain apple glittered in the moonlight. She squeezed it tight until the glass stem cut her palm like it had done so many times before.

"One apple, one apple oh god only one apple!"

Maria stared out the window. How long did she live with this? How long would the Fuehrer hold the gun in her mouth? How much longer did she have to count? A billion stars, a thousand rain drops, endless pebbles on the sidewalk.

"Gallons of blood, broken teeth..." she whispered.

The blood dripped from her thumb. One drop, two drops, three drops, a hundred drops, a universe of blood drops on one, two, a hundred carpet fibers. There were too many numbers in this room! Next to the apple she kept a bible. Maria ran her fingers over the worn cover.

"Speak to me in this madness." she whispered.

She clutched the apple and the bible and fell onto the bed. Blood mixed with tears. Maria wanted to count them but that would be impossible.

"What do you want me to know? Dear Lord, what fruit would you have me eat?" She squeezed the apple and re-opened her wounded palm. "Have I probed too far? Have I gained the knowledge that only you should know? What would you have me do?"

God didn't answer her. Instead, he left her stranded in the madness. The only thought that appeared was of the great Fuehrer. But she knew it was for a reason. And so, all she could do was wait. Curled tight into a fetus, miscarried 62 years after its birth. She waited on that bed like Jesus in the garden. She waited for every angel to walk into that room, she waited for Cain to beat her like Abel; she waited for God to speak to her, she waited for her madness and the world to end. She counted every piece of earth she saw, she wanted to die but instead fell asleep.

IV
Two Weeks Later

The sun was hot. It burned Bridgette's neck through the window where the shade of her large hat did not fall. She waited for the train to come to a stop, the steel beast slowly dragged itself a few more feet, crawling to the station then finally stopped moving.

"C'mon *Tante* Maria." Bridgette helped her aunt gather her luggage. "Let's see where you're going to live." Maria knew it would come to this. She had become a burden on her niece. But the madness swelled like a broken knee and her thoughts became uncontrollable. Everything needed to be counted because somehow, in some unexplainable way, the Fuehrer demanded it.

Pastel green wallpaper decorated the entire place. Maybe in another time, Maria would have enjoyed this place. It would be a serene place to die.

"Well Hello Maria we've been expecting you." A middle-aged woman in a nurse's smock gently took Maria by the hand. She was younger than Maria but the sincerity in the woman's voice soothed her a little even if she didn't show it. Bridgette went to the desk and filled out the necessary papers. Like a robot, she circled and checked the appropriate boxes. Mechanically, she signed over her aunt's life.

"Can we have a minute alone." Bridgette asked the caretaker.

"Absolutely. I'll be at the desk."

Bridgette took both of Maria's hands and whispered to her softly.

"I am so sorry." She started to cry. "I didn't want...You were like another mother...I..." she couldn't finish. She pulled her aunt into her chest and cried. Maria didn't respond but she knew. She knew this was the only way it could end. Bridgette said goodbye one last time and left the asylum.

V

She had been here a few days. The pleasant pastel green soothed her better than the medicine. But only to be interrupted by the radio, by the beloved Fuehrer.

"Adolph Hitler has acquired France for the glory of the third Reich! Hail Hitler! He will restore this beleaguered people's former glory! The world will tremble at our power!" The radio broadcast echoed throughout the common room. Maria slumped in her chair while Hitler advanced on the rest of Europe. That same fear overtook her. But she was weak.

"Time for your medicine dear." A nurse approached Eva with a spoonful of medicine. Maria quivered and counted to herself. Counted something.

"Mrs. Altendorpher! You look terrible! We must get you into bed! Here, take this first." The nurse gave her the spoon. She couldn't understand the pain, the fear. But it didn't matter. No medicine could help. No rest. The Fuehrer tormented her and there was no cure. All she felt was fear, a terrible foreboding.

"How was she when you left?" Eva asked.

Bridgette poured two cups of tea as she spoke to her neighbor.

"The same as always. She didn't even say goodbye. I just hope they can take care of her better there. The staff seems capable. I think she will be better off in the asylum. But I still feel horrible." she said quietly.

"You made the right choice." Eva took a sip. "Your aunt was mentally ill; she was in the beginning stages of senility or dementia who knows. It was only a matter of time before she totally collapsed, and you would not have been able to help her at all then."

"I know you're right, but still, it's hard to deal with. I just hope I never end up like that."

"It's a scary thing." Eva said. "Honestly, I think I would rather lose my body than my mind. But, then again, I guess you don't know any better if you do lose your mind."

"I agree." Bridgette stared out the window. No matter how much convincing she heard, she had sent her aunt, her own blood, to live in an asylum. The guilt was unbearable, like a cross crushing her shoulder blades. But like a dutiful soldier, she sat quietly and drank her tea. She did what had to be done.

VI

Paul Eckhart tugged nervously at the swastika pin on his lapel. He adjusted the Reich armband on his sleeve and cocked his gun. The full moon shone over the asylum like the eye of God. All was quiet at fourteen hundred hours. That's why they always come in the early hours of the morning.

"Okay boys you know what to do, clean house!" The general knocked violently at the door.

"Open this door! Open it now."

Slowly the door creaked open. The elderly caretaker stood half-awake in her nightgown.

"What seems to be the problem." She asked him politely. But, as her eyes began to survey the soldiers, she knew who they were and what they came for. The general didn't answer her question and pushed the caretaker out of the way.

"Okay boys, round 'em up! Put them on the trucks and kill anyone who gets in the way," he screamed over the caretaker as if she didn't exist.

Looking up at the general he was not a human. The caretaker rose to her feet. "No! These women are sick! Where are you taking them! You monster! You animals! Leave them alone." she grabbed his arm.

The general gave the caretaker a violent backhand. As she fell to the floor her nose sprayed blood on the tiles. He grabbed her by the shirt and pulled her up to his face. "If you say anything else, I will make you the soldier's whore!" He dropped her on the floor.

The soldiers pushed one sick woman after another like a line of school children forcing them into the back of a huge cargo truck.

"Eckhart!" The general screamed "Ride in the back with the women, keep an eye on them."

"Yes sir." Eckhart said unhesitatingly. As he climbed in the back of the truck he fooled everyone into thinking he was a good soldier. But instead of hailing Hitler, his mind focused on the biblical passage Mathew 25:30. It suited him well, so he memorized it. *'And throw this useless servant into the darkness outside where there will be wailing and grinding of teeth!'*

When he saw the people he had to kill, the passage popped into this head. Not for them but for him. He hated the agonizing moans; he hated the cries of pity, the wailing and grinding of teeth. And he was the useless servant; serving an evil master and not the god he loved.

"Oh God, I am so sorry, please forgive me!" He began to cry. The moon hid behind a cloud and as the old cargo truck rolled away, Paul Eckhart tried to hide with the moon. But he couldn't run away. He had a family who he had promised everything would be alright. His beautiful wife, his daughter and son. His blonde hair and blue eyes elevated him to a superior race. Nervously he fingered the crucifix in his palm. Maria, who was sitting beside him, caught the gold reflection in the moonlight.

'What shall we receive good at the hand of God, and shall we not receive evil?' The passage from Job rang true in his head. Paul Eckhart had lived a tough life but a good life. He provided for his family until these Nazi bastards slapped that dreaded swastika on his arm. Now, this superior being in the eyes of his new God-Adolph Hitler-had to shuffle off helpless women to be slaughtered. He had to accept the bad along with the good like 'Job.' These horrible sins would have to be lived with for all eternity simply to feed his family.

"Do not cry." Maria gently placed her hand on his.

"Woman! What are you doing! *Du Spinnst!*" Eckhart whispered as he recoiled his hand. And for a few moments, madness subsided. Maria could think clearly. She now had a purpose.

"You must be strong." she put her hand on his again. That crucifix was her sign. "Forgive them; they know not what they do." she whispered.

Eckhart stared in amazement. "Luke 23." his voice trailed off.

"There is a bigger purpose." She whispered gently "the body tears like paper but..." she pointed to her head "the ideas live on."

"What ideas?" He asked nervously.

"My madness is a warning. And now I die because of it. But that is fine because the idea will pass to you."

"I don't understand..." he said.

"Humans count their pain in milligrams. They number their hospital doors. Every day is a tally mark on the prison wall... She was beginning to understand.

"Woman, what are you talking about?" he asked frantically.

"There is no end! We count to infinity! I have spent the last years of my life counting and am no closer to an end!"

"I still don't understand! *Ich verstehe nicht!*" Eckhart said. He gripped her hand tightly.

"You don't have to understand. I don't truly understand. All I do is bear the madness and trust in God. It is not for us to understand but merely for us to carry it on." She handed him the tiny porcelain apple. He took it like a communion tablet.

"What is your name?" He asked quietly.

"Maria Altendorpher." She replied.

Eckhart stared at her and then back at the porcelain apple. What had she given him?

"I used to be a professor of Mathematics at the University of Berlin. The apple was a gift from my students years ago." she paused a moment then spoke again. "But I went too far and that is my reminder."

"Too far?" He asked.

"I wanted to know the end. Infinity beckoned. I was unable to control my thoughts, I went mad and now I will die, the great Fuehrer has seen to it himself..." she couldn't finish.

"Maybe I can sneak you out..." Even though Eckhart knew that was impossible.

"No. This is my cup. Shall I not drink from the cup my father has given me? The body will rot but the thoughts..." she pointed to her head "are attached to the numbers, they will go on infinitely-or until they find something."

There wasn't anything else for them to say. Soon, Maria would meet her death. She would drink from the cup God had given her. She would be one of the bodies in the Fuehrer's pile, but the ideas, her madness, would never die. It had a purpose now. A purpose even Hitler was powerless to stop. Eckhart handed her his crucifix.

"Be strong." he whispered.

The truck came to an abrupt stop. Small clouds of dust rose to sting his eyes.

"Line them up!" The general flung open the back gate of the truck.

VII

Some woman cried, others were oblivious when the butt end of the rifles hoarded them into the tiny shower room. Crusty nozzles arched off the wall like frightened cats. Eckhart wanted to gag from the stench, but he dared not flinch.

"We have room for a few more! We can get them all in one shot, less mess to clean up." The general ordered.

No matter how many times Eckhart did this he never became accustomed to it. He didn't understand how anybody could. But then he looked at those pigs. They enjoyed this. They enjoyed slaughtering defenseless women or skeletal Jews. Sometimes Eckhart wanted to put his general in here. Or put the gun in his own mouth.

"Lord forgive them, they know not what they do." He repeated it as he shoved a short gray-haired women in. "You will be in paradise today," he said to her. She clawed his arm pleading as the door shut.

"Forgive me Lord." he whispered. "I know not what I do."

All this time Maria Altendorpher never once broke eye contact with Eckhart-even as he shut the door- he could feel her eyes. Through the tiny glass window amidst all the crying, amidst the wailing and grinding of teeth, Maria simply stared at Eckhart.

The slight bulge from the apple stuck him in the leg. Fuck the Nazi's. Fuck Hitler and the Reich. Now something would live on. Maria would die shortly but her spirit would live on.

"Petersen!" The general barked at the soldier standing next to Eckhart. "You have the honor tonight."

Private Petersen, a stocky soldier with black hair, and no more than 19, walked over to the large, rusted handle on the side of the chamber.

"Is everything secure?" Another man who stood by the gate, checked it one last time and gave the thumbs up to the general.

"Hail Hitler!" Eckhart yanked on the rusted handle. It easily slid down like it had done so many times before.

"I love watching these invalids choke, it gives me a hard on!" The general gave Eckhart a hard slap on the back. Usually, he did not have the stomach to watch this. It was the expressions that haunted him. Faces twisted like corkscrews, yellow teeth shown through the gas. Eckhart wanted to turn away but this time, he had no choice. He couldn't break Maria's gaze with a hammer. Through the green cloud Maria Altendorpher stared at Eckhart stronger than any Gestapo gun.

"Hey Eckhart, I think that one's staring at you!" He pointed to

Maria who began to choke.

Eckhart grinned but did not break stare with Maria. He watched as the veins tightened in her neck like telephone cables. She began to hack blood and part of her lung. Little drops splattered on her chin. She dropped onto the concrete floor. And yet, her eyes stared intently at Eckhart. Even after her head smacked on the floor, her dead eyes still looked at him. They whispered to him, to make sure the knowledge would be passed on.

"We count our pain! Number sadness and yet it never ends! It goes on infinitely, past any human thought, the numbers go past the skin, past the sky, and the numbers never end!"

"Petersen, close the valve!" The general yelled.

Petersen waited a few more seconds before pushing the rusty level into place.

"Okay boys, we'll turn the air on, wait a few minutes than send the Jews to clean up the bodies."

Eckhart reluctantly opened the large chamber door. No matter how many times he did this, he could never get used to that sight.

"Look at this one" Petersen gave Maria a hard kick to the ribs. "Catholic idiot, only Catholics carry these," he bent down and picked the crucifix out of her fingers. "I'm gonna sell this, put it to some good."

Eckhart helped Petersen drag the bodies from the chamber. A sickening screech of teeth dragged on the concrete.

What the fuck is that sound?" Petersen dropped the corpse and walked around to its face. "It's those fucking teeth," In one violent motion, the butt end of his gun shattered Maria Altendorpher's front teeth across the floor. "Much better," he said with satisfaction. Now, all Eckhart could hear was the sick thud of tender jaw skin scrapped away on concrete.

Animal! Petersen could never understand this! Eckhart turned away from the butchery only to see the other dead. In a place like this, Maria's secret gave him hope. A hope, a dream of triumph, among the horror of the only world he knew.

'Horror! Horror! How horrible it will be on earth!' He recited the passage from revelation in his head. *'They will want to die but death will flee from them!'* He piled the bodies atop each other. What horror! "One, two, three..." He whispered silently to himself. Maria was right! Eckhart looked out the window-the same one that Maria looked out before she choked-and saw a gang of bony Jewish prisoners dig a grave for these bodies. No matter how many he counted there would be more! Thousands and millions of corpses in an endless parade of horror.

Eckhart felt the porcelain apple in his pocket. Maria had given him a purpose.

"Let's go. I'm going on a cigarette break." Petersen dropped the corpse he was dragging. "Get the Jews in here to clean this shit up."

Slowly, his cigarette smoke rose to heaven. Eckhart looked at his hands. The swastika was tight on his lapel and the apple stem stuck his leg. What had he done?

VIII
1 Week Later

"What is it?" Eva asked.

"It's a letter from the asylum."

"What does it say?" Eva asked. The daily tea talks always calmed Bridgette down but today nothing could prepare her. Bridgette waited a moment to reply. It was her fault.

"It says that Maria is dead."

"My God"," Eva got up to console her friend.

"I don't understand," Bridgette said. "When I left her last week, she was healthy. Maybe there's some mistake."

But Eva saw the tiny swastika at the bottom right-hand corner of the letter. There was no mistake. Bridgette took a sip of her tea. Her aunt didn't die a natural death. There was no way to prove anything. But deep in her heart Bridgette knew that her aunt was taken. That's how it happened. One day someone would be gone as if they never existed. Maria Altendorpher didn't die, she simply didn't exist anymore. Bridgette had heard the rumors of death camps and the cruel experimentation. Hitler hated Jews, Catholics, communists, gypsies, intellectuals, homosexuals, and anyone non-Aryan. Especially a senile old woman. Hitler and his Aryan race would have no use for an invalid. Eva and Bridgette sat quietly. There was nothing else to say except Hail Hitler.

IX

"Anybody got any cigarettes?" Ron Poole walked nervously around the bunk.

"Hey, I got some," another soldier threw him a box with three cigarettes in it.

"Thanks Pete," Ron pulled out his lighter and inhaled that sweet tobacco.

"I am so ready for this," Lieutenant Pete Pulaski said to Ron. "I can't wait to get off this godforsaken island and kill some krauts!" But

Ron only looked out the window. His thoughts were with his wife.

"I just want the orders ya know," he lit his cigarette. "I wanna go in there and kill all those Nazi bastards! Every single one of them!"

"Amen to that!" Another soldier in the back shouted.

"Hail Hitler," another one mocked.

"Hail this!" Pete grabbed his crotch. "Before I kill Hitler myself," Pete stood up "I want to cut off his arms and let him suffer."

"Cut off his balls!" A soldier yelled. "I just can't wait to kill a Nazi; I just want these fucking orders!"

Ron nervously smoked while he rummaged through his pocket. His fingers grazed over the worn photograph. "Randi," he whispered to himself. His wife always made him smile.

"Poole you in?" Joe held up a deck of cards.

"Ah Yeah. Deal me in." He needed to be distracted.

Pete shuffled the cards and distributed them as he talked. "I got the new titty mag. Wow; did you see the tits on her?"

Mike, another soldier chimed in "Yeah on Ms. July!"

Pete nodded his head. "I can't wait to get some ha-ha! But first I want to kill me some Nazi's!" He looked over at Ron, "What's the matter man? You've been quiet all day?"

Ron stared at the picture of his wife.

"You going soft?" Pete lightly punched him in the arm.

"I didn't want to say anything in front of the guys. In fact, I didn't want to say anything at all but..." he paused a minute.

"What's up man?"

"I'm scared."

Pete waited a second. Then finally he spoke. "Man, if you're scared of fighting it's not a big deal, were all scared..."

"I'm not scared of fighting." He said without emotion. "I got a letter from my wife today."

Pete waited for the rest of the story.

"Randi's pregnant."

"Oh man congrats!" Pete slapped him on the back. "Do you know what it's gonna be?"

"Randi thinks it's gonna be a girl but she's not sure."

"This is good news, what's the problem?" Pete asked.

"Of course, it's good news. And I'm happy but..." he paused a moment. "I feel guilty."

"Guilty over what?"

"Guilty and scared over bringing a child into this." The all too familiar and clichéd thought occurred to him. He was sure other fathers thought the same thing. But truthfully, how could he bring a daughter into this? His eyes settled on Pete's gun.

"Into what?" Pete asked. "Into this world?"

"Yes."

"Man, don't feel guilty. This world isn't a bad place. But the fucking Krauts are trying to destroy what we've built. We're trying to make it a better place for your girl. Don't you forget that. Go out there and fight hard. And when this is all done you love and spoil that kid every chance you get."

Ron snuffed out his cigarette. "You're right. It's just tough, I dunno. I'm sure other fathers have felt this before."

Pete's face lightened up again. "Of course, I'm right. I'm always right! Hey man you just remember what I said. You wanna play another game of cards?"

"Nah, I'm gonna lay down."

"Okay," Pete went back to the game. I'll pick you up when we go to eat.

"Sounds good," Ron laid back on his pillow.

X

"What did you mean?" Eckhart nervously fidgeted with the apple. "Maria, what did you discover?" He pondered her secret in solitude. Now, the lord God gave him a purpose. Like the tax collector, Jesus dined with him, a sinner. Jesus lived in the apple. Eckhart was to spread Maria's message across the universe. The Nazis exterminated her but that was irrelevant. Skin was useless. All that mattered was the idea that she wanted to communicate to him moments before her death. She had discovered a secret passage in humanity's numbers.

He read the faded inscription on the apple to himself. "One, two, three..." that's all it said. What was she counting? Eckhart surveyed the dark landscape. She must have seen hundreds of trees, a thousand blades of grass. He held out his hand. Ten fingers, a hundred hairs...

"What did you discover dammit! Tell me! Tell me!" he pounded the dirt. "What!!" But it was not for him to know; simply just to carry.

Then he heard the general's, hoarse voice scream in the night, "Americans! Americans! the general's voice pierced though the outskirts of the camp. Eckhart instinctively grabbed his rifle and ran back to camp.

"Mobilize! Mobilize!" *Schnell! Schnell!! Achtung!!*

When he arrived at the camp, he heard shouts and orders, cocking triggers, loaded guns but strangely all he could think of was the prisoners. This was his day of reckoning. The final judgment. An apocalypse in every American's gun.

XI

"Finally! We got the order! The first squadron is deployed!" We're moving in 15 minutes!" Joe pulled on his coat.

"Here we go," Ron whispered quietly to himself.

"I'm saving one bullet for Hitler himself." Pete put a .38 super in his front pocket and patted his chest. "Fuck that dirty kraut! Fuck all those dirty krauts!"

Ron nervously fidgeted with the picture of his wife Randi. He closed his eyes and whispered to himself. "Please God, give me strength."

His squadron waited for the call like the guillotine for the condemned. "Let's go! Move out!" the general barked.

The blade had fallen; it cut him off from the life he knew. He rose with his gun.

"Nazi Fucks!" We're not the pussy French!" Pete sprayed machine gun fire into the German camp. The mission was simple. Storm the Nazi camp outside of Munich and liberate the prisoners-if indeed there were truth to any-rumors that swirled around the American camps for weeks. Rumors of German torture camps and forced labor, of heinous experiments. No one knew for sure.

A bullet whizzed by Pete's ear. "You fucking Kraut!" Pete fired two rounds into the chest of a German soldier. He was on the radio trying to call for back-up. Pete stood over the dying man. "You piece of shit! Where is your general?"

Petersen spit on Pete's boots. Pete drove his boot heel into Petersen's wounds. He twisted the flesh like a skin ribbon.

"Where is he!"

"Hail. Hit..."

Pete shot him beneath the right eyeball. Petersen let out a sickly yelp before Pete kicked his ribs and put another bullet in his chest for good measure.

"Hail that!" He spit on Petersen's corpse.

Ron cautiously walked among the debris with his gun poised. Suddenly, he felt a trickle of hot blood in his jacket. It wasn't too bad, just a flesh wound. Instinctively he whirled around and fired.

Eckhart dropped to one knee and then fell into a semi-comatose heap. Ron took a step forward ready to finish him off, but the man was trying to say something. Ron's German was rusty, but it sounded like the man was praying.

"Father, why have you forsaken me."

He was reciting the bible...

And then, an uncontrollable rage rose in him. How could this man who killed defenseless women, a man who just tried to kill him, pray? Ron walked up to him. "How do you call yourself a Christian! You murder rape and torture! You are an animal! And now you want pity! Now you want forgiveness!" He dug his gun so deep into Eckhart's temple he saw the bruises already starting to form in the moonlight.

"*Ich*...never wanted...this..." Eckhart's English was choppy but understandable.

"Bullshit! You just tried to kill me!"

"No...I did not fire..."

Ron snatched his gun and opened the clip. No bullets had fired. Ron killed an innocent man. But no, he was a murderer. He killed the innocent.

"It doesn't matter." Ron pressed harder. "You are not innocent."

"No, I never wanted *dass*," he pointed to the gas chamber.

"Bull shit. You are a murderer. An animal. And now you've lost. Your savior Mr. Adolph Hitler has led your country into shit! Europe is dead! America has the balls now!" Ron was about to pull the trigger but noticed a small porcelain object rolling out of Eckhart's pocket.

"What's this?" Ron went to reach for it, but Eckhart snatched it with what little strength he had left.

"Maria Altendorpher..." he choked out.

"Who is Maria Altendorpher?" Ron should have killed but held off.

"I never wanted this; I didn't want her to die but...I had to...my family..."

Ron pressed the gun harder. "Fuck you, you're still a killer."

"But..." he gasped "She had a... *geheimnis*...a secret...that will outlast her bones..."

"What the fuck are you talking about?" Ron shouted.

Eckhart reached over and then stuck the apple in Ron's hand. As Eckhart pulled his own hand away a trail of blood appeared on Ron's fingers.

His speech was mixed between German and English. "The numbers, find them! Find what *sie gefunden hat*. Find the last number, find infinity, find the last number, *unendlichkeit, die letzte nummer*!" His teeth cracked when they hit the rocky ground. But it didn't matter now, his task was done.

Ron remained poised over Eckhart's corpse with a bloody

porcelain apple and a message.

"Find what?" he asked the corpse. "What did she find?" he rummaged through Eckhart's cloths and yanked his dog tags off.

"Find what Mr. Eckhart?" He said again to a dead man.

"Oh man I must have killed a dozen krauts!" Pete lit a cigarette.

Another soldier yelled from the back. "You're full of shit! You got maybe three!"

"Fuck you, Joe!" Pete shot back.

Ron didn't want to hear any of this. He crawled into his bunk-still with Eckhart's blood on his hand. An inhuman Nazi had asked his killer to find something, to uncover something that neither of them had any clue about. Ron cleaned the apple off (but not his hands) and put it in his bag. *'That will make a nice present for Janet.'* He thought of himself and his unborn baby girl.

Part II

I

1951. Western New York

"Hi daddy!" Janet ran into her father's arms. Ron picked her up and whirled her around in the air. Her chubby cheeks barely contained her smile.

"Guess what I did today!"

"What sweetheart?" he put her on his knee.

"I picked out dandelions and lilies for you!" She pulled a crumpled, misshaped bouquet from her pocket.

"Oh, thank you sweetie, you are so cute!" he hugged his daughter tight. Her green eyes were marbles or smooth rocks.

"And guess what I'm going to do tomorrow?"

"What?" he loved their conversations.

"I'm going to make you a surprise!"

"What is the surprise?"

"Daddy!" She yelled "If I told you, it wouldn't be a surprise!"

"Okay cutie I guess I will just have to wait and see."

His daughter gave him a mischievous grin. She crawled off his lap and a sharp pain shot through his sternum. She didn't see her father wince.

"Daddy I'm hungry." She stood with her hands on her hips.

"Okay sweetie, how 'bout ice cream?"

"Yay!" she jumped up and down "Ice cream! Ice cream!"

The pain in his chest did not subside. It hurt to sit; it hurt to stand. He was dying.

"Daddy what's wrong?"

"Nothing sweetie. Chocolate or Vanilla?"

Little Janet thought for a moment. "Strawberry!"

"Strawberry it is," he scooped her into his arms.

The war existed in him. There was shrapnel in his leg and now a nagging pain in his chest. It probably was cancer. Six years later, Hitler would finally kill him, just not in the way he had thought. The porcelain apple caught his eye. It always did. The red gleam reminded him of Eckhart's blood which was still caked onto the stem.

"Go see if Mommy wants any."

"Okay daddy," she ran to the kitchen.

The apple was a sort of symbol to him. It represented something he didn't understand but was somehow connected to, interwoven into this unknown phenomenon by chance.

"She wants a banana split."

"Okay Sweetie, let's go." He buckled her into the car seat.

Maria Altendorpher had a secret. She passed it to Paul Eckhart who didn't understand but wasn't supposed to. All he had to do was pass the secret, pass the apple on to whoever was supposed to have it next. And Ron wasn't the one to break the secret. He was a carrier like Eckhart. Who was he supposed to give it to?

"Hurry daddy! I'm hungry!"

"Okay. Okay, hold your horses," He smiled.

II

A Few Weeks Later

Ron Poole had a beautiful family. A gorgeous wife and two amazing daughters. And even after all these years, his long dead friend's words stuck with him.

"Don't ever feel guilty."

He was glad to bring Janet into this world. And he had fought to make it a safe world. He just so desperately wanted to be alive to see it. The pain ripped through his sternum again.

The pitter-patter of tiny feet down the hallway was unmistakable.

"Daddy!" Little Janet burst into the bedroom and flung herself into his arms.

"Daddy! I missed you! How come you didn't come to church with us?" her mouth arched into an exaggerated frown.

"I can't move too well sweetie. Daddy's chest hurts." His sternum ached from the impact, but he would rather die than tell his daughter to get off.

"How was church?" he asked.

"The priest read a story about Adam and Eve, but he used a lot of big words that I didn't understand."

"Do you know the whole story," his chest burned, but again, he would die before sending his baby girl away.

"Not really," she snuggled onto his lap.

"Well," he began "Before there were any people on the Earth, God lived by himself."

"Who made God?" she asked.

"No one sweetie, he has always been."

"But how, who made him?"

"Well," He didn't know how to explain this to a six-year-old. "He is not human. Nobody more powerful than God exists so nobody could have made him. He has always been alive."

She gave him a puzzled look. "Daddy, I don't get it." She frowned.

The familiar pain ripped through his heart again. "Well sweetie," some things are not meant for us to understand. Instead, we just have to believe," He could tell his daughter was not satisfied with this answer. Truth be told, neither was he, but that's the way it was. Her little mind churned like an engine. Ron knew his daughter was special. She did not just take the world as it came to her. She tore it apart like a lion and questioned everything.

"Okay," she said with a frown. "But maybe one day I'll be smart enough to understand."

"Sometimes it not about being smart. Sometimes all you have to do is use your imagination."

His daughter beamed that familiar wide grinned smile at him.

"God was lonely," Ron began again. "So, he made the earth and all the plants and animals, but he was still lonely."

"Why daddy?" He could have taken a pet." Ron leaned down with the sharp pain in his chest and kissed his daughter's cheeks. "You are so cute!"

"Daddy stop it! Your beard is scratching me! Finish the story," she pushed his face away.

"Well, he was still lonely after he created all that, so he decided to make a person. Do you know who the first person was?"

"Adam," she beamed up at him.

"That's right. But then God realized that Adam would be lonely so..."

"He made a girl," she finished his sentence.

"Yes, and her name was Eve," He couldn't help but smile.

"So, the first man was Adam. Then he created Eve. God made a beautiful garden called Eden and that's where Adam and Eve lived. God told them they could eat any fruit they wanted from any tree but..."

His daughter's little eyes grew wide with excitement.

"The only tree they couldn't eat from was the tree of knowledge in the middle of the garden."

"Why not?"

"Well, if they ate the fruit from that tree, then they would be like God. And nobody can be like God."

"Oh no!" Janet's eyes grew wide.

"One day, Eve was by herself in the garden and all of sudden, she saw a snake!" Ron lunged at his daughter.

"Eww Daddy! Stop it!"

"And the snake said to Eve, why don't you eat an apple from this tree. Eve told the snake that they were forbidden to eat the fruit of that tree. Oh no the snake said, God doesn't want you to eat it because he is afraid that you will be smarter than him. Eat it and be like God, you don't need him if you eat that fruit."

"So, Eve ate the apple. Then Adam came over and she gave it to him."

"Oh no! What happened to them!"

"Well, they got scared and hid from God."

"Well, that's just stupid," she rolled her little eyes "You can't hide from God!"

"That's right. God found them and he knew what they did. But he asked them why they were hiding, and they said because they were embarrassed because they were naked. But God asked who told them they were naked..."

"Now they were smart because they ate the smart apple."

"That's right sweetie. Then they confessed to God."

The pain became tolerable. Not because it subsided or lessened but because he was distracted.

"What did God do to them?" she asked.

"Well, he kicked them out of the garden."

"Oh no," she frowned.

"So, you see baby, no one can be like God. Adam and Eve disobeyed him, and he punished them for it. They should never have eaten that apple. There are some things we cannot know. The apple represents the things we don't, and can't, know. Sometimes people want to know things they're not supposed to; like Adam and Eve."

"Now it makes sense daddy. You're so smart," she hugged him.

"No cutie, you are the smart one."

"Daddy! Look!" Her little finger pointed to the other side of the room.

Ron strained his eyes. In the dusk sunlight a red object glittered.

"The apple daddy! You have one just like it."

Ron stared in amazement at the apple.

"Sweetie, can you get me the apple."

"Okay daddy," She walked over to it and handed it to him.

"Daddy, I am hungry." she said.

"Okay sweetie, go in the kitchen and I'll be there in a minute to make you a pb and j sandwich."

"Okay," she skipped down the hall.

Ron held the apple in his hand; he squeezed until the stem cut his palm. Was it some type of omen or just a strange coincidence? Ron was not a superstitious man, but something felt strange about the apple, almost mystical, almost sinister.

"One two three... infinity," he whispered the inscription. "What is it Maria?" he asked no one; but half expected an answer. "This is crazy." He shook his head and put the apple back on the shelf. "I'm going nuts." He went into the kitchen to make Janet a sandwich.

III

The windows shook violently. Ron heard the rain whip like tiny pebbles against the glass.

"Honey, can you give me a hand with the air-conditioning. I want to move it into the den." Randi walked over to window unit.

"Sure." Ron said. But he was slow to rise out of his chair. His knees felt like wet cement, hardening, unable to move. As soon as his wife saw him get up from the chair, she knew it was a mistake to ask him.

"Okay, I'll lift the heavy end with the compressor." Ron began to settle himself under the heavy unit. "I'll walk up the stairs backward with it, so let me go first."

His wife settled under her end and they both lifted. Ron unsteadily walked up the stairs. Randi could see a vein beginning to rise under his skin. His arms quivered under the weight of the compressor and each step was an unsure one.

"Honey I'll just call my father he can come tonight..."

"No. I got it." He said it firmly, trying to convince her.

He toiled up the steps, against the carpet, against the pain in his knee, against the weight of the compressor. Each step was slower. Until finally his feet would not obey, the bones stayed in the socket, unable to lift the burden.

"Ron!" She felt the light end of the air-conditioner slip from her hands. The compressor knocked the wind out of her husband as he fell on the step. He had lost. His legs protruded from under the heavy unit like scattered tree limbs. He was brittle, pathetic.

"I'll push it off you, but you got to push up!" she screamed frantically.

For a moment it looked as if he would lie there forever, with this huge weight crushing his sternum. And then she saw the man she married. With a new strength he pushed against the compressor just enough for her to get it. The unit tumbled down two steps before it stopped. Randi collapsed next to her husband, exasperated.

"I love you." It was all she could say.

He remained silent. But in that silence was an awful truth. Yet, an undeniable one. He was going to die. His body would give out. Death is only a word until it comes for you. Then it's real. His death would be the realest thing he ever felt. Strangely enough, he thought of the porcelain apple. He thought of how it was given to him. The pain ripped through his leg but that didn't matter. The apple had a secret. It had to. Why else would he think of it now?

"I love you so much." His wife whispered, almost inaudibly. But he didn't say anything back to her. For the entirety of his life, he gave all to his family. Maybe, just maybe, the apple was the last thing he had to give even if he didn't understand why. He hugged his wife as tight as his feeble arms would let him.

IV

Little Janet curled into a fetal position. Her soft blonde hair rested gently on the pillow. She dreamed of ice cream and daddy. But something else began to churn in her mind. For weeks she thought of God-infinite, beginning-less and unending; it confused and excited her. Her six-year-old brain could not comprehend the existence of something that wasn't born and that wouldn't die.

Ron stumbled over to the couch. He could barely breathe and didn't want to wake Randi with his incessant tossing and turning. He was dying. Whatever was wrong, it was killing him. He survived the war but ironically it was going to kill him now. He wouldn't get to see his beautiful baby graduate or go away to college. No, in a short time he would die, he would rot and be useless.

Not useless! He clutched the porcelain apple in his weak fingers. Like the others before him in this cosmic chain he too had a purpose. Throughout his life he was not overly religious. He went to church and raised his daughter Catholic. He was not overly intellectual. He did his job, supported his family, protected his country, he did the things required of him. And now in the final moments of life he had one last calling, perhaps the most important one.

Again, the unmistakable pitter-patter of pajama feet crept nervously down the hall.

"Daddy?" Little Janet whispered into the darkness.

"Over here sweetie, on the couch."

Janet crawled into her father's arms and laid her head on his chest. Ron smelled the strawberry shampoo from her hair and kissed her on the cheek.

"What are you doing up daddy?"

"I know baby, I couldn't sleep."

"Are you hurting?" He didn't need to see the eyes staring at him, he knew how beautiful they were.

"Sweetie," he took a few moments to finish a sentence now. "I want to give you something very important."

She picked her head up and her hot breath caressed his face. "What is it daddy?"

He handed her the apple. "It was a very special gift that was given to me, now I want to give it to you. If you look at it," he held it up to the moonlight "you can see what's engraved on it."

She whispered the numbers aloud "one...two...three... when does it stop?"

"No sweetie the numbers never stop. They go on forever and ever..."

"Like God," her innocence and simplicity amazed him.

"Yes, exactly like God," God was a number.

"This apple and those numbers are very special. They hold a secret..."

"A secret?" her eyes grew wide in the moonlight. "What is it?"

"Well, that's it. I don't know it. I just know that there is a secret. And one day you will figure it out."

"Me?" she asked.

"Yes. Because you are so smart." He kissed her on the forehead. He told her the story of how he got the apple. Of course, he edited it and made it kid-friendly. Randi could fill her in on the gory details in a few years. His work was done. He had passed on the ineffable cosmic secret. And somehow, he just knew it would end with Janet. Somehow, he felt that Janet would discover what Maria Altendorpher had died for.

"I love you Daddy," she hugged her father.

"I love you too sweetie." All he could do was hug her back and wait to die.

"From ash to ash, dust to dust now Ronald Poole, soldier of Christ, father husband and friend return to the God that created you," the preacher spoke over the rain wind gusts. "In the name of the father, son, holy spirit, Amen."

Baby Janet looked on as the dirt covered her father's casket. She didn't cry because she didn't understand-not yet. The apple sat in her pocket like gasoline, ready to burn.

"C'mon baby," Randi wiped her eyes. "I'll take you for some ice cream."

"Okay mommy."

Ronald was gone. Janet held the only piece of him that mattered.

Part III

I

1973. In college town in Western New York.

The professor droned on about parabolas. Janet shifted uncomfortably in her seat. Twenty-one minutes until this god forsaken lecture ended. She didn't know why she came to class. She had an A.
"If you connect point A to point C through the curvature..."
She checked her watch again. Nineteen minutes. Her thoughts wandered to her thesis. That's what was important. Her friend Lisa leaned over the desk and whispered to her.
"We going to the library tonight?" she asked.
Janet nodded her head.

They said she bordered on lunacy. No doubt she was the smartest person in her graduate class. But they all thought her nuts. And they were probably right. Since her childhood, the thought of infinity fascinated her. Through high school and college, mathematics became a language. It spoke to her in syllables of numbers.
"Okay Poole, time to go home, library closes in an hour."
Janet looked up from her notebook and smiled. Lisa gathered her coat and umbrella.
"Bye Poole, have a good weekend."
"You too," she went back to her notebook.
Lisa paused for a moment. "Janet, seriously, you have got to take a break. Go out, get drunk, something."
Janet had heard this refrain many times before. Instinctively she repeated her usual tape-recorded message from her brain. "My thesis is almost...."
"Poole that thesis is impossible." Lisa cut in. "I don't care how smart you are. It can't be done. Remember Cantor."
"I'll do it." she said bluntly. But the thought of Cantor always loomed in the back of her mind. And Lisa never failed to remind her of the brilliant mathematician who supposedly drove himself mad trying to discover infinity.
"Goodnight," Lisa smiled and walked off.
"I'll do it," she said to herself. Fuck Cantor. He just wasn't strong enough. He was a headcase too.
There was something different about Janet Poole. There always was. She had friends, in fact she had a lot. She went out, she partied, she got drunk, but there was a different part to her. Through high school and

college, and now graduate school, she was just different. A half hour left until the library closed.

The cold apartment made Janet shiver. She threw her keys on the nightstand. They slid off and hit the floor.

"Dammit," she didn't bother to pick them up. In the kitchen she fixed herself an amaretto sour and sipped it on the couch.

'Only you would work on a paper till 1:30 on a Friday night.' The ice clinked in her glass. Nothing moved in the apartment. The silence always irritated her, so she talked to herself. One bastard beam of lamplight stretched across her floor, barely illuminating her one-bedroom apartment.

II

"Hello," she groggily answered the phone.

"Janet, are you up?"

She looked at the clock. "Mom, it's 6:45."

"Are we still going to the grave?" Her mother asked undeterred about her comment.

Janet awoke as if a bucket of ice water was dumped on her face, as if she had been kicked in the ribs. She flipped the calendar on the nightstand. It read June 5th.

"Yes," she answered with no hint of sleepiness in her voice.

Tomorrow would be his birthday.

"I'm sorry to call you so early but I wanted to catch you. What time did you want to go?"

"Um, how about noon."

"Okay," her mother agreed. "Call me later."

"I will, bye mom."

"Bye Janet."

She looked at the clock again, 6:51. There was no way she could fall back to sleep. The sun broke into light slats on her bed sheet as it came through the blinds. She grabbed her towel from behind the door and stumbled to the shower.

'Once again, you're pathetic. Awake at 10 to 7 on a Saturday morning.' She said to herself. But truthfully, she could not fall back to sleep now. Tomorrow was his birthday. Every year on his birthday her mother and her always went to the grave.

The water beat on her head. It felt good.

'Might as well get some work done if I'm awake,' she always talked to herself. When you're alone most of the time, you get to know

yourself well. Sometimes too well. *'I'll go back to the library,'* she debated with herself.

She turned the water off and dried her hair. She put her eyeliner on, purple lip gloss. Her blond hair hung loosely across her slender shoulders. Perfume emanated. She walked into the living room and instinctively, almost subconsciously the picture of her and her father caught her eye. She was six years old and sat on her father's lap. Her chubby six-year-old face stared back at her slender 27-year-old face now, and it almost said, *'I have him; I'll have him forever, frozen in this picture like a Grecian urn.'*

She didn't stare long. The red light on her answering machine flashed like a dragon's eye. She scrunched her nose and pressed the message button.

"Hey Janet," she didn't have to hear the message. "Gimmie a call tonight." The disinterested voice said into the machine. "Bye."

He could wait. Strangely his voice angered but excited her at the same time. She didn't like him but liked having him around. When he was around, she wasn't alone. And he felt the same about her. Again, instinctively, she looked back at the picture of her father. She was never alone but alone all the time now.

III

"Can I help you ma'am?" The pharmacist called Janet to the desk.

"Hi. Um Poole, Janet. I dropped off my refill yesterday."

She hated this. The entire pharmaceutical staff knew she was nuts.

"Hold on one second ma'am." He returned a moment later holding her medicine, her salvation in an orange bottle.

"That will be 15 dollars."

She handed him the money.

"Thank you" she took the bottle of whatever pill it was now. But nonetheless they were her bible. They gave her peace. When she was young, she prayed every day, prayed to God for her father back. God didn't listen. Then the thoughts began. Horrible, uncontrollable thoughts that attacked like a lynch mob. Later they would be diagnosed as anxiety. But to her child's mind they were nothing short of hell. She prayed to God for them to stop but again, He didn't listen. So eventually, she said fuck him. She didn't need God. She shoved the bottle in her pocket. Her daddy always said she would be special.

"Where can I find a text on Archimedes and Pythagoras?"

The librarian gave her a puzzled look. "I'm sorry, what book were you looking for?"

"I am looking for two books, the first is *The Sand Reckoner*. It is by Archimedes. The second is *Fragments*, the writings of Pythagoras.

"Can you spell those names?" The librarian asked.

Janet spelled them out and the librarian looked for it in the card catalogue.

"Um, third floor, section 385.25."

"Thank you," Janet said as she headed to the stairs.

The smell of old carpet comforted her. She was in her own world of mathematics. It eased her like the medicine couldn't. Somehow, she felt the numbers were tied to her thoughts. Somehow mathematics could ease the thoughts that haunted her for her whole life.

She sat down at a table in the far corner and opened the book on Archimedes and silently read to herself.

'The question has been asked if all the sand in the world is of an infinite number.' Infinity. That word gave her a shudder.

*'Or, if the number is a finite number that can be represented. I intend to give a range for this astronomical number. '*Mr. Archimedes your sand grains don't come close to infinity. But it will make a good introduction. She thought to herself.

She then flipped the pages of Pythagoras.

Pythagoras and his followers grappled with the notion of the infinite because it challenged their conceptions of an orderly universe.

The number of sand grains in the universe didn't come close to infinity, and Mr. Pythagoras was too weak and stupid to follow it through. Just like Cantor. Janet Poole had been fascinated by this concept since her childhood. Since her father told her of God. The same God that didn't listen. Archimedes, Pythagoras, they all had a secret. They wanted to use numbers to infiltrate the finite universe.

They did not go far enough. She came to realize infinity had more power than God. God was a joke compared to infinity; infinity perhaps is the next stage of evolution.

'C'mon fellas, give me something to work with, some evidence,' she whispered to herself.

But they always left her in the same spot. Every single time. They left her with an improbable thesis. No, not improbable, just not enough evidence. She needed something more. Once again, she read her thesis out loud to herself, realizing the impossibility of her task.

'Infinity is a vast place, a stretch of universe uncharted by the human mind. Yet, the beginning of infinity surrounds us every day. Infinity

starts with the finite. Our own counting numbers, our two legs or ten fingers can start an unending torrent of numbers. The question is...is there an end?'

And that's where she drew a blank. She could start infinity but never finish it. Her brow ached. Maybe she should give up the thesis. Rational meaning becomes impossible; no human mind could conceptualize it. George Cantor tried, of course he was also bipolar. Pythagoras saw infinity as a threat. Janet reached into her pocket. The familiar apple rolled through her fingers. It kept her on task. The story of Maria Altendorpher and Paul Eckhart was her bedtime tale. And before he died, it passed to her.

She whispered the engraved numbers to herself. *'One, two, three...What did you want me to find dad? What did Maria discover?'*

She stared at her books like she had done so many times before and began to write the first letter of the Hebrew alphabet, the aleph. It was George Cantor's symbol for infinity.

'You're not gonna change the world today, Janet. Not today.' she whispered to herself and packed up.

"Hey Joe."

"Oh, hey Janet," He sounded distracted.

"Ah..." she trailed "Diner tomorrow?"

"Yeah," he replied unenthusiastically. "I'll get you at eight then?"

"Sure." she said. "Call me before you come."

"Okay I will. See you tomorrow."

"Okay bye." Janet hung up the phone. Another exciting date with Mr. Wrong. She poured herself an Amaretto.

IV

"I'll pick you up in ten minutes?" Her mother asked.

"Yes. I'll be ready."

She leaned back onto her couch. Every year at noon. She looked forward to it but at the same time dreaded it.

"I bought a nice arrangement of flowers," her mother said.

"Yeah, I like the tulips."

The emotion had been stripped from this day like an orange rind. Both women sat in silence. The flowers were more alive than them for one day of the year. They pulled up to the cemetery and Randi eased the car into park.

"Can you reach and get my basket in the back seat." Randi asked.

Both women silently approached the grave. Like the funeral procession all over again, like some sick rehearsal every year on June the 6th, both women stood in their own world of sorrow. Randi prayed. But Janet never prayed. Instead, she always remembered something she had read years ago. A poem by Sylvia Plath. And ever since then, she always recited it to herself when she stood over the grave.

Slowly the passages came back to her like a Hail Mary. "I never could talk to you. The tongue stuck in my jaw...I have always been scared of you..."

Yes, she was scared of her father. No, not scared but fascinated by his secret. And of course, she could never talk to him. "You died before I had time."

She never had time to ask him what he wanted her to know. Instead, she was left to decipher his secret.

"Daddy you can lie back now... Yes daddy, lie back. I will figure it out." She gently rubbed the apple in her pocket. "I will find it!"

Her mother gently took her hand.

"Do you want to get lunch?"

"Yes," Janet whispered. She didn't dare cry.

Neither of them spoke. It took a while for them to loosen up. In the awkward silence Janet could only think of the only thing she ever thought of. Obsessive-Compulsive thoughts raged inside. The ancients used to call them scruples. She called them hell. Did her father leave her with this? Or was this a chemical imbalance.?

"You are a special girl," her father's words echoed.

Yes, I am daddy. She saw numbers that didn't want to end, they laughed at her insanity, all the thoughts congealed in her skull. Dammit Daddy! What is it?

"What do you want to eat?" her mother reached for her hand as the thoughts stretched across Janet's brain and momentarily pulled her out.

"Um, I just want a sandwich."

"Okay we'll go to the deli."

"Sounds good. I think I'll get a turkey on wheat." Janet tried to sound normal. The thoughts subsided. At last, a welcome distraction.

V

His cologne diffused throughout the car. "Hey," he gave her a kiss on the cheek. "Dinner?"

"Yeah, that sounds good."

"I say we got loaded tonight."

Janet didn't need encouragement to get drunk. "Please let's; I got stuff to make Amaretto sours."

"Okay, I got some gin," he said.

"What did you do today?" the conversation was always forced, like someone held a gun to his mouth and forced the words to leave.

"Not much," she answered. "Worked on my grad paper and went out to lunch with my mom."

"Cool." he said disinterestedly.

Janet looked out the window and thought of the grave. Joe didn't deserve to know.

"I'll take a bacon cheeseburger and a miller light," he handed the menu to the waitress.

"I also got a bottle of Cuervo at my house." he said.

"That works."

She didn't like Joe. He bored her. And he could never understand her. But the sex became a welcome distraction, and the alcohol. She sipped her martini. They were temporary deterrents from the infinite madness. The one she lived with and the one she would always return to. But when they were used up, her empty gas tank screamed for something else.

His stubbly face scratched hers. But it didn't matter. His kisses were rough and forced but that didn't matter either.

"I want another shot!" she pushed his face away and poured the golden Cuervo and held up the glass.

"This shot is for..." she closed her eyes, held up the glass and involuntarily swayed. Joe began to slide his hand up her thigh.

"It's to my father... " she playfully slapped his hand away.

"Let me make a toast first." He began to kiss her arm.

"To my father who..." His hand slid to her crotch.

She looked at him. "Let me make a toast goddammit!" The alcohol always made her angry. Angry that her thesis was impossible, angry that she was lonely, angry that her father had died and left her with a horrible secret. Joe recoiled his hand and stared at her. she wanted him to be mad. She hated him, she used him. She wanted an excuse to hate him more. Scream at me! Hit me! Kick me out! Anything!

"I want to make a toast to my father. Today was his birthday."

"Oh," As Joe turned his head, Janet saw him roll his eyes. He turned back around and began to caress her again.

"Asshole!" she threw the Cuervo in his face. "Don't you ever speak about him like that! Ever!"

"First of all, you fucking bitch, I didn't say anything about your father. And you can get the fuck out of my house." He said all this without emotion. "I just wanted to fuck a smart bitch."

She smiled as she walked out the door.

VI

Of course, it had to rain. But she didn't care. She hated Joe. No, hate would mean she had an emotion toward him. The word was indifferent, she didn't care. He had nothing to offer her except a distraction. She stumbled back to her apartment.

The thoughts began again. The booze and medicine and sex stopped working. But infinity remained unaltered and untouched. She fiddled with the keys. The apartment door flung open, and she slammed it closed.

No more distractions.

'*Goddammit what is it!*' she stumbled over to the nightstand.

'*You died before I had time!*' Plath's words, spoken through her mouth. She grabbed the picture of her father and stared into her own six-year-old eyes. Her father's soft smile seemed on the verge of whispering his secret to her-like it always did.

'*Goddammit daddy!" One two three! What did you give me!*'

She squeezed the picture frame so hard it cracked. The shards sliced into her palm. Undeterred she pulled the picture closer until her mouth touched the glass.

'*I can't do this anymore!"* Again, Plath's words surfaced in her mouth like driftwood. '*Daddy. Daddy You bastard. I'm through.*'

She pulled out the replenished medicine from her purse. '*I'm through with this,*' she put all the pills in her mouth at once. The familiar chalk taste spread. The saliva pooled under her tongue, almost enough to swallow. That picture was taken the day her father told her the story of Adam and Eve. Why did she remember this? The pills began to dissolve. Oh, how sweet it would be! That sweet death would liberate her from the madness... Adam and Eve. The apple. It gleamed in the lamp light. One two three, infinite. She spit the pills out.

'*Apple...*' she whispered. The forbidden fruit.

She repeated the bible passages to herself.

'*And the lord cast Adam and Eve out of the garden because they had tasted the forbidden fruit from the tree of knowledge, they wanted to be like God.*'

Even with its dull finish, the apple sparkled.

'*It's not a symbol,*' she twirled it in the lamplight.

'*It's a warning!*' she said in awe. Maria Altendorpher passed down a secret and a warning. '*What daddy! What was she warning us about!*'

For all her G.P.A's and scholastic awards, SAT scores and straight A's and dean's list, she could not understand this. But they were only numbers! They were not what she needed. Her eyes closed and even though her father had been dead over twenty years, he could still teach her. '*Sometimes you have to use your imagination.*'

'*Daddy, daddy...*' she began to sob. She fell to the carpet with the apple and broken picture frame. '*A warning for what...*' her voice trailed.

VII

She woke up on the carpet. Instinctively she went for the aspirin. This was a routine. Another drunken night and another morning with a hangover. She didn't have sex but remembered a fight with Joe. She also remembered she had caused it and that she couldn't care less.

The sun hurt. She closed the blinds.

'*What did you do last night Janet?*' she said to herself.

The apple sparkled. Oh yes, now she remembered. The pills were in a pile on the floor. Probably another pretend suicide.

'*Oh Daddy,*' she whispered, '*What is it?*'

In the morning for just a few seconds after she awoke, there were always a few seconds of solace, a few moments where she didn't remember the thoughts, when she didn't miss her father. And now they returned. Her head throbbed and she wanted to vomit but then, like some awful sunrise ... it became clear.

Yes, the apple had been a warning. Eve took the apple because she wanted to be like God, but no one could be like God.

'*That's right sweetie,*' her father seemed to speak from the broken picture.

But like Paul Eckhart, Janet was forced to take the apple. She heeded no warning, forced by her own madness, she pushed further and explored this awful discovery. She lied inert, simply staring at her paper, trying to make sense of something, of anything. And then, after what seemed like centuries, like the slamming of gates with Eden still in view, she saw something. She half-raised her head.

'*Wait...*' she whispered. '*So simple...*' her words trailed in amazement. The simplicity became overbearing. Paradox is the atom of the infinite. Alpha is the Omega. Logic died here. Her thesis barely scratched the surface. She needed to go so much further.

Maria Altendorpher had discovered something that threatened humanity's precious sanity. That's why Hitler killed her. Janet understood. Maria gave her two choices- a secret and a warning. The apple told her to stop and not go through with this; it told her to forget this unknowable secret-it was not for her. But like Eve, she would sin, she would take the apple and be cast out in the garden, cast into an irrationality of some never-ending number. But Altendorpher had discovered... the last number.

Janet's head throbbed. She had used her imagination like her father told her. The last number? How could it be possible?

'*Tell me daddy! What is the last number!*' They all told her it was impossible. But she knew it, she used her imagination and not a calculator. Eva had tried to discover it too.

"The last number is God!" she shouted to her father. "The last number is that never-ending picture of us daddy! It's heaven and holocaust victims!"

Hitler killed Maria for it. Her father killed Paul Eckhart. And then her father died. And now she, a 28-year-old obsessive-compulsive grad student, knew the last number. She always knew it was never a number.

But it was forbidden! No one could be like God! But like the old crusty philosopher had said so long ago, '*God is dead.*'

'*I did it Daddy!*' she clutched the broken frame to her chest. A few blood drops stained her blouse.

Outside a car drove past her house. As she climbed up to the window, she saw a couple holding hands on the sidewalk. This early June day had been unseasonably warm. But Janet saw something different. Two legs, four wheels, one sun, everywhere she looked on this earth she could start counting. All the way to-

The last number.

Janet curled into the fetal position. She had discerned a pattern in the madness. Some type of hidden architecture of the last number. But she felt a peculiar foreboding. No, the last number was elusive, like a jellyfish. She had only begun.

'*One two three to God, to the last number. I did it daddy. I did it.*' she whispered. But suddenly, she felt sick. Vomit burned in her throat

and splattered on the carpet. Infinity was not a neat term like God or the last number. No, it was inconceivable to her feeble human brain. Not describable by words. It made scrap metal out of her G.P.A and Deans' lists.

The apartment had a pulse in tune with her heart. Slowly the walls expanded and contracted in this cardiovascular symphony. She curled up tighter. Infinity had numbered teeth, fraction jaws that left her partially digested. There was still more. So much more. Maria had known more. She lost her sanity and died for more.

"What else daddy? Goddammit! What else! Why did you curse me! What the fuck am I supposed to know!" she vomited again and passed out.

VIII

Janet rubbed her eyes. She'd been lying there for hours. She had a life that needed to be lived. But infinity beckoned like cocaine. It gave her a fix of the eternal. She remained prostrate, sprawled on the floor like a junkie. How could she ever live her life now, after she had a drop of infinity? How could the boring existence of amaretto sours hold meaning?

Eight pm and twilight sparkled in the apple.

But the delightful horror of infinity never ended. Instead, it extended as a geometric line into eternity, raping her. Straight lines never ended. It terrified but excited her like a car accident. Impossibility had been discovered. She reached her hand up towards the desk and felt for a notebook. She began her new thesis. An avalanche of papers and post-its rained down.

"I am surrounded by pockets of infinity." She shuttered. "Corners of walls extend forever. My own limbs start a number sequence that does not end. Infinity lurks as rapist, violating our consciousness. The last number is out there, under the logic, but it's not a number..." These were her words, this was the truth. And suddenly she was not alone.

"Daddy!" The hallucination of her father sat down on the floor. She knew he wasn't real but that was irrelevant. His fingers gently caressed his daughter's hair. He gave her the strength to finish what Maria Altendorpher had started over fifty years ago.

"I have discovered pockets of infinity within our finite world," she said. A slow terror overtook her. The pockets were everywhere. Everywhere! In the walls and tables, in the simplest arithmetic problems, even in the straight lines of her finger bones. She wasn't safe here.

'Daddy, you can save me! Please daddy you can protect me like when I was a little girl,' she whispered. *'Protect me from infinity! Please Daddy,*

the medicine doesn't work anymore!'

The hallucination of her father looked at her a long time before he spoke. "No sweetie, not yet. You still have more to do."

"Daddy! Please! I want to live with you! We can live together forever!" she stared at the corner of the wall and watched it extend through her father's dead heart. "I found it like you said I would and now I'm tired of this! Please!"

He moved closer to her.

"Sweetie. Now you need to understand."

"Daddy please! I can't!"

"Sweetie, you have always known."

She wiped her eyes. "I don't understand!"

He spoke in that gentle voice which always soothed her. Her head throbbed like a second heartbeat. The vomit swelled as a tidal wave in her throat. Infinity sickened her, but she needed to be strong. Gently, she touched the corner of the wall. It filled her with terror and joy; it filled her like nothing she had ever known before.

"Trace the pockets and they will lead you to..." she whispered to herself. And suddenly, as if it were spring, she saw infinity sprout. The lines and corners in the wall extended throughout her apartment. But they soon twisted into gas chambers somewhere in the universe, endless sequences of numbers wrapped around her neck like Gestapo hands.

"To the last number." She pulled herself up to her desk. She put her notebook on the now empty desk and began to write.

"The pockets lead to the last number..." Her eyes burned from tears, but she kept writing. She had no choice "And the last number is..." She pounded the desk in frustration. She knew but could not write it.

"C'mon sweetie, you know it," her father held her hand.

She gripped the pen so tight in her palms that it re-opened the wounds. She could barely breathe; her entire existence would be written into her next few sentences. She thought harder.

"The last number is not a number," she almost collapsed out of her chair "it's not meant to be counted. It's a virus. It's a rapist," she choked. Pills, sex, grad school and Amaretto Sours were useless.

"It is the forbidden fruit." No matter how high she counted, she only found holocausts and crucifixes, extending into forever. Clutching the paper, she was alone again. Her father had vanished, ebbed back into the ocean of her psyche.

"Daddy, protect me, save me from this!" But he was dead.

The apple glared as the eye of an unpleased God. She had disobeyed. All that remained for her was the delightful rape of infinity.

Part IV

I

2006, Western New York

Every time he blinked a tear of sweat pooled in his lashes. He felt the beads run down his nose and drip into his mouth. His armpits and forehead were saturated, and a strong vinegary odor rose from his shirt. He looked at his hands and then down at his chest, then back to his hands again. The shirt felt like a second skin, he peeled it repeatedly futilely, knowing it would only stick keep sticking. His hands glistened in the sunlight. He wiped his eye sockets only to have them fill up again. He tore his shirt off and slid out of his pants. But it didn't matter, even without the second skin, the perspiration continued. Slowly he lowered himself to his knees and put his hands together. He did not believe in God, but for some reason, he remembered the words to the Lord's prayer he had recited as a child.

"Our Father..." he croaked out, but the fear and the guilt did not subside, they only augmented, his stomach twisted like tin foil.

"Who art in heaven..." prayer was always the last option. By this time, it usually was too late to do anything else. The words sounded like a eulogy as he spoke.

"Hallowed be thy name...," thy kingdom come? He wanted the kingdom to come right now, like a fucking train engine hurled from the moon, please let the kingdom be done right now! Smash the useless world around John Spinoza, Jesus come down with that train and break his neck he thought, anything to alleviate ... *This*

The sun rose like it had for centuries. Lately he rose before it, just a minute or two before, covered in sweat, and most of the time, like today, wishing for Jesus to hurl a train.

II

"Okay ma'am if you sign here and here- "John slid the paper over the table. The plump woman, in her mid to late forties, smelled faintly of cigarettes, As John watched her sign the papers he noticed the lines in her hand. Deep grooves stretched across her skin as tiny spider webs. A few freckles spotted each knuckle and, in the light, he saw the beginnings of a yellow nicotine stain between her index and middle finger.

"Okay Mrs. Tarbarini, now this new account will have increased interest and will yield a higher profit than the previous account. However, there are stricter penalties for overdrafts, as well as an account minimum." He handed her a packet. She hastily took it from him and rose from her seat. John rose with her and extended his hand. She hurriedly shook his hand, gathered her things, and left the office.

John sat back down. He let out an exasperated sigh.

"Five o'clock," he said to himself. "Finally."

"Hey you," John's co-worker, Elaine. walked over to his desk. "What's up?"

"Casino tonight?" she asked.

"Yeah, I'm going. What time is everyone meeting?" He wiped his forehead, and Elaine noticed his saturated hand as he quickly stuck it in his pocket.

"Um...I think around eight," she said. "You look a little stressed; you okay?"

"Just a long Friday." He said "And very rude people. Oh well."

"Oh well," she smiled. "I'll see you tonight."

John gathered his things and left. As he opened the door, a snow gust stung him. And the sudden urge to scream with a tightening in the stomach. But he composed himself. Even in sub-degree temperatures, a small bead of sweat formed on his forehead.

"Whose driving?"

"Um...I'll drive, you drove last time."

"Okay cool, what time are you gonna be here?"

Mike hesitated for a moment. "Around quarter to eight." He said into the phone.

"Okay." Said John. "See you in an hour." He had an hour. An hour. Would that be enough time? Maybe he could hide in the casino, among the throng of people, but not here, not alone in his apartment. The dirty sofa would give him up for sure. Images became oceans of color, tidal waves among his couch that crushed his ribcage. Trapped under the swell, he saw pieces of his furniture floating by. No. He was fine. The feeling would ebb and recede. It would leave him twisted like driftwood on some beach, but ready at 8:15 pm.

III

At a Mental Institution in Western N.Y.

Janet Poole sipped her water. The plastic cup crinkled where she bit down on it. She bit it until her teeth hit her lips. But she kept biting, making her lip bleed. It would end like this, in here. She held the cup to the moonlight. The cracks where she had bitten looked like animal teeth marks. She wanted it to be over. But it was Tuesday night. Brook would be here soon. At least when she was there the pain subsided just a little, a youthful energy rejuvenated her. Like clockwork, her niece opened the door.

"Aunt Janet," she walked over to her aunt and gave her a kiss on the cheek.

"Hello," Janet said softly.

"I brought you the macaroons you like," Brook handed her aunt the box. "Did you sleep at all?"

"A little." Said Janet, "You know I don't sleep much."

"Are they still bad?" Brook pointed to her aunt's head.

"They come and go," Janet gave her niece a faint smile.

"I brought you some books too," Brook reached into her bag and handed her two hard cover novels. She looked good for her mid-sixties. She had slight crow's feet indentations in the corners of her eyes; lines of age stretched across her cheeks but there was still youthfulness to her. But it was a youth she had been robbed of, a youth she never really got to enjoy. Janet's auburn hair turned grey before it should have.

"How was traffic?" Janet asked.

"It wasn't too bad. It didn't take me too long to get here, just some normal rush hour congestion by the bridge."

Janet propped herself up. "How is your thesis going?" she asked.

"It's almost done." Brook said. She pulled a chair over to the bedside. "I wanted to thank you again for talking to me about it." Brook crossed her legs and then uncrossed them; sentimentality always made her uncomfortable.

"It is nice talking to you. I hope my information helped."

"Yeah, I have to write a few more journal entries, then I can put everything together."

Janet lay back and stared out the window. She watched the snow gusts in the moonlight. She enjoyed being a help to her niece. Even if it meant bringing it up.

"Can you answer a few questions?" Brook asked. "Do you feel up to it? If you do, I can finally finish this and stop bothering you."

"Yes," Janet said proudly. "And you're not a bother."

"Okay," Brook opened her notebook. "Basically, I just have one final topic for my paper. It focuses on the aspect of mind and body. Right now, you look healthy. We have intelligent and coherent conversations." She paused for a moment. "So, what is it? I mean what makes you..." she couldn't say it.

"Insane?" Janet gave her niece a slight smile. She only smiled to put her at ease.

"Well, for one thing I am a good faker. Even before I committed myself, I always could pretend to be sane. I paid my rent, got good grades, went around with guys..." she grinned "I could always put on a front." Brook returned her aunt's sly grin at the mention of guys.

"How did you do that?" asked Brook. "Why couldn't you believe what you pretended?"

"It's not what you show to the world but what you think about the world." Janet cringed. "It's not what do during the day but the thoughts you go to bed with..." Janet's skin reddened. She became choked-up and hesitated for a moment. Brook sat quietly.

"It is the thoughts that separate..." she blinked hard.

"It's the thoughts that make me, that can make a person, insane." The word sounded evil.

"Thoughts?" Brook asked.

"Thoughts are all I can say, it is all you will understand." Janet said without looking at her niece.

Janet sensed awkwardness. "If you don't want to say anymore..."

"Apples and infinity," Janet blurted out.

Brook was perplexed but not surprised. She had grown used to her aunt's seemingly random ideas.

"The apple," Janet reached into her nightstand and held the object. "I tried to find the last number..."

A small vein pushed under her forehead. Sentences became fragments. Brook knew she shouldn't have asked. But she wanted to finish this. And something in her aunt's story that intrigued her almost haunted her.

"The last number...it poisoned me, it wasn't a number, it was a thing, but all I have left from it are thoughts, numbers and lines that never end, of infinity..." she began to cry.

"Okay, it's okay. I'm sorry, I shouldn't be asking you these questions."

"No," Janet wiped her face "You need to know these things. Besides, I can't die with all this shit."

"You won't," Brook hugged her aunt. This was wrong and she felt bad as if she only used her aunt. It wasn't true. Over the past few months, they had grown especially close. Her aunt's illness became her illness in a way. They almost suffered together.

The vein twisted out of Janet's forehead.

No, they did not suffer together. Brook only observed it. But no one could truly know what Janet suffered.

"I've seen the last number..." Janet's vein almost broke the skin. Janet became frenzied. "But that's impossible! It can't exist!" She squeezed the porcelain apple until it cut her palm.

"Please stop, stop, it's okay..." Brook gently swayed, rocking her aunt like a baby. She had never seen her aunt get so upset. Janet finally calmed down but sobbed on Brook's sweater. She waited a long time to speak again. Slowly, she picked up her head and looked her niece in the eye.

"I found it. I found the last number. Just like Maria. I took the apple. I saw infinity. It..." she stammered "it is a nightmare, an endless holocaust, killing anyone who dares to know!" she plunged her head down into her niece's chest. A nurse opened the door, but Brook gestured that everything was fine.

"I'm sorry; I shouldn't do this to you." Aunt and niece remained motionless, consoling each other.

"No, it's good, it puts me to some good use," Janet said with a grin. She still trembled but Brook could see that she had relaxed a little.

"Stop it. Please don't talk like that." Brook cradled her aunt's head.

"I would like to read it when it's done." Janet said firmly.

Brook shot her a cautious look, but Janet spoke before she could protest.

"I deserve to see it."

Brook had no argument to that.

"Of course." She said finally, hesitantly. Then she spoke again. "Listen," she began awkwardly "I don't ever want you to think I just use you as a resource or..."

"Stop," Janet smiled with red eyes. "I know you don't. I like to help." And as if there was nothing, as if she hadn't been crying or insane, she talked of something else. "Do you want some tea?"

"Actually, I would, do you have that lemon kind?" Brook asked.

"Yes, I do." Janet said. "Why don't you fill up the pot and I'll get the tea." Janet took out a small box and Brook walked over to the sink.

"And let's eat the cookies you brought." Janet said as she poured the water.

IV

Intricate patterns danced in the bulbs. Arrow and word filaments blinked. John strode at the entrance of the casino like it was a new and brighter Eden.

"Big money! Double down!" Mike said as he pushed open the door. A haze of cigarette smoke greeted the men as they walked into the casino. Mike searched the crowd for his co-workers. He spotted Elaine by the slots. A few drops of martini sloshed onto the side of the cup as she walked over to them.

"I won sixty bucks!" She yelled drunkenly.

"But I spent it all on drinks," she took a sip of her martini.

"What took you guys so long to get here? It's past nine." She gave them an exaggerated frown.

"Fashionably late." Mike grinned.

"Okay Mr. Popular, over here," Elaine gestured with her thumb. She stood up with effort. "Time to lose more money," she walked over to some of her other co-workers at a blackjack table. John drifted off to a nearby craps table. He looked amongst the throng of people and suddenly felt ... Stranded.

As if all the sound in the world weaned and fell mute, remaining was the thong of people who flapped their mouths uselessly, skin flaps randomly fluttered in front of teeth in all directions.

"Bets down," the dealer's hoarse but methodical voice dragged him back. Mechanically he shuffled the cards, Jacks and Queens, aces, jokers, they flashed randomly, red, and black, twos and fours, threes, fives tens, twenty-five-dollar chips, two ice cubes clinked in a scotch glass.

"Sevens," the dealer said methodically.

John laid down another chip and the symphony began again. Content laughs of drunk women, clacking chips, sucking, and shuffling of plastic-coated cards, ten-dollar bills, twenty, fifty, hundred-dollar bills, the ring, whoosh and ring of the slots, slot bells...

It became too loud.

Stranded in noise-

"Sir..."

Cigarette smoke and dirty carpets, coins pouring into metal tins, white teeth, fake jewelry...

"Sir, your bet please." The dealer said, obviously irritated.

"Oh, sorry," John responded sheepishly.

And then as expected, fifty dollars lost, five fingers empty, grasping another chip, melted ice cubes, a suffering cigarette that died in an ashtray, extinguished,

And that was him, a suffering cigarette being put out in the casino ashtray, extinguished.

"Hey," a voice startled him out. A woman sat down next to him.

"Hi," he gradually drifted back.

"Win anything tonight?"

He glanced at the woman and noticed her already short skirt hiked up a bit. Her creamy white leg glowed under the table, and he had the urge to run his hand over that soft skin.

"I'm two fifty in the hole," she said. "And I am going to win it all back with this throw right now." She put down her last chip.

"With that throw, huh?" John smiled.

"Damn right. This is my lucky chip. I guarantee this chip..."

"Fuck!" she knocked back the last of her scotch. "Oh well, not gonna win anything tonight, but I am going to get another scotch."

John watched her blond hair dangle on her shoulder. From the corner of his eye, he saw Mike pounding the blackjack table. A little further away, Elaine stumbled to the bar.

"John Spinoza," he extended his hand, almost instinctively.

"Karen Eppi," she shook his hand.

"I'm down a hundred myself," he said.

Her skin began to pull him away from the distractions, chings, bells, coins in metal trays, that same stupid drunken laugh, a river of glistening sweat, coins, soft plastic cards tapping the felt ... Could he tell her all this? No, instead he let it disappear.

"You're a strange one," she smiled.

"Excuse me?" he said with a bemused grin. "And you're a forward one."

"You seem to be in la-la land."

"Just got a lot on my mind" he smiled.

"Want to get a drink at the bar?" she asked.

"Sure."

He walked with this stranger named Karen to the bar.

Her breasts bubbled out of the top of her blouse, pushed together, advertised for sex, sweating sex with scotch, soft breasts glistening in the artificial lamp glow.

Just like his bank account number. How the hell could he think of his job at a time like this?

"Do you live around here?" she asked.

"About a half hour away, what about you?"

"I live a few miles down the road. I have a tiny shit hole apartment." Her red lips curved into a grin.

"Like I said, you are a forward one."

"Hey, I tell it like it is," she held his hand.

"What do you do?" she asked.

"I work for a bank" he answered.

"Ohh a banker," she rolled her eyes. And John couldn't help but admire her spunk.

"And you?"

"I am an executive production assistant," she smiled proudly.

"A what?"

"I manage the Macy's in the mall." Her grin widened.

"You are a riot," he said.

"Yeah, I hear that a lot." She finished her scotch. "Okay what do you say we try to win back that money?" Before he had time to respond, she grabbed his wrist and pulled him back into the forest of coins and human sweat.

V

All her journals were spread on the floor. This was her Friday night. Spent with psychology journals instead of friends-instead of a man. But in a strange way they comforted her like those things which she lacked were unable to do. She glanced over the words, analytic, subconscious, Freudian and they excited her, pathetic as it was. As a child when she visited her aunt for the first time, she felt a strange sensation. She felt *'a something else'* that her aunt was a part of. Something irreconcilable to Brook's sheltered world. She didn't know why her aunt was in a hospital; she didn't look sick. But as she grew older, she understood the meaning of sick. Sick was not just throwing up and staying home from school. Your head could be sick as well, like Aunt Janet's. It wasn't until she was nine years old that she felt the full force of that something else that only Aunt Janet was privy to. Little Brook held her mother's hand. With her other hand she grasped her favorite teddy bear. Mom and Aunt Janet talked like they usually did, of family and new books when, suddenly Aunt Janet's face stiffened.

She began to twist. A vein tightened her neck. Her fingers dug into the bed linen, and little Janet noticed the rug burn on the fingertips. Her back arched and she began to scream. Finally, the nurses and orderlies came in, but Janet continued to scream herself hoarse until her vocal cords were ready to rip, she kept repeating- "I've seen it!"

And then, it stopped.

She overheard the nurses talking later on. They said, "something must have set her off." It was Brook's first encounter with this something else, which she would later learn was called insanity.

Yes, her aunt was insane. But insane was only a word. But to Janet, it was a *world*. A world that existed alongside her own orderly world. Sixteen years later, she was writing her thesis on sensory experience and the function of the mind. Her notes were scattered everywhere; bits of information were scribbled in the red margins of papers. Textbooks and case studies were open to specific pages. She knew almost all her books by heart. She rummaged through the pile to find a particular paper. "Got it," she whispered triumphantly to herself.

The paper was barely legible, but she knew it would be the bread and butter of her thesis. She read the terms out loud like she always did, to let them sink into her memory.

"The notion of the human mind possessing certain innate ideas at birth has been debated for centuries."

Innate ideas. The thought still fascinated her. Could a human be born with innate ideas, ideas that already existed in the brain? If so, did they figure into mental illnesses like in the case of her aunt? She needed to narrow down her topic considerably and concentrate on one aspect, these were only the preliminary stages, but those topics were endless to her. If the mind did have innate ideas who put them there? And why?

She had studied a plethora of philosophy as well and she was inclined to agree with the German philosopher Immanuel Kant's assessment. She believed that maybe humans weren't born with innate ideas, but rather that the human mind was "programmed" in certain fashion. She quietly read her scribbled notes. *Programmed with space and time.*

Perhaps the mind was pre-programmed from birth to perceive the world with space and time. From those conceptions, then maybe the mind constructs its own useable universe, or maybe space and time were just stories we told ourselves. She remembered reading somewhere that stories were like the atoms of the universe, maybe space and time were the tales we invented to make the universe more tolerable. Stories of an ending, which masked infinity.

She had hoped that by becoming an abnormal clinical psychologist she could more easily understand the mind, but as she studied, and she probed further, she only encountered more difficult questions and impossible solutions. Why bother with space and time? Why exist? Sometimes she hated all this shit and agreed with Rousseau that-people should give up philosophy and become shepherds.

"C'mon guys, gimmie something," she said to herself. Time. Space. Notions that people take for granted. Yet she wanted to expose them, analyze them and then... and then what? What else could she do after that?

"Brng! Brng!" The phone interrupted her thoughts. She reached over and hit 'talk'.

"Hey mom," but even before her mother responded, Brook already knew the conversation, like it was on tape.

"It's Friday night" her mother began. Go out, do something, don't tell me you're staying home again..."

But Brook cut her off before she went anything further. "Stop. You know how much work I have to do."

"It's Friday. Take some time off. You can't be that busy. Please, don't be a hermit."

"I saw Aunt Janet today," Brook said, changing the subject.

Reluctantly her mother asked. "Oh." Her tone flattened. "How did she look?"

"Good. We drank tea, talked a while..."

"I haven't been up there this week; I'd like to go on Sunday."

"Call me if you do." Brook said.

"You want to go again?" her mother asked.

There followed a long silence on the phone. Nothing had to be said but Brook knew exactly what it meant.

"Mom Stop it!" she didn't want to yell.

"I'm just worried!" Her mother retorted. "I am still your mother, and I can still worry about you!"

"Look, I'm sorry for yelling. But I hate it when you insinuate that. I'm the sane one, remember? I'm trying to help the insane, not become one."

"If you see something too much..."

But Brook cut her off "I know. You become one. It's like telling a cop he'll become a criminal."

"No. It's different. Never mind. I'll call you this weekend."

"Okay, Goodbye."

Brook returned to her notes. She poured herself a beer. The gold bubbles rose and popped, rose, and streamed up to the surface and popped as tiny tarps.

She repeated the terms over to herself.

Time. Space.

Humans inhabit and occupy space. We live in space; we use it to think. She leaned back on the sofa and tried to envision a world without space.

Space. The space in her apartment, from wall to wall, between the thin film of beer bubbles there was space. In between teeth and atoms, between the moon and her aunt. She, Brook Oliver, occupied a certain space. But what if she didn't have to? What if over there was over here? And this "necessary" space merely separated her from her own heart?

A methodical tick from her Mickey Mouse clock echoed, it passed seconds, each tick, each tick, tick, tick, she was 24 years old-

24 years had passed since her birth,

A trillion years from the creation of the universe (in space) and so each tick left her one second removed, further from the birth moment, heading toward,

She closed her eyes.

Heading toward-...

What?

Where was time bringing her?

Did it tick the world into hell? Or maybe closer to some other creation, some better creation? She hated to admit it, but sometimes she thought her mother was right. As if someone turned the lenses, she came into focus.

The scattered papers returned on her floor. Space and time became necessary again. Programmed and required for her mind to function. She took another sip. The alcohol made the world real; made it settle into place like her butt on the sofa. She began to write.

VI

"How many is that for you?" she asked.

John finished the last of his beer. "I believe that makes nine beers and two scotches." He said proudly.

"You don't even look drunk," Karen swayed on the bar stool. Her eyes looked like depressed tongues.

"I'm buzzed," John lied. He was hammered but didn't show it.

"Well," Karen spun her stool around and lodged her knees into the side of John's thigh. She leaned close, and he felt her hot breath on his eye.

"I got a secret," she whispered.

"Yeah," he turned his head to face her. "What's that?"

"I think," she licked the corner of her mouth, "you're hot."

Her lips took him by surprise; they were soft and warm against his. It only lasted a few seconds, but when she pulled her face away, he saw a drunken smile. She wanted more.

"How 'bout another beer?" she ordered two more.

John contently surveyed the bar. Out in the casino he saw Elaine, sloppy drunk, losing money at the blackjack table. Mike was at the craps table, furiously throwing the dice. Karen put the money down for drinks. Her hand drifted towards John's leg. She smiled at him. John smelled alcohol and spearmint. Her breasts pushed over the top of her shirt, the tops were cleaving over and tempting. Her lips were fluffy and warm; skin poured like cream onto delicate bones.

Did you drive here?" She asked him in slurred words.

"No, you?" John asked.

"We can take a cab. I live about five minutes from here. I rode with some of my girlfriends."

He noticed how she subtly invited him to her place. He was going to get laid.

"Do you live alone?" he asked her casually.

"I have a roommate but she's in Boston this weekend."

A quarter of her beer remained and about half of his. He chugged it in one short gulp. She followed behind him.

"Want to go?" she took his hand and led him before he answered.

"I just got to tell my buddy that I'm leaving."

"Okay," she said, "I'll get the cab."

John sifted through the crowd of people, bustling through alleyways which collapsed after he squeezed past. He reached the craps table. Mike didn't notice him.

"I'm leaving." Mike didn't respond.

"I'm leaving." He repeated but this time gave Mike a hard shove in the ribs.

"Geez! Okay man!" Mike said irritated. "Who are you going with?"

John pointed across the room to Karen. "That blond chick over there."

Mike smiled. "Good job buddy, call me tomorrow let me know how it goes."

"Of course.... Later bro." John made his way through the crowd. But as he elbowed though, he began to sweat. Beads pooled in his eyes. He blinked furiously but it irritated him more. He stopped in front of a woman with a pink dress. Her hair looked like little sausages dangling from her bowling ball shaped head. She reeked of body odor. John tried to go left but the woman jumped because she won a big hand. Her arms flailed in excitement.

"Harry, I won! Harry! Harry!"

Her husband, presumably, stood next to her. He was much smaller. The fluorescent light refracted off his bald head except for the few spotted patches of hair. His glasses slipped on the bridge of his nose. John tried to maneuver to the right this time, but she reached to grab a cocktail from a nearby waitress. The same tidal wave from before swelled in him, the woman became a hippo. He was paralyzed by this massive thing. The light clack of coins formed a wretched symphony and he, John Spinoza, had to listen, the hippo would not let him leave. He wasn't supposed to feel this in the casino. The casino was meant as distraction. A distraction of what he did not know. Flesh was all he knew, the wrinkled, oily flesh of the hippo. Sweat pooled in the fat folds behind her neck. He was not supposed to feel this now, only when he was alone-

"Excuse me!" he shoved past the hippo so that she gave him a dirty look. But she soon forgot this when her husband won another big hand.

"You ready?" Karen surprised him. She put her hands on his sides. And he wanted to fuck her right there, in the middle of the casino, tear her clothes off and expose those huge breasts, he wanted her to cleanse the awful stench of the hippo, but even if he fucked Karen he would still sweat,

"Cab's here," she gently led him to the open door. "Thirty Fifth and Seals Road." They didn't talk on the ride to her apartment. Instead, she slowly slid her hand into his crotch.

VII

Karen's hand had been on his cock since the cab ride. As they stumbled into her apartment, she undressed. It looked like a crime scene. Bras and panties were indiscriminately scattered on the floor. As he kissed her breasts he caught a whiff of her perfume. And finally, the tidal wave receded a bit. The fat hippo reluctantly began to walk away in his thoughts. He firmly squeezed her and kissed down to her stomach. Her skin rolled in his fingers like cream, he felt her, smelled her perfume, tasted that cream skin, but all the while there was:

A noise.

A faint repetitive clicking, through the kisses and moans.

Something was ticking; yes, it ticked.

A cold metallic sensation brushed against his ear, it was her watch, and it ticked as she straddled him, as he sweat, it ticked, ticked as their bodies interwove like tapestries to hang in reality for this one moment, the sweat would make them slide off the wall-

"Oh My God!" she yelled.

The sex ended.

But there was still that ticking.

"Oh my god! That was amazing!" she rolled over onto her back.

Spinoza stared at the ceiling. He lay in sweat and the feeling returned. He was dissatisfied. Not with Karen but with something. Her heartbeat but that wasn't it, it was that her heartbeat within the open space of her chest.

"So, are we gonna do this again? Karen lit a cigarette and smiled at John. "I usually don't do this but wow, "she shook her head "it was great."

He wanted to roll his eyes but smiled instead. In the moonlight the shape of her breast protruded. It felt good to alleviate, to forget, even for a few moments, but as she laid back down, he felt it. It. Jesus in the closet, waiting to yell surprise, life's a joke! You're going to hell! Karen cuddled up with a pillow and closed her eyes. And, any minute, John expected a butcher to crawl from under the bed and hack his bones and lungs, then stomp, stomp on it, push it together, and eliminate the spaces-

"Are you going to bed?" he asked. No butchers. No Jesus. Just Karen.

"Yeah, you gave me a workout," she smiled and rolled back over. He lay down, still unsatisfied and fell into a restless sleep.

VIII

A 3 a.m. moon was no friend to Janet Poole. It never had been. Instead, it became an interrogation lamp. An unforgiving light bent on her, forced her to give up the secrets and thoughts which tormented her. And the stars were eyes, silent but expecting, an audience of eyes that watched the drama, watched the thought exorcised in the hospital room.

"Please...God..." was all she could choke out between the sobs "Make it...go away." But the exorcism commenced, vivid remembrances of that night elbowed their way to the top of her memory. Janet curled into the fetal position.

"I...see...the...end, but that's impossible. There is no end there is only..." Plus, one, plus one, plus one."

She remembered the night when her dead father spoke to her,

she remembered seeing infinity bloom, lines in the furniture continued endlessly, she counted limbs, one, two, three, four and it started... Infinity.

Every atom and hair on her flesh began the madness, lines from her notebook paper extended as a devil horn and somewhere in the universe they twisted into a gas chamber. The last number was a joke, but she didn't laugh. She only saw something that could not end. She only always saw... One more body, one more fucking number.

"Go away..." but her voice was too feeble. Clutched in her palm was that God forsaken apple. It was a warning. A forbidden fruit.

"Do not enter this garden," it said, "do not attempt to eat the fruit of infinity. It is not an apple but a human head, bite the nose and feel the warm blood rush down its endless lines, veins of notebook lines..."

Goddamit! No! It was only a porcelain apple! A piece of rock! And infinity was only an idea, not an actual place! She should have done something with her life, put her knowledge to some good use, instead she wasted it on this idea of infinity, this awful meaningless idea...

But there was redemption.

Brook would be the savior. She was practical. She wouldn't waste her energy on a fantasy but instead channel it into psychology. She used her knowledge to help people, not to discover a meaningless idea. She would be Brook's case study, her source of information. Her madness could help Brook understand. Somewhat satisfied, she lay back on the pillow, with the faceless nose of forbidden fruit in her mouth. As the blood washed down the straight lines of her mattress, she finally slept.

IX
Saturday Morning

Brook arranged her note cards in a discernable order. She hadn't made much progress last night. Instead of a beer, she poured herself an orange juice. She sat back on the couch, like she had done the night before, and like the night before, she still felt alone.

The phone rang like a life preserver.

"Hi," her mother's voice threw a line to her.

"Hey mom," even though they disagreed it was nice to hear another voice besides her own.

"Do you want to go today?" her mother asked pleasantly, as if the argument the last night hadn't happened.

"What time do you want to go?" she asked.

"I was going to go around noon. Do you want me to pick you up?"

Her mother asked.

"Yeah that would be perfect."

"And then afterwards we can do lunch?"

"Let's try that new deli across the street. The Italian place."

"Okay," Courtney said to her daughter. "I'll be there soon."

"I'm gonna take a shower, see you in a bit," she hung up the phone. A warm bagel smell diffused through the apartment. Condensation spread like spider webs on the windows. Brook walked with her bagel to the couch and heard a barely audible creak of floorboards.

"Shit." A purple bruise began to form from where she banged onto the table and the bagel fluttered helplessly to the floor. Cream cheese stuck in the carpet fibers.

"Klutz," She muttered. Her knee throbbed. As she looked around her apartment, she never realized how small it was.

"Hey you." Courtney reached over the metal girder of the hospital bed and hugged her sister.

"How are you guys?" Janet smiled.

Brook felt awkward, awkward like a fart in church, watching her aunt, standing over her, condemning her to this institution.

"Brook, would you like some of that tea? Courtney, you should have it too. It is really good."

The two sisters involuntarily stared each other down. The sane one pitted against the freak, like an old western showdown. The one with a family and one with only her hospital bed. And Brook became the spectator.

"Can you get the tea ready?" Her mother called to her. Brook nodded and began to microwave the water.

Courtney settled into the chair as Brook prepared the tea.

"Listen," as Janet sat up the sheets ruffled and pulled off one corner. She didn't notice.

"I want to discuss my will with you to here."

Courtney shot her sister a look of disgust before speaking.

"Absolutely not," she sounded more like a mother than a sister. "You are physically healthy and hopefully in time you may actually leave this place and live a normal life."

"A normal life." Janet gave a scornful laugh and shook her head. It seemed as if she was having a conversation with herself before she spoke to her sister. "It's never too early to think about a will. I just want to be certain..."

"What kind of attitude is that?" she cut her off. Courtney became agitated. Brook became a bystander.

"Let's face it, without the mind..."

"Stop! Just stop it! It's a ploy! You want everyone to feel sorry for you! Well, I don't! You refuse to get better!"

Janet lay back on her pillow in defeat. Courtney stood smugly over her; sanity had triumphed again. But Brook did not think it was a ploy. She looked into her aunt's eyes and saw something. She had seen plenty of her case studies, but her aunt was different. In her aunt she saw madness. Not some lunatic like in a movie, but a concentrated madness, madness with a purpose.

"You're being irrational." Janet said bluntly.

Brook wanted to laugh but remained quiet. She was the only one who saw the irony of a mental patient calling a sane woman "irrational."

"I want to talk about it." Janet composed herself.

"Well, you can discuss it with her." Courtney walked out of the room.

Brook set the tray down and handed her aunt a cup.

"Please," she placed her hand on Brook's. "Please listen to me."

Brook pulled a chair up to the bed.

"I'm not well. I can't go on like this."

Brook's eyes opened in terror. "What are you trying to say..."

"I don't mean that," Janet sat back and gave her niece a slight grin. "I just don't know how much longer I can live with this," she shuttered. "With these thoughts," The look in her expression was unmistakable, she became agitated. "With..."

"Calm down, don't do this," she squeezed her aunt's hand.

Janet took a breath and composed herself. "I just want to make sure that when I'm gone, everything will be taken care of."

"Okay," Brook said.

"I want you to go to the bank and just make sure that my will is set."

"Wait," Brook smiled. "You've already done the will?"

Janet smiled back at her. "I'm insane, not stupid."

"But what do you have, I mean you've been here for almost 15 years?"

Janet gave a chuckle. "I didn't win the lotto or anything, but I have some things that are important to me, that I want to make sure wind up with the right people."

"You're definitely not stupid." Brook smiled. "What do you want me to do?"

"BB and T bank." She scribbled the directions on a piece of paper. "I've taken care of everything by phone but they need a representative to sign for it. They might give you a little hassle, so just make sure you have two forms of I.D."

Brook nodded her head but then shot her aunt a curious look. "Wait, you have everything set for me to sign?"

"I made you the main beneficiary."

"Really? Why"

"Well, don't get your hopes up, I don't have much money." Janet smiled.

"I still feel weird talking about this" Brook gazed absent-mindedly out the window at some passing traffic.

"Well don't." Janet said, "We all have to die," she said pleasantly, "I just wanted to make sure everything is set."

"Okay, just let me know what I have to do."

Janet handed her niece a card with the information on it. And then, they didn't speak about it anymore. Brook put the card in her pocket, and they spoke about life. They talked as if Janet were normal and only knew normal things her whole life. They laughed and joked. They watched television and dozed off. A few minutes after they dozed off. Courtney entered the room. Brook awoke with a slight startle.

"Mom! You scared me."

"Looks like you fell asleep."

"We dozed off. How long were you gone?"

"About twenty minutes. I got a coffee. Do you want to get going?"

"Yeah, I'm hungry," Brook got her stuff together and hugged Janet.

When Courtney re-entered the room, she had caught both of them sleeping. She gazed at her sister and her daughter, just for a few moments, and couldn't help but feel as if she were the outsider.

X

"What happened to you on Friday?" Elaine walked over to John's desk. He rubbed his eyes.

"I wasn't winning, so I left." he grinned at her.

"That's not what I heard," she widened her eyes. "I heard you left with someone," she gave John a devilish expression. "But it was probably better than my night, the only action I got was puking in the parking lot."

"You were pretty drunk when I last saw you," He rubbed his face and the stubble from his five-day old beard left short red track marks on the back of his hand.

Mike walked over with a cup of coffee. A drop sloshed onto his tie. "Shit," he muttered. He quickly wiped it off. "I think we should try that new bar that just opened."

"Which one?" Elaine asked.

"It's right down the street." Mike gestured with his free hand.

"Oh Yeah. I heard about the place. "Elaine moved a hair out of her eyes. "It's called Backwoods or something?"

"Foxwoods," John interjected. He swiveled his head around the desk inadvertently and he noticed his flip calendar. Tuesday. January twenty-sixth. Tuesday- the word sat in his stomach like a bad oyster.

The crowd at his desk stood upon like Gods, Gods of coffee and cubicles. On the far side of the bank, John noticed his boss. Clean shaven with a red tie, methodically clacking away as if his life depended on it, as if the universe depended on it. He slightly hunched over the cabinet. In between the crook of his arm and the file drawer a weird polygon shape formed. His red tie dangled in it like a noose. John felt that tie around his neck, his feet kicking in the space less polygon-

"We should try that place on Friday. They have drink specials for the grand opening." Mike said.

"Yeah." John said. He felt a breeze as the door opened. A woman walked in. She looked no more than 25 with blondish hair which she kept in a ponytail. John straightened up in his chair as she approached.

"Guys watch out, someone is coming."

Elaine and Mike, both, shot him a jeering look.

"Haha, okay Mr. Spinoza." Mike put a mocking emphasis on the *'Mr. Spinoza'* as he and Elaine walked away.

The woman paused a moment in the foyer. She scanned the area for an open desk and John waved her over. She gave a slight nod and slowly approached him.

"Hello." John said cordially as she sat down. A few snowflakes brushed off her shoulders. "Hi," she said back.

"My name is John. How can I help you?" he asked her.

"Well, my aunt recently drafted her will. She made me primary beneficiary and I must sign off on it. I have all of her information."

"Okay. I just need to see two forms of I.D. Technically she is supposed to be here with you but it's okay for now."

"Thank you. I appreciate it. She..." Brook hesitated "couldn't be here."

Her eyeballs formed perfect circles, like tubes down to her heart.

"I'm sorry, I didn't catch your name." John extended his hand, as did Brook. "Oh, I'm sorry. Brook Olivia." she shook his hand back.

He wanted to jump into those tubes and splash in her heart. Instead, he finalized the will. All the numbers on the will were counted and measured, expanded infinitely, numbers as veins, now like blocked off throats.

"Well," he began, "it seems as if she had drafted this about six years ago."

Brook sat calmly in front of his desk. He couldn't help but notice how good she smelled and how curvy her body was. But what struck him the most was not anything physical but her eloquence. It was the way she carried herself. The numbers on the computer screen vanished, and the evil polygon closed. All that was left was her, an angel in cotton.

"Like I said, I'm really not supposed to give you a copy of the will, so just don't tell anyone. " He smiled.

She grinned at him. "Promise."

"I'll just need you to sign off on a few things." He pulled two papers from his desk and marked the spots. She leaned over slightly to sign them. He desperately wanted to say something- anything to her. He wanted her to stay. Frantically he searched his mind,

"Do you go out around here at all?" He cringed. That sounded dumb. His face burned like a hot iron, he felt so stupid but to his surprise she responded pleasantly.

"Um," she smiled. "If I go out, I go to Murrays."

"Is that the pub a few blocks from here? On Cross street?" He asked.

"Yeah, it's kind of a dive, but the beer's cheap." She gave a little chuckle. "But I usually don't go out, I'm kind of a dork."

"There's nothing wrong with that, I was only asking because I'm kind of new around here. I mean I go out with the guys from the bank, but I was wondering what else there was," he felt himself begin to sweat. She gracefully opened her purse and folded the forms.

"Well maybe I'll see you out sometime. John, right?"

"Yeah", he said sheepishly.

"Well okay," she rose out of her chair ready to leave but he stopped her.

"Wait," he said. "Um, I know this is kind of forward, but here..." he hastily scribbled his cell phone number on a piece of note paper. "It's my cell. If you ever want to go out, give me a call." He felt sheepish and awkward, but she did not change her disposition. She smiled gracefully and stood up. That same piece of hair hung down over her eyes. "I will."

she said. "Okay, Goodbye."

"Yeah, bye," he muttered to himself when she was out of ear shot. He settled back into his chair.

XI

"Don't stop, please don't stop!" Karen moaned. Wisps of her brown hair stuck onto her forehead. Strands of moonlight hung from her face as if it were white hair.

"You are amazing." she whispered.

"So are you." he smiled back.

She cuddled tighter into the crook of his arm, but he still held her limply. He did not have the courage to hold her close, instead he let her wallow in his limbs. She gave him a kiss on the cheek and closed her eyes. But he didn't, he couldn't hold her tight. Instead, he counted the moonlight butchered in the hanging blind-slats, splattered on the wall. A singular sweat bead formed on her nose. It dripped into the corner of her mouth. He saw things that Karen didn't, but nonetheless, they were there. And to John the bead of sweat became vital, at that moment, it was vital to his existence, and he didn't know why. The butchered moonlight made it glow; made it contort into something heinous; it slithered down her chin like a transparent eel. The urge to break her jaw, which resembled an eel, almost became intolerable. He had to squish that eel to save the universe! His fist tightened. A vein in his neck began to surface but there was no eel, only sweat! Yet, it slithered in the space he hated, the only space he could know, the only space he could perceive, the one he was born with knowing. Slowly he unclenched his fist. A hot gust of breath from her mouth exhaled onto his other hand. The eel was only sweat.

He wanted Karen to be Brook. But she would never be.

"Are you sleeping?" she whispered.

"No."

"Me either, I think I dozed off, but I can't fall asleep." She turned and faced him.

"I always have trouble falling asleep." He said dully.

"My cousin had insomnia. It was really bad. She could never sleep. You should go to the doctor."

"I can fall asleep; it just takes a while."

"My cousin went three days without sleeping."

"I'm lucky that I eventually do fall asleep-"

She cut him off mid-sentence. "I saw her after that, and she looked *awful*."

She didn't see him roll his eyes because he turned his head

slightly.

"It's so nice, I put my head down, five minutes later, I'm passed out. Like I'm drunk."

He noticed the slight curvature of her breast, like a flesh hill peeking out of her sternum. They were fake. This time she did notice his eyes.

"Could you tell they were fake?" she asked bemused.

"Ah...I wasn't sure." he said.

"It's great. I used to go out and no one talked to me, now I can't go anywhere without getting free drinks. I wanted to do that since I was fifteen. I always had small ones." She grinned in the dark.

His gaze wandered to the corner of her eye where a small chunk of mascara congealed and clung to her lash. Karen. Karen with fake tits. He repeated the name in his head. She was a balloon. He could almost smell the stink of polyurethane breath, puffed up, painted and able to stretch into any form she needed to be. He wanted her to be Brook ...

Brook. Brook.

But why? He met her once. It wasn't love at first sight or anything sentimental but there was a grace in her, an eloquence. Even for the few minutes they spoke, he could recognize her sincerity, flesh with bones, not some carnival balloon. For some reason, he could tell Brook was unable to be twisted and painted. And it made him angry, sick, almost to the point of vomiting. All he had was this. She thought he was caressing her breast but all he was doing was acknowledging the rumpled plastic,

"I still can't sleep," she said mischievously.

Without thinking he spun on top of her, this is what she wanted, all she wanted, all anybody wanted, another way to pass the time. And so, he fucked the balloon in sweat, specks of mascara flaked onto the pillow, she moaned, all he could do was fuck, he was meant to fill space, and so he did.

XII

"Our father, who art in heaven," she recited the prayer to herself. The words were automatic and familiar, like digestion.

"Thy will be done on earth as it is in heaven."

She stopped. The lord's prayer butted against her teeth. They were a lie!

She repeated the lie. "Thy will be done on earth as it is heaven."

No, it wouldn't! His will was infinity, and it cannot be done on earth! But it starts here, she examined her hands, 10 fingers, two hands, two ears, she traced the rigid steel in the hospital bed. But it was a straight line in line with eternity. The apple was still a warning, even after 60 years Maria Altendorpher's apple weighed heavily on her branch of a heart. But Janet was no tree of knowledge. She was a mental patient obsessed with ....

Infinity.

She reached down into her nightstand. The worn papers crinkled as she brought them to her bed. She whispered the thesis to herself as if it were the lord's prayer.

"Pockets of infinity exist within our finite world..." years ago, she began this odyssey. But the higher she counted the further away she was. But what good was her sane world to her after infinity? Who cared for bureaucratic degrees with nicely written titles?

"This certifies that Janet M. Poole is a fucking lunatic on this the seventh day of fuck. Eleven, seven, two thousand five."

Number mud clogged existence. She flailed in it, but still it dripped, it stank, splattered on her diplomas. It could not be like this forever. Infinity saw forever and she dared to follow it on earth. But she only found gas chambers, apples, swastikas, dead fathers, and higher numbers. Flowers of lines.

Why did he ever give her that godforsaken apple? She hated him for it but at the same time, she couldn't have been more grateful. The world she abandoned had been dried of blood. It was the world of diplomas, slumped over a toilet, vomiting its nourishment like a bulimic teenager. And she stood in the emaciated skeleton. She longed for the infinite blood that began with her straight knuckle bones; but the skin pulled tighter on her ribs, the existence she was taught to love and abandoned coiled around those ribs, the same ribs that poke through her skin.

XIII

"You shouldn't just storm out like that." Brook sat down across from her mother.

"She's my sister. I've known her a lot longer than you. Trust me she is not as sorrowful as she comes off."

"I know but you could at least humor her a bit. All she wanted was to make sure her will was set. She already did it."

Courtney shot her daughter a quick look, "You mean she had it all prepared? Then what did she need us for?"

"I don't think she was asking as much as telling us. She just wanted me to finalize it."

"Unbelievable." Courtney shook her head. "Listen, I know she has had it rough. The last half of her life has been basically one long stay in that place. You know. You've seen it, she's been in and out of institutions."

"I know but..."

Courtney cut her off. "She had no grip on reality."

"Mom, she's in a mental institution. Of course, she doesn't..."

"No, that's not what I mean." Her mother retorted. "She is very coherent. What I meant is that to her everything is a poem or a movie."

"What are you talking about?" Brook asked with annoyance.

"She doesn't understand that life isn't a movie. The world doesn't care if she discovered some great mathematical problem. She's a dreamer but she is not practical. And that has been her problem her entire life."

"You two just have opposite personalities." Brook said.

"No. I live my life while she just imagines hers. When the taxes are due, I write a check, she screams about infinity or something ridiculous."

"So, you think this is some kind of act? Some kind of ploy to escape from life?" Brook asked.

"I didn't say that. Whatever she suffers from is legitimate. I think she has very serious problems. But when the bills are due, problems don't pay them. She is unable to live in a rational society..."

"Rationality can sometimes be subjective." Brook said, almost condescendingly.

"Don't use your psychology on me," her mother snapped. "What it is, it is. And like it or not, subjectively or not, you either adhere to it or spend the rest of your fucking life like her." Courtney never cursed.

Brook and Courtney sat quietly at the kitchen table. Brook poured herself a glass of iced tea. Awkwardly the subject changed.

"I wanted to invite you and dad over for dinner on Thursday. I was going to try that recipe you gave me."

"You mean the chicken and stuffing one?"

"Yeah."

"What time should we come?" Her mother asked.

"I get out of work at five." She deliberated in her head. "Why don't you come about seven-thirty?"

"Do you want us to bring anything?"

"Um..." Brook thought again "why don't you pick up a bottle of wine."

"Actually, your father has a bottle of aged red. We'll just bring that."

"Sounds good," she placed her empty glass in the dishwasher. "I'm gonna get going."

"I thought you don't go into work until nine?"

Brook hesitated. "I told you I wanted to go to the hospital again."

Courtney hid her agitation well. "Tell her I said Hi."

"Will do. Love you mom." She reached over and kissed her on the cheek.

"Okay everything is taken care of. I talked to the bank." She pulled out two papers. "They guy wasn't really supposed to give them to me, but I think he thought I was cute." Her face turned red as she gave her aunt a quick smile.

"Thank you. I also had a little money which I am giving to you. Use it on something nice. But enough with the will." Janet hurriedly stuffed the papers in her nightstand. "How are you doing? How is life?"

"Well," Brook smiled "Not bad. Not too interesting either."

"Do you still work at that office?"

"Yeah, I still work at the counseling center. Hopefully after I finish my master's I can get an actual counseling job but right now I'm working my way up."

Janet leaned in a bit. "And what about your love life?" She smiled at her niece and forgot about infinity for a moment. "You are so pretty. I hope you have a boyfriend."

Brook hated this. This conversation.

"No not yet." She said sheepishly.

"What about those guys you dated during your undergrad?" Janet asked.

"Didn't work out with them." Brook smiled.

"You know, you shouldn't spend all your time with college and papers and books. You need to learn how to love or at least have some fun."

Brook hid her irritation. "You don't learn how to love, you just do it. But you have to learn knowledge."

"Take it from me. You must learn to love because love is stronger than knowledge. It will win every time."

It was conversations like these that reminded Brook of why her aunt was in this place. She tried to humor her.

"Love will win every time? You sound like a pop song." She grinned.

"You are still young, and you don't understand. Love never ends, whereas knowledge does. Love is ... Infinite."

She couldn't finish her own sentence. Brook sensed her agitation. "Lay down and relax. I'll make some tea and then I have to go."

"Okay." Janet said distantly.

The tea calmed her down. After a while Brook hugged her and left for work. But she still was slightly irritated. She hated that conversation. She looked back at Janet one last time before she closed the door. Janet looked in her direction but past her. And Brook saw an old woman, haggard and beaten. She saw someone who did not fit anywhere in the world, not even in her hospital bed. And yet, it was her aunt, her family. Janet blinked and Brook turned away. This was the last time they were to see each other.

"This is enough." Janet whispered to herself a few minutes after Brook left the room. Janet began to knot and twist the bed sheet. Infinity would finally end.

XIV

Wind rattled the door. It slammed the glass against the panes. Brook forcibly shut and held the door closed to lock it. Quickly she buttoned her jacket and walked to the car. The heat blasted her, and she felt warm. She felt safe against the blizzard winds outside. The heat reminded her of red fire against the swirling white snow. Her icicled blood thawed and released in metallic veins. She waited a moment in the oasis of her front seat. There was something lonely in this parking lot. As she put the car into drive, the lonely demon screeched between the gears. Claws scratched at the glass, but only she heard this thing; only she felt its alienation. As she drove away it followed her. She was alone. Alone in the snow and cold, in her car. And when this demon finally confronted her, she would welcome it because it would at least be something. But she wasn't that lucky, she knew even this thing would not attack her. She truly was alone. The irony was that all day she tried to help others, tried to rescue them for their mental hells. And yet now she was pursued by her own lonely demon. No one was safe. She was just stronger than others. For now.

The floors creaked when she stepped. As usual, she spread her note cards on the carpet and began talking to herself.

"The human being is learned through experience. However, it learns to learn by innate programming and instinct. Space and time are among them."

She placed that note card down and picked up another one.

"I believe that certain mental illness is caused by a disruption or inadequacy with this innate programming."

She picked up another card that had been put aside. And the

passage was scribbled more hastily written than the others, it almost looked ominous. But she read it despite her fear.

"What if these instincts could be," she paused a moment. She was lonely, yes, but the blood became oil. There was no one there to save her but she felt pain, she felt the absolute need to know "What if these instincts could be re-programmed?" A terror overcame her. She should not dabble in this. Leave the mind be. The mind does not need to be re-programmed! Just be there in case it falls, pick it up and help it function rationally. But rationality was subjective; it was based on space and time.

"Stop!" she said to herself aloud. For a long time, she held the note card. It became heavier and the words made less sense. Who was she to try and change it? She crumpled the card. The mind did not need to be re-configured, just helped.

"Stick to the basics," she said, "stick to the thesis."

She went about arranging the cards in a feasible order for her to visualize the flow. But she couldn't. Not tonight. It didn't come. Instead, the cards were tonsils, useless and exposed-except-the one crumpled in the trash. The forbidden one the one that excited her the most. But she feared it as well, she was afraid to be alone with that card, with the idea.

Her aunt had been alone with ideas... She walked to her purse and rummaged through it. This was stupid. But she needed something. Something to alleviate the fear and loneliness of her empty apartment. Something to distract her from the crumpled paper. She dialed the number and let it ring.

"Hello," a strong male voice answered.

"Hi John um I know this may be awkward," she felt dumb but continued anyway, she didn't want to go back to that crumpled paper.

"This is Brook. I don't know if you remember me. I was at your bank the other day, you gave me your number..." she waited for his response.

"Hey," he said awkwardly, but pleasantly.

"You told me to call you if I wanted to go out sometime. I was kind of in the mood for coffee," she kept tripping over her words "Would you want to meet with me at that Mason Green, the coffee shop?"

"You mean the one on Pleasant Street?"

"Yeah, I mean if you can't make it tonight we can do it..."

"Tonight is good. What time?" he asked.

She waited a minute to speak. "How about eight?"

"That sounds good," he said. "Listen," now it was his turn to be nervous "I'm glad you called." He cussed silently to himself for sounding stupid.

"Okay, I'll see you there at eight" she said cheerily. "Bye Bye."

"Okay, see you soon, bye." They both hung up the phone.

Brook stared at the phone. She knew this was stupid and especially out of character for her, but she couldn't stay here.

XV

Seven fifty-five. Neither of them wanted to look anxious and get there too early. John sat in his car with the air-conditioning on. Winter did not matter to him. He was nervous, he felt the slippery layer of sweat despite the blast of air. He nervously scanned the parking lot. Finally, he saw a red Honda. Its headlights grazed him. He shut his car off and walked over.

"I..." she said sheepishly "I hope you don't think this is weird."

"No. Seriously, I was happy you called." He held the door for her. "That's why I gave you my number."

"Okay good." She gave a curt smile, and it made her left dimple visible.

"Can I help the next person in line?" The cashier looked towards John and Brook. They stepped up. John motioned for Brook to order first.

"Hi. I'd like a mocha chino and chocolate biscotti."

"And you sir?" she looked at John.

"I'll have a cappuccino with skim milk."

Brook shot him a sarcastic smile. "Skim?" she asked.

"Ever see an old out of shape former football player? They get fat." He patted his belly. "I have to make sure I keep my figure." He smiled back.

"Gotcha," she paid for her coffee. "Want to sit there?" She pointed to a table by the window.

"Sure." he also paid the cashier.

At first there was a slightly awkward silence between them. They both seemed to be captivated by the slight snow that began to flurry outside. John finally broke it.

"Well since you already know what I do for a living, how about you? What do you do?" He took a sip.

"Right now, I work at a counseling center. I'm also working towards my Master's. Once I get that I want to start doing clinical psychology."

"You mean like the office with the couch" he smiled.

"Something like that."

"What made you want to become a psychologist?" he asked.

"I don't know. This sounds kind of corny, but the mind has always fascinated me." She took a bite of her biscotti. "What about you. Do you work at the bank full time?"

"Yeah, for right now. I'm going to take the L-7 this spring. Hopefully pass and get my broker license."

"Oh," Brook squinted her brow and cringed at him.

"Bad experience with the stock market?" he asked.

"No nothing like that" she gave a chuckle. "It's just that you deal with numbers all day long. I *hate* numbers!" she put an emphasis on the word hate. "I barely passed math in high school."

"I'm guessing you were a history and English person."

"All the way." She said "And then later on psychology. In college, as a freshman, I had to take one math class. I squeaked by with a C. I still don't know how I got that. I'm definitely right-brained."

He sipped his cappuccino. "I did alright in the other subjects, but math was my thing, and then accounting a business in college."

She smiled and shook her head. "Numbers are too boring for me."

"I don't know, it's weird. I love numbers because they are concrete. They don't lie. They are what they are. But in English there are thousands of different answers for everything. I need clarity and for things to be clear cut."

"I'm the opposite. I like a variety of answers, or being able to come up with something new..."

A little piece of her biscotti flew from her lips because she talked faster. It landed on his shirt.

"I am so sorry!" she managed to say in her embarrassment. She reached over the table to brush it off his shirt. Her face was red, but it helped to lighten the mood. John had a huge grin on his face the entire time.

"I'm relieved." John said.

"Relieved?"

"Yeah, I thought for sure that I would be the first to spill something or have the chunk of food in my teeth." He laughed.

Brook wiped her lips with an exaggerated motion before talking again. "Well, now it is your turn to do something dumb." She grinned.

"Don't worry, just give it time." They exchanged smiles and both relaxed a little. A chemistry began to form. Not love but an unsaid understanding and a comfort with each other.

"So anyway," John said "Where do you work?"

"It's in the next town, by the super Wal-Mart, in that plaza."

"Oh, ok I think I know where that is."

They talked long after their drinks were gone. Brook fidgeted with the empty Styrofoam cup. John leaned back in his seat. They talked as if they had known each other forever. As he leaned back into his seat, the familiar sensation grabbed him, with his eyes he traced the steel pattern in the table. Each criss-cross formed a tiny singular space, a thousand spaces, infinite spaces packed into the steel wheel. Singular oceans ebbed under the empty cups, he did not want to drown...No, he would not drown, not here, not tonight. This stranger as his life preserver, he would not drown! For some unexplainable reason, in this coffee shop, he recovered. He felt it, whatever it may be, but it ebbed back enough for him to raise his nose above the water.

She looked at her watch. "Wow, we've been here two hours."

"Yeah, we should probably get going," he said.

But neither of them wanted to leave. In each other they had found something rare. Someone to listen, to joke with. Someone to understand. They reluctantly stood by the entrance.

"Well, I'm glad you called." John finally said.

"I am too, don't take this the wrong way but," she paused "I felt very relaxed around you, very comfortable."

"Yeah, it was like we've known each other for a long time." John did not want this to end. He searched his mind for something to say "Well, how about you call me, and we can do this again."

"Okay," she extended her hand to shake his.

"See you soon." he said as he walked to her car. From his car he watched her drive away.

XVI

The room took on a whole new appearance. Janet had fooled everyone into thinking she was not a threat to herself. She counted the specks in the ceiling. Life to her had become infinite and uncertain with always one more terror to add. 62 years was considered relatively young but what is 62 years out of infinity? Nothing. She held makeshift ligature in her hand, 62 is infinity and it is nothing. She fooled them into thinking she was not suicidal. She reached over into her nightstand. The papers were yellow. She unfolded them to reveal... madness But it was not madness, it was dreams she could not possibly have and that drove her mad. The wind felt cold, but it felt good. It revitalized her. She wondered if she could float. The noose felt good around her neck, better than anything she had ever felt. No one heard her kick and flail.

XVII

Lucinda Ramos mixed her coffee like she performed every action in her life, methodically. Sweat-stink on latex became habitual. She peeled off her glove. It was sad, but she knew every corner and dirt spot in this break room. The coffee was bitter, but it was coffee, and it kept her awake. Her English hadn't improved much but no one talked to her anyway. She knew how bad she looked. Her black hair draped in a knotted crow's nest over her olive skin. Her black, stained apron draped over her breasts just as the scraggly hair over her eyes. She brushed her apron off and readied her cleaning cart. The linen and shampoos were in order. As she wheeled it down the hall the left wheel clacked annoyingly. She checked the clipboard for the schedule.

"A-128," she said quietly to herself and drove her cart down the east wing. Each room slowly disappeared behind her. The same monotonous tile pattern repeated under the wheels as she rolled to room A-128. The key jiggled in the door handle before the door finally gave. Methodically she reached for the broom and dustpan. She felt a slight breeze.

"Oh..." All she could do was repeat the sign of the cross. She stumbled back, tripped over the bed wheel, and landed hard on her butt.

"The lord Jesus..." but she couldn't form the sentence. Janet's corpse dangled silently, almost peacefully. Lucinda crawled back on her hands until she hit the wall. But she could still see the trickle of blood which escaped Janet's mouth. In that instant, Lucinda prayed to God harder than she ever had. The worst part about the whole scene was that Lucinda could swear that there was a faint smile on Janet's face.

XVIII

"We going to Foxwoods this weekend?" Mike asked.

"Sure." John answered disinterestedly. And frankly he surprised himself by answering at all. The world seemed to be something different today. John yawned in exhaustion; he tired of trying to find meaning with it. Customers shuffled in, tellers clicked on keyboards, white teeth beamed under red lips, asking for loans, muscled tongues flattened into words. And when detached from it, from all its clicks and conversations, they all looked ridiculous. Everything appeared to be something other than it was intended to be. John felt his telescope eyes focus and bring a distinctly different world into view.

"You alright man?"

"Yeah, sorry, just didn't sleep well." John looked at his watch. "We going on break now?"

"Yeah" Mike grabbed his coat. "I wanna smoke, let's go outside."

Both men walked through the re-focused world, but only John had telescope eyes to see it. To see all the bodies in space, all the numbered plots dancing to a stupid symphony of car exhausts and cash registers.

Mike took a long drag on his cigarette. "Foxwoods should be cool."

"Yeah, I heard it was."

It began to flurry. John felt a vibration in his pants.

"You're blowin' up." Mike pointed to his cell phone.

"Yeah, I am," His phone tailed off. When he saw the number on the I.D. his eyes lit up.

"Brook," he said excitedly.

"Whose Brook? Is she the chick from the casino?"

John ignored him and checked his voice mail. As he listened, his happiness changed to worry.

"Who is she?" Mike pestered him.

With an exasperated expression, John turned to his friend.

"She was a customer that I had a couple of days ago. We went out to coffee."

"Coffee?" he interrupted.

"Yeah, it was great. We talked for like two hours."

"Wait." Mike cut him off again "Is this the chick you've been fucking?"

"No." John said. "That's Karen, she's from the casino."

"So, what's up with this girl?"

"I dunno, something was wrong, she didn't sound right. I'm gonna call her back."

"Okay man," Mike flicked his cigarette on the ground. "I'll leave you alone." He walked back inside. John dialed her number.

XIX

"Listen, I'm sorry if this is weird for you..." Brook took a breath, "but seriously. I just needed to talk to someone neutral. And the other day, we just clicked so well..."

"Hey, I don't mind. I'm glad you came to me."

"Really?" she said.

"I know we only had one date, but...I don't know it felt different. I mean, didn't you feel something?"

Yeah, that's why I knew I could call you."

John nodded his head in agreement. "If it not like love at first sight or anything corny like that, but it was just..."

"A feeling," she said.

"Yeah, kind of hard to explain I guess."

"It's my aunt." She took a sip of coffee. "When I first came to the bank and saw you, she had wanted me to finalize her will but," she adjusted her shirt. "Yesterday a cleaning lady found her..." there was a pause.

"Dead?" he speculated.

"Hung herself. The police came and ruled out foul play. She used a bed sheet." Brook's eyes began to water.

"My God..." John trailed off. "Don't they try to watch out for things like that at an asylum?" He asked. He hoped he did not sound too insensitive.

"It depends. She was not deemed a threat to herself. No one foresaw this. While suicide in mental institutions is rare, it happens. She's been in Bergen Pines for years now. When she was 24, she had a mental breakdown. After that she was in and out of hospitals, shuffled between counselors and finally committed."

"What was wrong? If you don't mind me asking." John leaned in slightly. Brook wiped her eyes.

"She...this will sound odd...she was obsessed."

"You mean obsessive-compulsive?"

"Kind of. But she didn't wash her hands all the time or became obsessed with dirt, it was nothing like that..."

John waited for her to finish.

"She became obsessed with..." again she paused "infinity."

"Infinity?" repeated John.

"It's kind of a long story. During high school and college, she got straight A's. I mean she was brilliant. She decided to get her master's degree in abstract mathematics..."

"Abstract mathematics?" John asked.

"Yeah," Brook hesitated. "I'm sorry, I still feel really stupid. This is the third time we've met and were discussing my dead aunt," she forced a laugh.

"Seriously, it's okay. I mean, if you'd rather talk about something else, that's fine too. But trust me; I'm glad you've called."

Brook smiled warmly. "Thank you. It's just that I was close to her. I mean my mother used to take me to see her a lot."

Infinity. It sloshed around in his head like blood. He needed more.

"She was obsessed with infinity?"

"Yeah. When she was in Grad School, she tried to find the last number for her thesis."

"The last number?" John asked. That hit him like a bat to the teeth. The last number? He repeated it to himself, over and over.

"Everyone told her it was impossible, but she did it anyway. But in the end, it gave her a breakdown. She tried to figure out infinity and failed. I told you it was weird."

"Hey, I'm a numbers guy remember?" John smiled.

"Oh Yeah," she smiled. Her face was red and puffy.

"I mean, I didn't deal too much with abstract stuff like that but..." he trailed off "I know numbers can be downright impossible. If you study them long enough, they play tricks on you. Like I said earlier, I like the concreteness of numbers, but there is a whole other side to them, an irrational side...

"She used to say things like that. I remember one time when I was young, my mother and I visited her, and she had an episode right in front of me. She began to scream and beat her fists. The nurses had to restrain her. The whole time she was yelling 'I've seen the last number!' and 'apples and swastikas' over and over until she was hoarse."

"Apples and swastikas?" John asked.

"Oh, that's a whole other part of the story. Trust me, you don't want to hear that part."

But there was something intriguing in her story. He leaned closer to her. "I do, I want to know more," he said eagerly.

"Her father was a vet. He fought in World War Two."

"He died?"

"Well, he died a few years afterward," Suddenly she felt strange talking about this. "He got cancer from shrapnel in his leg."

"Oh wow."

"Anyway, he was in a raid of a concentration camp in Germany and he and his platoon killed a bunch of Nazis." She closed her eyes and tried to re-configure the story in her head. "The story I got was that before one of them died, he gave a red porcelain apple to him."

"Wait," John tried to clarify "The Nazi gave your aunt's father an apple?"

"Yeah, I know it's confusing" Brook smiled. "It was a granite apple given to the German soldier by a woman he had put in the gas chamber."

"Holy Shit." John face contorted. "Was she a Jew?"

"No, she was in a mental institution."

John gave her a puzzled look.

"I know it's crazy, two aunts, two mental institutions...a great aunt actually."

"Like it's contagious or something." John said. But he felt stupid after he said it. She didn't seem to notice.

"Well, it runs in my family. I did some genealogy research and a few of my other relatives have had mental problems. It's another reason why I am so interested in it. Anyway, no one really knows the whole story. But eventually my aunt's father passed on the apple to her when she was a kid."

"What's so special about it?" John asked.

"I'm not sure, but I think it had something to do with counting or numbers... On the back it has 1,2,3... engraved on it with three little dashes- Oh wait a minute!" she exclaimed. "Here," She rummaged through her purse and handed the apple to him. "I forgot I had it with me."

John twirled the apple slowly. It felt heavy and strange.

"So, this apple was passed on a bunch of times and finally wound up with your aunt?" he asked.

"Yes, and everyone who's had it has died and or gone crazy. My Aunt Janet killed herself. My mother is afraid of it. She won't speak to me about it. That's why I got all my aunt's personal stuff in her will. She wanted me to finalize to make sure I was getting everything."

"What do you mean your mother is afraid of it?"

"Her and my aunt were just totally different. Polar opposites. My mother is concrete, by the book, two kids' husband good job. My aunt, well, she went crazy. My mother is scared for me."

John raised his eyebrows. "What is she scared of?"

"You want to hear more of my family history?" she grinned with her puffy face.

"Well, I feel bad if you'd rather not talk about it... "

"Actually, it's good for me..." she chuckled "It shows me how crazy and coincidental the whole thing is. Are you sure you want to hear this?"

"Seriously, I don't mind." And he was sincere. Most of the time he faked concern to get laid. But this time, this time was different. The story sucked him in.

"My mom worries about me because she thinks I'm identical to my aunt. The way I approach psychology is the way she approached numbers. She thinks I'm going to go crazy because I get too into it."

"Like how?"

"Well, she doesn't know the details, but I do get into it, I probably am slightly obsessive over it..." she paused "It's complicated. And I have talked too much; what about you?" she tried to give him outs but he insisted on listening.

"Please, keep going. You're not sitting here bragging about yourself, droning on and on. This is an interesting story. It's weird but good." He smiled at her. "I mean it's a lot more interesting than my days' work." He felt a strange comfort with her. Almost enough to tell her about the thoughts. But no, those were his thoughts. No one could understand those. He wanted to concentrate on her anyway. Something in her story intrigued him. The obsession with infinity perhaps. He didn't know but he wanted to hear more.

"So, what are these theories of yours?" he grinned.

"Are you sure you want to hear this?"

He gave her an expectant look.

"Okay," she smiled "Basically, it's a theory of ideas. Some say we are born with certain things in our heads already, that we don't have to learn them. Whereas others believe we are a blank slate and learn everything through experience."

"What ideas can someone be born with?" he asked.

"Well, later on, a sort of compromise was reached. It's not so much that people are born with ideas but that their mind is programmed in a certain way."

"Programmed?" He repeated it to himself. The mind was programmed a certain way, "with what?"

"Well," she said. "Close your eyes."

He closed them and smiled. "I give up," he said.

"Okay, now open them."

"As soon as you open your eyes, you see space. You see division between yourself and other objects, you become aware of distance and separation."

"You should become a teacher." He joked.

She smiled at him. "Okay, now just sit there."

They waited. And waited. And waited.

"Time is the other idea. We instantly become aware of a type of progression, which we later learn is time." She felt like she was reading right out of a textbook. "In some way, space and time might be stories or fictions we created to comfort ourselves..."

Programmed. He digested it. We use space and time to perceive our world. Programmed. "What if we could re-program it?" he said out loud.

Brook put her coffee down and stared at him. It was a cold gaze. One that skinned him in his chair. The rest of the coffee shop danced with stupid patrons. They worried about useless things like being short changed and overpriced coffee. But between Brook and John a vein grew, a similar blood circulated the same obsessive fears.

"Stop it." She muttered. There was desperation in her voice, but John didn't hear it.

"What if, instead of seeing space and using it we developed something else, something new, we told ourselves a new story…"

"Stop it!" A few customers peaked their heads towards her. John sat, perplexed. And Brook felt that he spoke her words, her ideas.

"I'm sorry I shouldn't have yelled but…" she collected herself. "I mean, this is why."

"This is why what?" Her sentences became fragments. "What's the matter?"

"This is why she fucking hung herself, she tried to understand things she wasn't supposed to, like…" she paused. "infinity, like the last number. And I had the same idea, to try to reprogram the mind. But you can't mess around with this stuff…"

"I'm sorry," John said, interrupting her, stopping the conversation. An awkwardness was born, and it made the space between their bodies take on its own life. John wanted to recoil in his seat but stood firm. Spaces in his ventricles snapped closed like starving mouths to digest this one moment and all his happiness in it.

"But I think we have to evolve to understand…"

"No!" Once again, the patrons turned to look "We're not supposed to know!"

John twisted in his seat and the seat twisted. This woman changed.

He referred to her as Brook, but that was all. She became a stranger.

A few moments ago, she was a sun which thawed him, but she burned out into a black hole.

"But we can know!" he raised his voice. We must keep trying, keep evolving, it's our responsibility to know what we can't! We need new stories!" And suddenly he hated her. The thief. Yes, she was a thief. She tried to steal what was owed to him.

He knew the space around them, a division of earth into coffee shops and an endless parade of idiots that marched through time, but he had found a way to end all that and now, the last number, but she wanted to take it! He found a way to…

Reprogram it. To teach the idiots how to see something else, something better…

Brook fidgeted. "My aunt hung herself. For what? For some stupid number that isn't even real? For some stupid obsession? She wasted her intelligence, her whole fucking life for this..." Brook reached into her purse and pulled out a wad of crumpled papers "for this meaningless shit!" she threw the papers across the table. "Who cares about reprogramming the mind? None of it matters!" Red patches formed on her palm. She couldn't understand why she noticed the blood in her hands, but it revitalized her. "I can't waste my life on this..." She thrust the apple towards him. "She wanted me to have this. She gave me the apple and her unfinished thesis in her will..."

"So, she wanted you to follow her..." John interrupted her.

"No!" A small chunk from her mascara began to clot. "She wanted to warn me! She didn't want me to follow her, waste my talents! She wanted me to help people!"

John sat on the other side of the Grand Canyon from her. She cried. And then, she wiped her face, and it was over. "If you want all this shit, take it." She stood up and left a five on the table. "Thanks for the coffee." Her tone became cold. "I'm sorry that 'us'-had to be like this, I just..." she stammered. "It's just...I'm sorry." She ran out the door.

John sat dumbfounded. A few patrons turned to look at him. In less than an hour, Brook had come into his life and vanished. It wasn't love but a connection, and good or bad it existed for something greater than its parts. Like two asteroids that crashed in the depths of space, they met and parted but something had changed,

The apple and papers. Infinity.

Asteroids smashed the skull. Skull pieces floated in the space around them. In the space which he hated

Maybe it was obsolete. Brook was too afraid to evolve past-the space. Too frightened to re-program it. So, he would have to do it, alone. But with what?

He sat alone and scanned Janet's papers. He gripped the apple so tight it cut his palm. The last number was mouthwash, gasoline, and electricity. He stared at it, his eyes burned, and his thoughts didn't end.

Like infinity.

He looked up from the table. Everything he saw ended. He traced the outline of a woman. Her elbows, the coffee in her hand, her teeth, and all these pieces were measured and ended.

Not the apple.

And then it dawned on him. Why measure finite things with infinite numbers? Or even- the last number?

And suddenly, the room beat like a heart, the wall knocked him down as it contracted, and he stood in the artery of his table-apple.

Reprogram the mind, reprogram the universe with

Infinity! Yes! Infinity!

But how? He scanned the coffee shop, the idiots wouldn't know, they didn't give a shit. When they opened their eyes, they saw fractions. Finite shoes and empty mugs. No one cared about infinity except an old suicide victim.

John spun the apple around and looked at the engraving. 1, 2, 3...

And like an iron to the face, he knew." It's so easy!"

Infinity was the easiest place to get to and then the last number, he began to scribble on a napkin. 1, 2, 3... and filled up the napkin all the way to 4,956. He began to scribble on another napkin, starting with 4, 957. He could reach infinity; all he had to do was count.

XX

Brook angrily put the shifter in drive. She drove nowhere. Routes, exits and highway paved over hearts, blood in the gears. She drove to alleviate, tears dripped but she

Only saw her aunt,

Dangling

With no blood and no neck, just a bed sheet rope burns and

Infinity.

Brook was done. No more stupid theories. No more unthinkable equations. Her foot pressed harder on the pedal. The car whined with acceleration. She gripped the steering wheel tight until her knuckles looked like white paper. Life was finally life now, not some inconceivable thing anymore. Her aunt died for nothing.

For nothing. For infinity.

The only thing she loved about Janet was her noose. She imagined it pulled taut, but what it pulled had already been dead for 25 years or more. The abstract infinity killed Janet long before she died. She put her blinker on, turned onto the exit, continued going nowhere and felt happy.

XXI
Two Days Later

Napkins and ripped loose leaf papered the house, his counter tops and desktop were filled, he started to write on the wall.

4,765,894,034,941,211.

But he could always add 1.

Fuck infinity. He would find it. There had to be an end. Everything ends. He would keep counting until he found it.

Plus 1. Plus 1. Plus 1.

He was running out of room; it only took two days to fill up his kitchen. And sometimes sleep made him stop counting. And he would always wake up to ... Another number.

But now he slept.

The pen slid in his hand. A bit of ink dribbled onto his pant leg. He woke up from his sleep in a chair to the phone ringing.

"Hey you." Karen's voice sounded almost childish.

"Hey." he answered distantly.

"What are you doing?"

I'm thinking about re-programming my mind with infinity. I'm trying to replace the spaces and progression of time with infinity. I am trying to find the last number and I can't stop counting.

But instead, he said "Nothing much. You woke me up."

"Well?" she asked.

"Well, what?"

He wanted her to get the hint. He never called her. He thought maybe she would just stop calling. But every time she did call, he wanted to fuck her.

"C'mon, you know, don't make me beg. "She jokingly pleaded.

The urge to reach through the phone and strangle her became insatiable and he would have done it if it were possible.

"Come over. The door will be unlocked." he said dryly.

"You're bad, you know that? I'll be over in a few, let me get ready."

"Okay, see you, bye." It was said mechanically. Hopefully, the sex would distract him.

He wanted Karen to be Brook, but Brook was a stranger now. Brook not only wanted to measure space, she wanted to occupy it. And he wanted to evolve past it. But he felt extinction before evolution.

"Hey cutie, where are you?" The door creaked open; her voice stung him like a jellyfish. He hated her, but needed her, her breasts and softness; he needed to halt the extinction. He needed to alleviate ...

Infinity.

But, as she entered the room, she didn't notice any of the numbers. And he realized there would be no alleviation. She didn't care about infinity. He had to bear it alone. Because all his life he had a fear. A fear of empty buildings, a fear of meaningless objects, a fear of abandonment within space, but now it became simple, life was only...

Plus one, plus one, always able to add one more.

She didn't see the numbers in the dark.

The sex went as expected. A nice, fun, momentary distraction. Like alcohol or weed, nothing more. But infinity remained like it always did. Infinity like cancer, like it had with Maria and Janet.

Karen sat at the edge of the bed and began to fasten her bra. "How are you so good?" she asked.

John only half-heartedly paid attention to her. He really couldn't stand her, but he needed her, he needed her like a child needs a toy or some distraction.

"I have to go to work," she smiled as she kissed him on the lips. "Call me later?"

"Of course." He lied. And she knew it. But she was just as addicted to the sex like he was so she would keep calling. Perhaps she really wasn't that different than he was, each needing one distraction after the next, one debauchery filled romp just to deflect from the numbers. But no, she was not insane like him, she did not try to count existence like him...

"I am just going to make some coffee quickly." She interrupted him. He almost wanted to hit her for interrupting him, but all he said was "okay. I will be there in a second."

The smell of coffee diffused throughout the apartment and brought him back to sanity, at least somewhat. At least he could pretend.

"This is good coffee," Karen remarked as she took a sip. "Do you mind if I use one of your travel mugs?"

"Ah, no that is fine." He said.

"What's wrong?" she asked. "I do have to go soon, but you just seem sad, you seem off...is it me?"

And in that moment, he felt pity for her. She was beautiful, a great figure, soft skin, long black hair, blue eyes and an angular and inviting face. She smelled of lavender and soap. He noticed the waistline of her pants and how it sat erotically just above her butt.

"Nothing really..." he could never tell her. "Just been a little tired."

"Well, you are going to be tired today, after what you did last night." She smiled. "Let me know if you want to talk." She kissed him again and left.

He did not hate her. She just could never understand his thoughts. As she left, he sat alone. He listened to the hum of the traffic outside. Calmly, he rose and opened a locked drawer. He took out a gun and placed it in his mouth. The traffic continued to hum, and the sun shone brightly. The apartment still smelled of the good coffee. He took the gun out of his mouth, took out the bullets and sat silently for a while. His phone vibrated, he checked it.

Karen ☺ happy face.

She didn't love him, but she felt something for him. No, he didn't hate her, but he just could not see her again. Karen with the fake tits, Karen who did not listen to him, but he did not hate or pity her, he just understood. She was another point, another body, in space, another plot of lines searching for salvation, happiness and redemption. She would not find it in him though. And in that instant, it became clear, it was almost as if a vista opened before his eyes. He was no longer scared of infinity. He opened his laptop and began to search for real estate listings.

XXII

2008

Brook slid her engagement ring up and down. The white-gold disc glided on her finger. Her husband-to-be sat next to her. They both stared intently at the priest, both nervous, holding hands, with their ring nerves glittering in the stain glassed sun. The energetic priest, Fr. James swayed to and fro as he gave his sermon, which the crowd were also listening to intently. His voice peaked and volleyed to accent certain parts.

"Our Hebrew ancestors used a word called *hesed*, which translated as steadfast. *Hesed* is the type of love our Hebrew ancestors used to endure years of homelessness and slavery and hardship. And I speak about *hesed* at this feast between Brook and Michael, because it is the type of love which they must share, not a hallmark movie love, but a realistic love, a strong love, *hesed*, a steadfast love."

The priest's blue eyes were brighter than the stained glass behind him. Brook stared into that eternity of colors and sunlight. She squeezed Michael's hand and realized how happy she truly was, and how thankful she was for that happiness, because she knew how fickle it was. Two years ago, at her aunt's funeral, there were no colors, just a horrible black coffin, no happiness only her own madness. She couldn't see the rope burn on her aunt's neck at the service, but it was just underneath the long black coffin veil lid, like a permanent smile on her neck, which would be there until her skin rotted off. A rope burn smile on a miserable neck with both ends pointing to infinity, to a bottomless endless hell, a hell which her aunt Janet invented during her life. And it was that which killed her aunt, it was infinity, and the rope was only a hired gun. And two years ago, Brook thought it would swallow her. But infinity could not touch Brook in here, not now. It broke apart harmlessly into stain glass patterns. Hesed would protect her. Michael's grandmother made the sign of the cross and adjusted the microphone.

"A reading from Paul to the Corinthians." She stopped for a moment to clear her throat. "Love is patient, love is kind, love is never jealous..."

Brook's mind raced. It sifted through all sorts of thoughts, some not appropriate for a wedding day. She expected and accepted her mind to run wild today; the medication could not corral all the thoughts. She understood the stress of her wedding day would most likely aggravate her obsessive-compulsive disorder. She had lived with this affliction for most of her life. And on this special day, she would not let it ruin her. She knew the power of her thoughts; they almost drove her mad. She tried to reprogram it with something else besides time and space. But it was futile; it scared her, she had to stop. She gazed at the section with her family and felt the vacant spot where her aunt should have been, even though there was no space for her. Her mother cried happily, Michael's grandmother continued with the reading. Brook thought it sadly ironic that she used her aunt's little inheritance to help pay for the wedding.

"Love is never spiteful, it never rejoices in wrongdoing, or others misfortune..."

Michael smiled and squeezed her hand. She thought of this archaic Catholic service and how people went through the motions of the ceremony, but she actually listened or better yet, understood the words. But that is what OCD does: it makes one think, analyze and tear apart every single word, every action. This was no different. Paul's two-thousand-year-old words lodged themselves into Brook's brain, like the diamond into her ring.

And perhaps it was the dreaded OCD, but nonetheless, as his grandmother spoke, monsters and demons that once threatened her were now simply refracted into harmless stain glass light showers. She squeezed Michael's hand and realized that even the demons of infinity were no match for love, for *hesed*, which she and Michael now pledged to each other. In her temporary madness, she often wondered the reason for existence, the age-old question, and she realized it was love, but love was only a human word for god, love was *hesed* or Jesus on the cross, it was holding the door open for someone, it was a laugh, it was teaching someone, it was raising a child.

The demon of infinity and OCD were bi-products, extraneous roots in her math equations. The reason for existence was love, in an instantaneous flash she could re-program the mind with love, with *hesed*, a steadfast love to encounter the hells it must face. She didn't need philosophy or Phd's, Gpa's or cum laude, all those meaningless and empty things took their place among her white dress, she could just as well have worn sweatpants and wore a pipe cleaner for a ring, love is patient, love is kind, it is never jealous or boastful, she began to see.

She stared at Jesus on the cross, and even though Jesus was not a math professor, she learned from him, she understood, now the ceremony was not a mindless ritual, it had substance and blood (Christ's, Michael's and her own) in a delicate and beautiful symphony. Her love for Michael filled the empty zero of her, in a beautiful, mystical and cosmic fusion, in a reason for life, a reason to bear through any pain, *hesed* was Jesus' binary commandment of love, it was completion, infinite blood rushed through zero space in veins of a newborn, this was not so much a marriage as a birth, the newborn of Michael and herself, if only her aunt Janet could have been here.

"Will the wedding party please come forward."

Brook, Michael, the best man, and the maid of honor Elizabeth stepped forward toward Father James. His blue eyes were lost among the stained glass. He motioned to Robert, the best man, for the rings. The maid of honor fixed Brook's dress. Fr. James smiled at Michael and Brook.

"I, Michael, take Brook to be my lawfully wedded wife," the priest said. Michael then repeated the words. "To have and to hold, through richer and poorer, in sickness and health." Brook and Michael both repeated the vows to each other and placed the rings on each other's fingers. They held hands and Father James was ready to complete the marriage. He smiled and said, "Let no one divide what God has joined."

And nothing would divide them, not a knife or jealously not an event from the past, not a jackhammer. Brook quickly surveyed the church and saw her family, smiling, and in the far-off pew she even saw infinity and OCD, begrudgingly they accepted the union, the newborn, because even they could not break what God, what love had joined, even those hideous things, those extraneous things respected.

"I now pronounce you man and wife. You may kiss the bride."

And as Brook and Michael kissed their souls joined into a beautiful river, into Jesus on the cross and a newborn child, they joined into love, into a reason to exist at all.

XXIII

2012, A rural town in Western Maine

The harvest had been good this year, bountiful. John methodically picked the potatoes and carrots and blueberries. He placed each in a defined basket and brought them to his cellar. The air smelled sweet, it smelled like early autumn. John took a deep, long breath as he walked back up the stairs. The paint on his house started to peel just a little, but John thought it gave the old cottage a rustic look. He sat down on his porch and poured himself a cup of coffee, added a little skim milk and sat back on his old rocking chair. The sun began to set, and the sky flooded with red, orange and pink. His house, his property, his harvest, his coffee, gave him peace, a peace he had never known before. There were no more numbers out here, just his cottage, just his potatoes. A vibrant red cardinal landed on the rail. The red feathers stunned John, he lost himself in that vigorous red. The bird turned its head a few times and flew away. Steam rose gently from his coffee, and he thought of Karen. He thought of her from time to time. She had gotten married and recently had a kid. He was happy for her; she deserved to be happy. He scanned the yard, and his eyes settled on the old oak tree. A few feet below that he buried the apple that Brook's aunt had given her, he buried infinity and the last number in the black dirt of his home. He didn't forget about what happened, that would be a part of him forever, but he liked to focus on the tasks at hand, he harvested potatoes and drank coffee at sunset. In the winter he shoveled snow and tended his fire. He worked online, he was so grateful he could work a few hours a day online to earn some money, but he made more than enough to support his simple and solitary lifestyle.

Walden lay open on the small table. He thought himself a little like Thoreau, but living out here just gave him clarity. He had some contact, he went into town every week, sometimes he would see a movie. He did not want to be some survivalist or purist; he just wanted solitude. He lived alone but was not lonely. He differed from Thoreau, however. Thoreau did not go in search of the last number, but John searched for it along with H–, the priests of Palma Sola, Paul Eckhart, Maria Altendorpher, Janet, and Brook, but John found it or at least came close.

He sipped his coffee again and let the warmth radiate through his entire body. Living alone, here, in this place, allowed him to reflect. In some ways, he felt like he had detached himself from the world and become a solitary observer, the world's necessary solitary observer. And in this role, he came to some tentative conclusions. What he began to realize was that if space and time really were just programed into his mind, if they were just stories we told ourselves, perhaps space and time were not real, just useful fictions. If they were not real, then perhaps there was some type of existential unity of all things and space and time were artificial but necessary dividers. He read somewhere that is how God saw the world, in a unity that eluded our feeble understanding, but he didn't believe in God. No, there was just him, John Spinoza, sitting in this cabin. Space and time were stories we told ourselves, or they resembled theater stages or little cosmic sandboxes where we played and acted, and some people played better than others. On these stages, we slept, competed, fucked, and worked. Some people acted like high jumpers and others race car drivers, some executives and bankers and teachers, and some furniture delivery crew. But no matter what one was, they had to move in space for some duration, and they told themselves how important they were. Just like little rats scurrying in some vast desert, climbing over each other, biting each other's necks, putting each other in concentration camps. And this movement continued, one human died and another took its place, one number came after another in a tireless and nauseating progression, but John Spinoza figured out the secret. The last number, the end of infinity, at least for human consciousness, was perhaps the end of movement and duration altogether, maybe that would come on the last day of the universe, the beautiful moment before the universe died, or maybe it was just him, getting off the stage, sitting on this porch, in this cottage drinking coffee on a brisk fall evening. Maybe the last number was a real apple or potato or blueberry (not some fake apple), that is where all the movement of eons led to. Once the movement ended then we would evolve past space and time and all these stupid constraints. Maybe the last number could be a new story, but no one would listen.

So, he became a type of silent repository for all of Maria's and Janet's crazy thoughts, he held on to those thoughts, stories of space and time and the last number and infinity, so others could live a normal if artificial life. There are signs of infinity everywhere despite how much we ignore it, signs tucked away in all the obscure corners of the universe, like in the supposed rational numbers we created, maybe the numbers were just little bastards of infinity. H- figured that out centuries ago, Maria and Janet knew. But no one would inherit this madness now; it would die with him, John Spinoza. He thought of Brook. She had gotten married and

John hoped she'd found happiness. He could carry all of this for her, for Maria, and for all those that came before like H-, for everyone, he could carry it, like a gene, like a reminder.

Smashed and Glued

I
Bavaria, 1813

Houses always had a distinct scent when a body had been prepared for a funeral. Fredrich Gingale sat on the wooden chair and inhaled the dust. Mourners walked softly and prayed over the casket. They whispered silent inaudible prayers for a dead woman who could no longer hear. Anna Zolosky lay motionless with her hands crossed over her chest. Her thumb had withered into crinkled paper, sucked dry by some invisible force.

Fredrich approached the coffin again and kneeled before it. He almost bawled because she died alone. He wondered what that must have felt like. She probably choked out some inaudible phrases and then passed over. What was her absolute last moment of existence like? She had stood up and collapsed, bashed her head on the corner of the night stand but she was dead already! She had already died alone! Her body sat in the apartment for three days, it rotted until someone came looking for her, she...

"Hey, how are you doing?"

Fredrich's wife knelt next to him. She lightly touched his arm.

"I'm okay," he smiled at her. Her green glass marble eyes swam in her cream skin. He gave himself the sign of the cross and rose up with his wife.

They walked over to a station with fresh water. Janette, his wife, bent down and took a sip. Anna was Fredrich's step aunt. He felt most sorry for his stepfamily, especially his stepfather and his stepfather's father, but when he looked at the woman that used to be his aunt, he truly did want to break down and cry. Her life was lived for everyone else, no husband, no children, but all she did was help others, giving money to charity, building houses for the poor, and yet she collapsed, died alone and tragically.

Anna's father, Glab, approached Fredrich in his stern German manor. He solemnly shook Fredrich's hand, while not making eye contact.

"Thank you," he began to choke up. "Thank you... for coming, it means so much to me, to my family." Fredrich almost cried with him. He watched as this broken old man had to bury his eldest daughter. As a sign of stoic demeanor, he had asked to dig the hole in which his daughter would be buried. Glab walked into the washroom to avoid a total breakdown in front of Fredrich and his wife.

"I'm going to go outside and get some air." Fredrich kissed his wife lightly on the cheek.

"Okay, I am going to wait with your mother."

Fredrich quietly surveyed the outside of the home, he looked at the bricks and horse carriages outside, but that goddamn cold stung at him. A man across the street bundled his coat tighter and walked past. Confetti flurries danced, they took no notice that someone had died, died alone and tragic.

"Hi Fredrich," an arriving guest quietly shook his hand.

"Hi Ludwig," Fredrich courteously shook his hand and uttered a soft greeting.

The formality almost made him laugh, but it was necessary, especially at a time like this. But then, in the face of that laughable etiquette, Fredrich saw the lines of the earth congeal, snowflakes and a black dress rose in one gigantic swell and broke in his mouth. Anna was dead at 47. A life lived for everyone else but herself. When Fredrich prayed over her, he touched her wrinkled thumb, like a neurotic mental patient, he just had to touch it when he prayed, for no specific reason, he had to gently reach in and brush the paper skin. No one thought him odd, other people gently touched her hands as well when they prayed, but only Fredrich knew they were not her hands, they were something else now.

"Hey," Fredrich's stepfather, George, stood next to him. "I needed to get out of there," he smiled at Fredrich. "So sad."

"Yeah, how is everything?" Fredrich asked.

"It's going okay. My father is taking it hard." George remarked.

"Yeah, he came up and started talking to Janette and me and almost broke down." Fredrich relayed the story.

"Really?" George's eyes widened. "What did he say?"

"He was just thanking us for being here."

"Yeah, it means a lot to him."

Both paused. The cold settled on them.

"You know," George began "It's amazing. One day you're cooking dinner, going to work, whatever, the next day, you're in a coffin. We shouldn't worry about the little stuff, just look at Anna."

"It's a sobering thought. Everything we know in our life will one day be gone." Fredrich reiterated.

Both stood quiet once again, letting the light snow flurries dance on their shoulders.

II

"Did you try the bratwurst?" Fredrich's mother, Marie, asked Janette.

"It's delicious," she said. "But I really liked the bread."

Marie cut a piece of Bratwurst for her daughter, Christiania.

"It's good mommy." Christiania looked up at her mother.

"Did you try some?" Christiana asked Fredrich. He smiled at his half-sister before responding. "Not yet sweetie."

Marie, Janette, and Christiana ate and conversed. They talked of trivial things; everyone at the table did, like some giant distraction. How could they not? Even Anna's father talked politics with some of the men. But deep down, the suddenness of Anna's death left everyone helpless and alone, perhaps sorrowful for her, perhaps scared for themselves.

"Juliana, where did this meat come from?" Marie asked Juliana who was the hostess, and Anna's sister.

"I bought it from the new butcher in town. The meat is better there, I think anyway."

Juliana tried her best to be a gracious hostess. Everyone could see the family was trying their best to hold up and were doing an amazing job considering the circumstances.

The basement was warm. Paintings and bookcases gave it an intellectual but cozy feel. Elizabeth, Anna's other sister, called the children over, who were running around. It must have seemed like a picturesque Christmas scene, the falling snow, the full moon, the fireplace, ten children huddled around. But this was a funeral, Anna's family gathered together as was the custom after a funeral. Elizabeth, holding back tears, began to gently take out some of Anna's porcelain dolls from her bag.

"Okay children," she placed each doll on the carpet, "these were *Tante* Annie's, I want everyone to take one for Christmas, she would want all of you to share what she had."

The children, too young to understand the implications, greedily snatched at the free gifts. Perhaps they were better off not knowing the full gravity of the situation.

"Easy," Elizabeth guarded the dolls. "They are made of glass." But the children didn't listen. Fredrich watched them scramble for the best ones, but Christiana stayed back. She waited politely for her cousins to take first. Christiania surveyed the remaining dolls and made her selection. She reached for one doll, forgotten and turned over on its stomach. The doll was pale and wore an old-fashioned dress. Christiania gently cradled the doll and stroked its auburn hair. She almost looked like a doll herself. She had glassy eyes and white skin and pudgy cheeks. Fredrich wondered what she thought. She stood on some imaginary line, teetering between childhood and sorrow. She walked over to Fredrich, still cradling the doll. And in her simple tiny voice, she spoke to her brother.

"Where is *Tante* Annie?" she asked.

Fredrich scrunched his lips. Elizabeth did not hear her niece's question. The other children played roughly with the dolls, but Christiana wanted more than a toy, she wanted an answer. "Well," he sat her on his lap "When you die, your soul leaves your body and goes to heaven." She stroked the doll's hair.

"So, Aunt Annie wasn't in her body when we saw her today at the wake?"

"No...her soul went to heaven."

"What's heaven like?" Christiana asked.

"Well..." he paused again, "it's a place where you don't feel any pain. In heaven, Aunt Annie's knees don't hurt, and she isn't overweight."

"So, what happens to her body?" Christiana was relentless.

"Well," Fredrich chose his words carefully "The body stays on earth, and when the end of the world comes, Aunt Annie will get her body back, like a parking space for a horse when its owner goes into the market, so see, everything is better now." He gave his sister a slight, unconvincing chuckle.

Christiania's brow scrunched as she tried to process the information. Fredrich had given her a safety net, a story for her seven-year-old brain to comprehend. And he wished so hard that he could believe his own words, but there was no safety net, there, just an endless plummet with the endless echo of empty words.

She continued to stroke the doll's hair and silently ponder her brother's words. He knew that she wanted a better explanation, truth be told he was not happy with what he had said. She had questions that she wanted to ask but didn't know how to ask, didn't know what to ask, didn't know if she should ask, but he saw her little brain working out the secrets of the universe, and desperately Yearning for something so simple, yet so distant and alien; the truth.

III

A Few Weeks Later. A small town outside of Berlin.

Fredrich felt the rigors of daily life return. Taxes were due soon. The harvest would need reaping. He had to go back to school because his students depended on him. Anna died but he had to live. And with his return, Fredrich gradually came out of his funk. Funerals and other sad events played tricks on him, made him think crazy thoughts. But now he had returned to the hustle.

"Are you all signed up for your classes?" Marie poured her husband some soup.

"Yeah, I'm set. They start next Monday."

"What are you taking?" she asked.

"Um..." He had to think. "The Progress of World History, and..." he paused to think again..."the Degeneration of Thought and Progress of History," He shoveled a generous helping of soup and meat into his mouth.

"Those sound interesting." She nodded.

Sometimes he just liked to watch her. The way her jaw delicately chewed the meat, the way she stared off into space. He knew he was odd, but he couldn't help it.

"Yeah, I guess there's some kind of dispute between the two professors. One has these really upbeat and optimistic theories, I guess he is really proper and gentlemanly like, his name is professor Tegel, Sirus Tegel is his full name. But the other guy, I hear he is a nut. His hair is a mess; he's dirty, he's antisocial."

"What does he teach about?" Janette asked.

"His theories are completely opposed to Tegel's, he believes the only force in the world is random chaos that controls and perverts all."

"Wow," Janette, made a face. "That seems pretty pessimistic. Sounds like it will be a fun semester."

"I'm looking forward to it." He said "The only thing I'm worried about is taking two classes. That's going to be tough with teaching."

"Yeah, but you'll manage. I can help you cover classes if you need it." She said, "Not sure how your students would react if they had a woman teach them though."

"They might not be ready for that. But it is another reason why I love you," he smiled.

He stared at her again and just had to admire her. She probably could teach his class. He loved that she had been educated. He could never marry some typical *hausefrau*. He loved their conversations. And when she thought he was wrong, she fiercely disputed him.

She ate the last spoonful of soup in her bowl. "Have you spoken to your mother lately? How is your stepfather's family doing?"

"I got a letter yesterday. She said they are doing okay, considering. It's been tough on them. Glab goes to the grave every day. They all said it meant a lot to them that we made the trip and came."

"Yeah, it was important. I'm glad we went; I know it meant a lot to them. It was a sign of respect."

"Of course," she got up and began to clean her plate. "How is Christiana?"

"My mother said she's doing okay. Sometimes she asks questions, but she thinks that Anna's soul is in heaven with God."

Janette smiled. "Oh, by the way, I forgot to show you this. I packed it in the bag and forgot about it." She walked over to the mantle and gently took hold of a porcelain doll. "Elizabeth gave it to me...for the baby." Janette rubbed her belly. Fredrich smiled at his wife. "That was really nice of her, I wish Anna could have seen the baby, she would have spoiled it."

"Yeah," Janette smiled,

"It's like a bad omen. For her to die at the end of the year near Christmas. I don't know, it's eerie."

"I thought you don't believe in omens." She gave him a smile.

"I don't." He smiled back. "But it's still a bad omen."

They both lay in bed. The day's stresses would resume tomorrow. Now they had a few hours of respite.

"How is the baby doing?" Fredrich reached over and rubbed Janette's stomach. He gently laid his ear to her skin.

"I felt it kick some today." She said.

"Really?"

"Yes. It was amazing" she said.

"Isn't it weird...?" Janette could tell Fredrich was deep in thought and about to say something crazy "Anna dies, and we are going to give birth."

"So maybe it's not an omen, maybe it's just life," Janette said.

"Yeah," he laid his head softly back onto her stomach.

IV
Two Weeks Later. The University of Berlin

"So, you see," Tegel gestured toward the diagram on the board "History is a movement, a progression, it is heading somewhere. Now, I am not the only one to have theorized this. Aristotle believed existence to be teleological, or having a purpose. Empedocles believed existence to be a tension of opposites, the Stoics believed history to be governed by the logos." Tegel quickly scribbled the names of the ancient Greek philosophers on the board.

"But I am taking this one step further." He continued. "History is a combination of certain historical moments that form in opposition to each other. In this way, negative and positive moments compete, but overall, they work in a reluctant competition to create a new moment. An opposite tension then arises to the new moment and thus this process goes on ad infinitum to the end of history."

Tegel surveyed the class. It had swelled to capacity. Some students even sat on the floor. He was the hottest professor in the philosophy department, perhaps in the entire university. He tried not to exaggerate his own self-importance, and he didn't think he did. But students wanted to hear him. And he had things to say, some old, some re-interpreted, some original. His philosophy combined ideas from the last 3,000 years and he believed it would lead the German lands into the future.

"Right now, we are in an incomplete stage." He began again. "We are heading to the absolute, a rational union with the divine creator, but we're not there yet. We have to continually overcome ourselves and our base desires, our freedom has to evolve, nothing is given, and nothing is taken for granted. Only when we realize our incompleteness and strive to reunify with the divine, will the end of history come, and we, the masters of these ideas, will be the kings of our era."

The students listened intently. They copied down every word. They scribbled and looked up, scribbled, and looked down at the paper again. He was the disseminator, the purveyor of this guarded knowledge; he had the awesome responsibility of training the German youth.

Fredrich sat toward the rear of the room. He could not write fast enough to keep up with Tegel. He couldn't think fast enough, he felt like he was behind already. The other students raised their hands, but Fredrich dared not to, at least not yet. He felt out of his league, he felt dumb, but he kept writing.

"Yes," the professor called on a student with his hand raised.

"What is the driving force behind history, what actually drives the progression?"

Tegel took a moment to answer.

"The force behind this progression is what I call the word spirit, or the geist. This force is the collective human reason, combined with passion. This combination drives the historical moments and creates new ones; of course, always in accordance with divine reason, the logos if you will. This world spirit enables the progression."

Fredrich wiped his brow. He took a deliberate, prolonged breath. He felt intimidated. Maybe a doctorate wasn't for him. He could still teach classes but never be a full professor. The students next to him were much smarter than him. He barely got into this program and wasn't sure if he could make it through. The students all wore a smug look, a look of arrogance and almost of omnipotence.

"So, you see, all history, all existence, is progress. All evil and violence, while unfortunate for many, are not in vain, they have a higher purpose." Tegel enunciated the last words of his lecture slowly to give effect. Tegel waited for the students to write their notes. He adjusted his spectacles and straightened his bow tie while surveying his audience.

The corner of his tie made a perfect perpendicular triangle with the upper corner of his lapel. Fredrich looked at this man, this amazing piece of living geometry and wondered how one came to be so intelligent? Was he born gifted? Was he a hard worker? Did all his brains fall into line and follow suit on the path carved out by his bowtie? What kind of gift must one have to fill lecture halls day in and day out, Year in and year out? This man had some crucial knowledge of the universe, and Fredrich felt like he just couldn't grasp it.

"Well gentlemen, I think that will be enough for today. Read Plato's *Allegory of the Cave*, and the sections assigned from Kant's *Critique* for Thursday." Tegel gently closed his notebook and gathered his pens, ink containers and parchment. His white hair formed a neat cusp over his large forehead.

Fredrich began to make his way through the throng of students to the doorway. A swell of students had gathered around Tegel and asked further questions about the lecture. Tegel gladly answered them with patience and reserve. It was like a little unofficial fraternity. Fredrich never had anything to say; in fact, he didn't think Tegel knew who he was. Quickly, he scurried past the swell into the hallway.

V

Sethhauer hurriedly scribbled on his parchment. The candle waned as the moonlight dominated it in his tiny office. Sethhauer's hair flopped into his eyes, he brushed it away, but it fell back, and the whole process repeated. If he could have cut it off or torn it out from his head he would have, but that would have taken time away from his work.

His finger's gnarled around the pen like a Neanderthal's club. He squeezed it so tight he thought his fingers might bleed. The room was near freezing but that did not matter. In this cesspool that we called life, in this trash heap of existence, Sethhauer found a reason to exist at all, which was to destroy any shred of faith or happiness or hope in anyone else, they needed to see existence for what it was, misery and pain, and purposelessness. As he muttered words to himself, his breath rose in the moonlight.

"Excuse me sir..." Greta, the secretary startled him. "You should probably be leaving soon; the custodians wanted everyone out by nine."

Sethhauer, startled, interrupted and now furious, slowly looked at the woman. He wanted to strangle her. Bitch. He wanted to kick her old yellow teeth.

"I told you never to interrupt me!" He snarled at her. "I have told you this repeatedly!"

With an air of contempt, Greta scowled right back at Sethhauer. "How dare you! I was told everyone has to be out by nine! You miserable old cuss! Stay here and be locked in!" Her scraggly grey hair hung loosely over her shoulders. It simply looked like an extension of her veins which snaked off her face. Sethhauer truly did hate this old bag.

"Get out of my office! I will leave when I am a goddamn good and ready!" Veins rose and dropped in his neck, like a demented print board.

Greta stormed out of his office. Sethhauer sat for a moment, fuming. He felt sick and irritated. With one swift motion he punched the globe on his desk. The blue sphere spiraled out of its metal holder, which clanged loudly on the floor. The cardboard globe sliced in half when it forcibly struck the corner of a book. The beautiful world exposed its weary cardboard guts, for all to point and laugh at.

"I told you never...in here...do not come in...ever!" His words were choppy and incoherent. He looked for something else to strike; frantically his eyes scanned the small office, he grabbed hold of a statue on his desk and was about to shatter it but suddenly stopped. He slowly brought the statue down to his eye level. There was no more anger, no popped veins, no bitch secretary, just the miniature Buddha in his hand, which calmed him instantaneously. He gently placed the Buddha down and made sure it was set just perfectly next to his standing books. Quietly, he began to collect the pieces of the broken globe. The ugly cardboard frowns died in the trash can, died in obscurity.

Sethhauer sat back down and collected himself. He intently stared at the Buddha and felt slightly embarrassed at his reaction. He did not feel remorse for that old bitch Greta but felt embarrassed at acting like that in front of Buddha. Sethhauer began to write again, silently mouthing words to himself as he wrote.

"There is no progress...how can there be? That fool says progress...Progress! A reunification with the divine...the divine?!" Sethhauer clenched his fist. That goddamn charlatan Tegel had brainwashed everyone, he hijacked their brains. But anyone who believed his nonsense didn't have a brain in the first place.

"There is no progress... just a groundless, timeless, space-less, egoless will to live, the seed of all is chaos, is domination, is the blood in the drowning man's lungs...yes, yes, I know the truth, but who will listen? They want to listen to that phony, to that perverter..." His words became louder, but he didn't care. "Why will no one listen...listen to the truth, why will no..." Suddenly he felt the presence of another in the room.

"I am sorry Professor Sethhauer," Alfred, the head night custodian began. "Everyone has to be out by nine." Alfred's voice was uncertain and lost in the angry gaze of Sethhauer. He clenched his fist, then unclenched it, then clenched it again. The veins rose in his neck but then he noticed the Buddha. The statue looked blissful, and at peace with itself. The ancient Eastern sage had silent words of wisdom for his unknown Western follower.

Hurriedly, Sethhauer gathered his things and shoved past Alfred into the dark hall.

VI

"I was asleep when you came in last night. How did class go?" Janette buttered a piece of rye bread.

Fredrich hated being reminded of his painful failures. And he had a hunch this class would be one. But he always answered his wife's inquiries.

"Difficult." He set his books down on the oak table. Methodically he cut the cold pieces of dried pork into edible portions for him and his wife. He loved it when she came to eat lunch with him, but today he did not feel like talking. Lee Stousburg, a mathematics teacher, took his usual place at the table. The creature teachers of habit all strolled into the faculty room, with their soups and fish. The chatter of the school day emanated from the room.

"I went to the market today and got that liverwurst you liked."

"Oh good, I was going to ask you if you could get that."

She smiled at him. "No, you weren't."

"Okay," he smiled guiltily, "I wasn't. But I am glad you got it."

She prepared her coffee with sugar and cream. The smell diffused throughout the faculty center.

"What about your class? You quizzed them on the Roman branches of government, right?" she asked.

"Yes. Tomorrow I am starting the gladiator games. I think ..." But Stousberg interrupted, like he usually did. "Well, every one of my geometry students aced their quarter test. They really seemed to grasp isosceles and scalene triangles." He retorted smugly. "I think my students this year will make me look fantastic."

Only there was nothing to retort. Neither Fredrich nor Janette had questioned him. Fredrich grew irate. Was there any need for this jerk to interject and brag into a conversation that was not even directed to him? It seemed as if this situation happened increasingly more often. Friedrich politely smiled at Stousberg's smugness, eager to avoid a conflict, but Janette didn't hold back.

"Congratulations. But it must be easy since students have to be considered advanced to even take geometry. He has all the regular students." She pointed to her husband.

Stousberg gave him a snarl and continued eating. Fredrich was not sure how he felt about his wife defending his honor, but he loved her and loved how she stood up for him. She put that education to use. Stousberg turned to another math teacher to avoid the embarrassment of being shown up by a woman.

"They usually get into the gladiator section," Friedrich tried to ease the awkwardness. "The blood and the violence, they love it." He chomped off a piece of dried pork.

The blood, violence. He thought of Tegel. For Tegel, these unfortunate things have a place in the progress of man. The beaten and depressed serve a purpose, they help to drive history. He thought of the countless gladiators who died in the coliseum, he thought of the helpless Jewish captives who were dragged from Jerusalem and torn apart by wild dogs and applauded for it, he thought of the Christians burnt alive and used as Nero's garden torches. Were they all progressing?

"I'm sorry, I got sidetracked before. Why was your class difficult?" she asked.

"I don't know." He didn't want Stousberg to hear this conversation. "He is just a really good professor; his theories are amazing. But he has this small little posse that surrounds him after class, all these *Arsch Kussen* who just want him to know their names. I don't know. I'm going to stick it out."

"You are such a downer!" she lightly hit his arm. "You'll do fine."

He wondered whether he truly was a downer. But the class was difficult. If this were prehistoric times, he would not be able to bring meat home to his wife and children. But things were not simple like that anymore. Stousberg even sipped his meat soup like an arrogant snob. He thought of all the kiss asses that surrounded Tegel after class. He wanted to throw them in the coliseum and watch them be torn apart by dogs. What about Anna? Did Anna drive the world spirit? Were they now in a more advanced spot because Anna died? Was she progressing?

He cut another piece of pork.

VII

"What you see is not what is. What you do is not what you think. The joy you feel is only representation; your achievements are mirage."

The students were spread unevenly throughout the room. Some had their feet up on the empty seats in front of them; some had their books in the empty seats. Sethhauer had not shaved in days, his scraggly facial hair crawled over his dirty collar.

"All the apparent progress in the world," he accented the word progress, is a joke, a goddam joke!"

The students jolted out of their seats. One in the front row dropped his pencil.

"We all think we matter, think we are important, most importantly we think we are in control, but really, at the root of all our apparent success, is the core, the seed of the irrational, which dominates all."

Fredrich scribbled the lecture notes. Even if he didn't score well in his classes, it at least would be interesting. The apparent rift between Tegel and Sethhauer was obvious. Their theories were completely at odds with each other.

"Plato spoke of two worlds in the Allegory of the Cave, and he was very close to being right." Sethhauer's oozed arrogance. "Plato theorized an eternal world and a temporal world, a world of prototypes and world of copies. Where he was wrong, was in assuming that this other world of prototypes was a divine-like essence. The other world was eternal, but not in the way he envisioned. It is devoid of time, space, and ego. It is an eternal force, controlling all, willing all its desires through the human mind and animal instincts, through the plant's stems and gravity. Every single force in this existence is merely a tentacle of this eternal will, this will to live. The will tricks, controls and dominates all."

A student raised his hand and Sethhauer nodded gruffly in his direction.

"For Professor Tegel's class, we also had to read Plato..." At the mention of Tegel, Sethhauer's face tightened up. The student must not have been aware of the conflict, or perhaps he just tried to show off his knowledge. "It's just interesting how Professor Tegel's theories and your own theories are similar despite their differences. He believed the eternal world was a combination..."

Sethhauer's eyes bulged, and he spoke through his teeth.

"If you value your standing in this class, you will not mention him. That charlatan imposter philosopher," his words began to sound choppy again "he has hijacked your brains into thinking there is some sort of progress, some sort of goal. But you need to see! There is no goal, we are not headed to some enlightenment or realization or eternal world of the divine! There is nothing but the irrational, nothing but the will to live!"

The student tried to back pedal his argument. He did not want to incur the wrath of Sethhauer, which he had unleashed, but the time had already passed for that.

"Well, sir, all I meant was that there were some similarities..."

"What you meant," Sethhauer came up close to the student, "was to hold my theories in the same light as that imposter! I will not be made a mockery of! He has fed you lies! Given you something to believe in, something to sleep better at night! Like some narcotic! There is no goal! There is no progress!"

The student sat mystified, and while he no doubt was stunned by Sethhauer's rant, it had left Fredrich with a different feeling. Sethhauer had said there was to nothing to believe in, and Tegel's progress was simply a narcotic, it struck Fredrich.

"If none of you can see that then get out. Leave. I will not speak to imbecilic, brainless clones. Go and pack into his lecture like everyone else. Only listen to me if you dare to hear the truth. Leave. Get out!"

The few students that actually signed up for Sethhauer's class awkwardly piled out of the near empty lecture hall. Sethhauer sat stoically and watched them leave. They didn't want to listen to the truth, because truth is difficult, it is painful and hard to hear. These lightweights could only receive drugs in the form of lies, in pats on the ass, like a mother telling her son that daddy is going to heaven when he dies. They couldn't face the irrational in all its awesome terrifying force. They couldn't bear to look at their father stiff in the coffin and be told he simply was usurped back into the will.

When he looked out his office window, he didn't see humanity's amazing architectural or political achievements, he only saw them crumbling. He only saw the vultures tearing at a squirrel's carcass, not the miracle of life. Life is not a miracle; it is an aberration, a mistake, a jail sentence. And at times it seemed that only he, Albert Sethhauer could sense this, only he could see the pure beauty of his theories, only he saw the vultures, only he embraced the irrational.

The students were gone. He sat alone in the empty hall. But not alone, he sat with himself. He felt himself die little by little, his cells attacked each other, the will to live was cannibalistic, it fed on itself. He felt his own death and had to smile.

VIII

"Opa, I brought the flowers you wanted." Elizabeth placed the roses on Anna's grave. Glab helped her arrange them.

"Where did you buy these flowers? They are beautiful,"

"The flower vendor knew Anna. He donated them for her."

Glab had to smile. Only Anna could still receive favors after she had died. A twinge of pride bubbled up in him. He had raised her right. She helped anyone who needed it, she helped the stubborn who refused, she helped all.

Sometimes Glab wished for noise. People screaming, livestock, vendors, snotty children, whatever, something. But the absolute stillness forced him to stare at the grave, reading and re-reading the epithet, over and over and over again.

"Should we put the flowers on the dirt, or on the head stone?" asked Elizabeth. She could sense her father slipping into his trance. The tears began to well up on his old stubborn face.

"Opa, where should we put the flowers?" she asked a bit louder.

Startled, he looked up at her, like he hadn't heard what she said, like she had screamed in his face, like she was a stranger.

"Where would she have wanted them?" he asked despondently.

"I don't know Opa. She isn't here, I am asking you." Elizabeth said, a bit frustrated.

"Where do you think she is?" Glab asked helplessly, almost pathetically.

Elizabeth spread the flowers on the new earth under the headstone. She arranged them so each vibrant red petal showed.

"She has to be in heaven." Elizabeth answered. "If she's not, then I can't believe in God."

Father and remaining daughter held hands at the foot of Anna's grave.

IX

"What the hell happened in Sethhauer's class?" Poinmoms asked Tegel. Tegel poured a cup of coffee. He waited a moment to answer his former student, now a colleague.

"I don't really know the details. I guess one of his students mentioned me, and he blew up."

"What is his problem?" Poinmoms voice became agitated. "He

has had it out for you since he arrived. That arrogant bastard. I still can't believe he was even hired here."

Spencer, another one of Tegels students turned professor, shook his head with a look of disgust. "I heard the administration is looking for a reason to fire him. It shouldn't be long until he's gone."

Tegel and his colleagues, some of whom were former students, sat at the table in the faculty lounge in between their lectures. Sethhauer's recent outburst had given them fodder for their conversation. A general hatred of Sethhauer became obvious among the philosophy department. His gruff appearance and gruffer demeanor all added to this, and his controversial theories always sparked debate. But above all this was his unmitigated, unswerving hatred of Sirus Tegel.

"I really don't think it's anything I did personally." Tegel answered. "I seriously think there is something wrong with him. He needs attention; he wants to be an outcast, so he creates these abdominal theories to get noticed. And since I am one of the most popular professors here, he has targeted me. I truly do not believe that he can control his arrogance or his hatred. In fact, I rather feel sorry for him."

"Well, I am not one for pity." Spencer remarked.

Tegel smiled. "You'll learn it as you get older."

"Yes, but to act the way he acts is just despicable. Where does he get the right to insult and degrade a senior professor like you?" Spencer took another sip of his coffee.

A gust of wind blew into the room. Several candles were extinguished. No one had to turn around to see who had opened the door. They all could feel it. Sethhauer glared at all of them as he went to his locker. The conversation had immediately died when he walked in; it was obvious they had been talking about him. The only sound was the slurping of cold coffee.

Sethhauer crouched and retrieved some books from his allotted cubby hole. Spencer did not see his face as he crouched, but he knew that Sethhauer smiled. Then, Sethhauer slowly stood up. But instead of leaving, he stood motionless and surveyed the sitting faculty. And then, he let out a sickening cackle, not a human laugh, it sounded like hyenas and dogs, like things in a dark forest. Spencer and Poinmoms sat perplexed and frightened at this philosopher dog. But Tegel wore a curious look on his face, awaiting Sethhauer's rant.

"You think I don't know," Sethhauer snarled. "Go ahead and talk. All of you are brainless and have no balls. You sit and hang on every word *he* says" Sethhauer nodded to Tegel.

Spencer tried to defend his own honor. "I will have you know I am no one's puppet," he said smugly, "I have my own theories, unlike you I am not just a skeptic, I do not simply contradict what people say. I..." but Sethhauer cut him off.

"How many times have you ever disagreed with him?" He nodded to Tegel again. "I have watched you kowtow and kiss ass, never once offering any criticism, never once even hearing you ask a question! All of you are pathetic cronies!"

And with this truthful accusation, they all sat silent. Except Tegel. He retorted.

"What they have Albert, is respect. They also have a belief in something more than violence and chaos. They, like me, have a vision, a goal. What do you have but criticisms? You live a sad existence, and I truly feel sorry for you."

Spencer and Poinmoms sat motionless, awaiting the angry rant. They could see it in Sethhauer's face, the bulging eyes, the veins.

"You feel sorry for me?" Sethhauer exploded. He violently threw his books onto the floor. "How can you feel sorry for me? I am the bringer of truth! I am the light! I am the one who knows this existence! You are a brainwasher! A crooked evangelist!"

"My friend," Tegel gave a smug smile. You are no Jesus Christ; you are simply a broken man with nothing to believe in."

At this, Sethhauer no longer appeared human. He felt an animal instinct overtake him. He also knew that he had to be careful because he had been warned by the dean about his actions. But hatred knows no rules, no boundaries, or consequences. Animals only think about the present, and the present was in front of him; it sat in the form of Tegel.

"You prey on people's vulnerability! You seek out their need for something to believe in and give them a drug!"

"My friend, how can you deny progress and logic?" Tegel calmly asked. "I have read your theories, and I am still left wanting. Read your history son. China, India, Persia, Egypt, Greece, and Rome, it is all a progression. Despite the violence you love so much, overall, the condition of living has improved. Look around you, look at what you live in. How can you deny this?"

"First of all, don't you ever refer to me as your friend or as your son. And if you take off your horse blinders, you will actually see. This so-called progression is a trick, made to fool you. Your standard of living is a ploy. All your logic, all your progress is a tyrant! This used to be a world of Gods! But logic and progress have beat each god into submission, choked the gods until they crawled back into the netherworld. Logic has banished anything it cannot control; infinity, death and instinct are abstract terms, subjected to your progression. They have no real meaning anymore to anyone important. And in time, the chimera of logic will be beaten, just like the gods before it, in fact..."

"And why should they?" Tegel cut in. "Those abstract terms have no meaning I grant you that, but I am not concerned with words but with action. We are trying to make a better world. What are you doing? You are an ancient relic of a long-gone time, obsessed with the past's violence and struggle. We are the future."

Sethhauer fumed. "You are a Charlatan! I am the Gadfly! I am the one who brings the truth! I speak of the things that you are afraid of!

Poinmoms and Spencer sat mystified, stunned at the emerging duel. Sethhauer versus Tegel. Progress versus the irrational. Both titans stood bloodied in the awkward silence. Sethhauer gathered his books. But before he left, he glared at Tegel.

"Be wary, I will expose your fraudulence!"

Tegel smiled. "Son, you cannot expose what isn't there."

Sethhauer stormed out angrily.

X

The temperature rapidly dropped outside. Janette poked the ash in the fire, and she watched as the flame rose. The flame danced and flickered, and it always memorized her. Even as a child she used to love to watch her father stir the ash. The heat diffused throughout the house. The door creaked open and slightly startled her.

"Hey Fred," she called to him. He brushed the snowflakes off his jacket and walked over to her.

"Was the store open?" she asked.

"Yes, and I got the last loaf of bread." He set it down on the table.

"Excellent," she said. "I'll start dinner." She began to prepare the soup and Fredrich began to cut the loaf and butter it.

"You have class tomorrow, right?" she asked.

"Yes. In the evening. I'm so glad class is close that I can walk.

"Some guys I know travel over an hour by horse or foot."

"That's crazy, especially in the cold."

"I know." He ate a piece of bread.

"So, have things gotten better with class?"

"Yeah, I'm hanging on. This semester has been tough, but I am learning a lot."

"How are those two professors? The ones that don't get along." she asked.

"I think that's what has made this semester so interesting."

"What's been going on?" she asked.

"Oh, I didn't tell you!" Fredrich raised his voice in excitement. "Sethhauer flipped out on us and kicked us all out."

"Which one is he?" Janette asked.

"He's the negative pessimistic one."

"Oh. What happened? Why did he flip out?" she asked.

"A student started to make a comparison between his theories and Tegel's theories."

"Between Sethhauer and Tegel's?" she asked.

"Yes. And Sethhauer absolutely despises Tegel with a passion. So, the student tried to backpedal his argument, because he realized he had angered Sethhauer. Sethhauer looked like a dog. He just tore the kid apart. He started screaming at him, then all of us. I seriously was afraid; it looked like Sethhauer wanted to kill him. His eyes bulged, the veins in his neck rose, it was scary." Fredrich poured himself a cup of soup.

"Wow," Janette said. "So, he kicked everyone out."

"Yes, he told us all to get out. Truth is, I think Sethhauer is a good professor, his theories are interesting, but he's crazy. Sometimes it makes it hard to learn."

"Yeah, this whole thing sounds like it could be a distraction." She said.

"It can be, but it is also really interesting, I mean, it makes you really question."

"How so?" she asked.

"Well," he paused a moment. "Tegel's theories basically boil down to progress. Tegel believes that all of history is simply a progression toward a goal, to a reunification with the divine. Ever since the fall of Adam, humanity has been trying to get back to God. All of history is an evolution, a positive progression. All the violence and misfortunes are part of a bigger plan, a divine plan according to reason. Tegel believes that this time right now is near the end of history because everything is almost perfect. But Tegel does not believe this divine is the old God in the sky with the white beard. His vision of the divine is something akin to reason, all of humanities reason together."

Janette raised her eyebrows. "Perfect, here? If everything was perfect, we wouldn't be freezing and working for pittance at the gymnasium," she smiled. "He sounds like he's trying to justify things."

"Well, that's kind of what Sethhauer believes. His theories are based on an opposition to Tegel. Sethhauer believes that all Tegel's supposed progress is nothing but a joke, a mirage. At the core of existence is this irrational, chaotic force called the will to live, which controls everything. It swells and pulses, it manipulates and takes and takes and takes."

"Nice choices. An apologist and a pessimist." She grinned. He grinned too; he loved the fact that she could probably show up half of Tegel's kiss ass followers with her education.

"Basically, it boils down to progress versus chaos." He said.

Janette thought for a moment. She took in what her husband had just said. Progress versus chaos.

"And really," he swallowed a chunk of bread. "I look at it as trying to answer an age-old question."

"How so?" she scrunched her brow.

"Well, really, I mean, they are both possible answers."

His wife waited in anticipation.

"What is the purpose of existence?" He paused to give the question effect. "Why are we here? Are we masters of our destiny and enabling this divine progression? Or are we simply adrift in an infinite cold universe, puppets of some irrational force?"

Janette pondered her husband's words.

"I don't know what to think," he said "I mean, agree with some of their points and I disagree with others. Some of the students have aligned themselves, actually, most have aligned with Tegel. His class is jam packed; Sethhauer can't fill a lecture hall."

"I don't know what I think either," she tried to answer the age-old question. "If you look around, you see both sides. I do see progress, I mean, we are better off than we would have been a hundred years ago or two hundred years ago." She slowly chewed a piece of bread. "I guess we can appreciate Tegel's progression, being history teachers, but look what that progression has been built on. Look at all the suffering and violence. Look at how many people must die for us to progress. Look at how the rich exploit the poor, all the poverty and crime, so I can see Sethhauer's point too."

"So at least if I fail, I will learn something." He smiled.

Janette gave her husband a disparaging look. "You are not going to fail."

"We all can't be as good as Stousberg" he kept smiling.

"Oh, I didn't tell you! I saw his wife in the market. She doesn't know who I am, but I remembered her from a function you took me too a while back. She was gossiping with some of the others. Do you know what she said?" her voice raised.

"What?"

"I overheard her talking about how the history teachers have it the easiest."

Fredrich shook his head. "I almost feel sorry for him. He's pathetic, he's always trying to one up somebody and justify his own importance. He's nothing, he's empty, and everyone knows it."

"He's still a jerk," she said.

"I know," he smiled.

They ate the rest of their meal talking of trivial things, of students and quizzes and the upcoming baby, but their earlier discussion hung on his mind. He looked down at his wife's growing belly and wondered what their baby would inherit, a world of progress or chaos. Was their baby a link in some divine progression, or an appendage of the irrational will to live, an aberration? He tasted the buttered bread and felt the steam from his soup dish. He looked at his wife's delicate face, what was all this, what was existence? And then, something caught his eye. On the mantle, in the next room, he saw Anna's porcelain doll. What about Anna? Death, birth, butter, glass dolls and fish, everything became a question.

Or perhaps everything became an answer to which there was no question.

XI

Sethhauer sat calmly at his desk chair. He swiveled ever so slightly. Every time he moved, the chair creaked. Like the moan of a dying man, it sounded alien and out of place, it comforted him. *He balled up the official request of resignation and then unballed it.* The slow crinkle of the paper and creak of the chair sounded, echoed, ominously. In his heart he knew this day would come. It was inevitable. When he began his personal crusade against Tegel, he knew he would amass many enemies. The idiot cronies who blindly followed Tegel angered Sethhauer the most, those goddamn *Arschkusse*. No, no, that wasn't true. It was Tegel. That stupid old man, the goddam charlatan, selling his snake oil and pretending it was philosophy.

The look on the dean's face was so rehearsed. Sethhauer replayed this afternoon's conversation ever so vividly.

"Professor Sethhauer, you have previously been warned about your personal feelings toward Professor Tegel."

He balled the request again.

"You were also warned that if those feelings interfered with your teaching, you would suffer severe repercussions."

He balled it tighter.

"And it has come to my attention that there were two incidents alone in the past week. One in which you verbally assaulted a student for mention of Tegel, in which the student had every right to do so, and then the unprovoked outburst against Professor Tegel and your colleagues in the faculty room."

Sethhauer's face grew red. *His fist clamped around the request as tight as he could squeeze.*

"I have heard many positive comments about your teaching methods and theories. But the truth of the matter is that you roam this campus like a rabid dog. You assault anyone who does not agree with you, students, and faculty alike. I cannot allow this behavior to continue."

Tighter.

"I'm sorry Professor Sethhauer. I have to release you from this university. I will allow you to resign your post. If you do not resign your position by Friday, you will be terminated."

Sethhauer didn't say anything. He stormed out of the Dean's office and came back to his office-well, what used to be his office. And he had been sitting there for the last three hours.

The Buddha smiled at him, but Sethhauer couldn't be calmed. Even though he always knew the inevitably of this moment; it didn't make it any easier to take.

Tegel. Tegel. Tegel.

He repeated the name over and over. His hatred could not be appeased. Not even by the Buddha. All these idiots took their drug in the form of Tegel's theories. His nonsense cluttered the universe; it distracted people from the truth. But, then again, people do not want the truth; they want what is easy.

The creaking and crinkling continued to fill the room. Really, now, there could only be one way to prove Tegel wrong. There could only be one way to make him look like a fool; there was only one way to completely destroy his credibility. Tegel believed all was progress, even violence and suffering.

Really, the only way to force the truth on people was to tear its skirt off and rape it publicly, force it on the people. The only way to contradict Tegel's theories was to murder him.

"Fredrich..." His wife's breathing became irregular. He could only hear her breath in the dark room. Truthfully, it frightened him because he had not fully woken yet. The lantern had gone out long ago. The only source of light was a moonbeam on the floor.

"Fred...I think this is it!" Quickly, Fredrich shed his sleep. He scrambled in the dark room. After repeated attempts, he finally lit the lantern. A soft glow spread into the room. His wife's face appeared out of the darkness. Sweat marks glistened in the new light. Her teeth gritted and her eyes bulged. She was in the beginning stages of giving birth. The baby was coming early. They had arranged for the midwife to stay the next week, but also had this contingent plan worked out.

"Fredrich, the midwife...you have to get her!"

The midwife lived half a kilometer away. He didn't want to risk leaving his wife, but he couldn't deliver the baby. If he left now, he could get back in time. He kissed her on the cheek and left.

"Go...hurry!" she yelled after him, but her voice dropped like an icicle. He had gone already. He had forgotten his coat, but he didn't care. He stumbled through the snow to his neighbor's house. Violently, he banged on the door to rouse her out of sleep. Groggily, Ms. Whilem, an old widow, answered the door.

"Ms. Whilem, please..." he was out of breath already, "Janette, she is giving birth!"

Even before he said her name, Ms. Whilem sprinted up to his apartment. This was pre-arranged. Without acknowledging his own shortness of breath, he began to sprint to the midwife's house. The important thing was that she had a horse, and they could ride back. He didn't feel his shortness of breath, he didn't feel the cold, he didn't feel anything. All he could think about was his baby. Right now, a new life was being born, a new existence passed through his wife and crowned.

"Hey, you!" a police officer shouted at Fredrich.

"My wife, she's pregnant!" He screamed out the address. "Go there please, I'm getting the midwife!" The officer deliberated a minute. Fredrich realized how ridiculous he must look. Sprinting in his slippers and pajamas in the snow. The officer let out a grunt and decided to believe the crazy man. He saddled up his horse and went to the address.

He saw the midwife's house. If his wife was not about to give birth, he would have stopped to admire the serenity of this nighttime landscape. The snow, the moon, the cold all of it always thrilled him.

"Ms. Claudette!" He banged on the door. Instantly Ms. Claudette opened it, almost as if she had been expecting his knock at three in the morning. But she wasn't the most respected midwife for no reason. Hurriedly she gathered her things.

"Meet me at the stable around back." She said quietly.

He went to the stable and she came down a moment later. Quickly she readied the horse, and they were off.

XII

Sirus Tegel awoke with no purpose. Suddenly, he awoke, and he hadn't the slightest idea why. Groggily he lit his lantern and went to the outhouse. He then returned to his bed, but now awake, he couldn't fall back to sleep. So once again he lit the lantern, and this time went to the kitchen across the yard. He rummaged through his pantry until he found a pretzel. He did not want to wake the servants. He sat down at the table and began to butter slices of it, then returned to his bedroom.

Outside, snow flurries fell with no purpose. They scattered like confetti, but no one had married. All of the servants slept peacefully, so did the horses. This was not unusual for Tegel. In fact, these late-night awakenings had become more frequent. He looked down at the swirled butter and traced the lines with his eyes. Times like these he could truly reflect on his life and his life's work. His doctoral certification hung over his fireplace. He had graduated top of his class. He thought about all the students that piled into his lecture hall. He had purpose, he had meaning. His theories were becoming nationally renowned. He had been asked to write for numerous philosophical publications. Some had even called him the leading philosopher of Germany.

Slowly he chewed. The creamy butter coated the bread as he ate it. The patterns on his flannel pajama shirt criss-crossed into infinite oblivions he could not trace with his eyes. Right now, the world had grown silent and cold, the only real thing with meaning he held in his hand.

XIII

"You have it sweetie, push, push." the midwife calmly instructed Janette. Fredrich and even the police officer was frantic. But Ms. Claudette kept her head throughout the entire procedure. She gently cupped the baby's head and slowly assisted the tiny body out of the womb. Quickly, she washed the baby off and bundled it up.

Fredrich stared at his newborn daughter. She was beautiful. But it was the birth itself that amazed him. A new existence had appeared; a new life form had pushed its way through blood and bone to join the human race. And it sat in a pile of mush and tissue, but ready to live.

"My baby..." Janette said faintly. The midwife handed her the baby. Instinctively, Fredrich went over to his wife. He kissed the newborn atop her brand-new skull, ever so gently.

"Well Mr. Gingale, you have a healthy baby girl." Ms. Claudette shook his hand. Even the gruff police officer cracked a smile. "She's a beauty, pal. Makes me remember when mine was born." He also shook Fredrich's hand.

Fredrich stared at his baby and instantly loved her.

"Ma'am, are you leaving soon? If you want, I will ride back with you, so you do not have to go alone so late at night." The police officer said to Ms. Claudette.

"Actually, I am going to stay here at least until morning." Ms. Claudette responded. "But thank you for the offer."

The officer smiled at her and then turned to Fredrich. "Sir, I am going to get on my way, do you think you need anything else?"

Fredrich thought for a moment. "No officer, I think we are okay. Thank you."

"I didn't do anything. It was all her," he pointed to Ms. Claudette "and her" he pointed to Janette. Both women smiled at the compliment. "Once again congratulations to the new parents" he tipped his hat, "and good evening." He walked out the door.

"Your wife needs some rest Mr. Gingale." Ms. Claudette pulled Fredrich aside. "You and I will tend to the baby."

Fredrich went to kiss his wife good night.

"I want to...see my baby" she said exhaustedly.

"You will sweetie. But you need to sleep first. Ms. Claudette and I will tend to the baby." Janette tried to argue but fell asleep. Fredrich kissed her forehead and pulled the blanket up to her chin.

"She truly is beautiful, Mr. Gingale." Ms. Claudette held the baby and soothed it to sleep. "She looks very healthy. One of the healthier ones I've been around. "Here." She handed the baby to her father.

The tiny piece of life fell asleep in Fredrich's arms. He cradled her ever so gently. He gazed at this raw chunk of existence, like sinewy tissue that gives life to its predator, this baby gave a bit more life to a stagnant universe. And as he held her, he wanted to tell her that everything would be okay, that life would be good, like he had told his sister at the funeral. But he didn't know if he could lie anymore.

"Your name will be Sofia." He kissed her warm head. "It means wisdom." He whispered. Ms. Claudette looked at father and daughter from across the room as she readied blankets. She smiled as she folded.

XIV

"The world spirit had its first stirrings in China." Tegel paused for a moment. "It is in China where an autocratic government arose, under Shi Hunagi. And in this autocratic regime, we first have a true state and subordinate people. However, the people are forced into this state; their needs are subordinated to the state. It is an artificial state based on the sole will of the emperor. Nonetheless, it exhibited the first true break with our animal nature; it was humanity's first true government."

He loved to watch the students write. Their faces were so intent; they hung on his words. Because, and he genuinely believed this, these students knew the truth, and they sensed Sirus Tegel could give it to them. He spoke of China, India, and Egypt. And all the while his students listened.

Fredrich sat in his usual seat in the back. And, like always, he struggled to keep up. It seemed as soon as he finally comprehended one thought, Tegel and the other students were discussing another. Fredrich felt like he was five minutes behind everyone else.

"Next, we come to Persia. And it is with the religion of Zoroastrianism that man first has a glimpse of the divine. It is Zoroaster who first gave man the choice to inherit the light of the good. It didn't depend on the emperors, or on a caste system, it was only the light and the dark, and man had the choice to reunite with light."

Fredrich had been told that some of Tegel's theories were ethnocentric, and others were severe oversimplifications. And he tended to somewhat agree. He knew that no one else would dare contradict such a great teacher, and Tegel truly was an amazing professor. And really who was he to contradict Professor Tegel? He kept his thoughts to himself and kept writing.

A student toward the front of the room raised his hand. "Is it true that some of the later Persian emperors converted to Zoroastrianism?"

"Yes." Nodded Tegel. "Not only that, but the already existing religion of Judaism, and later Christianity would be heavily influenced by Zoroaster's teachings."

Once again, like eunuch scribes, the students copied down Tegel's words. And while Fredrich did the same, a twinge of anger rose in him. All these supposedly brilliant students were nothing but copycats. Cristof Horbis, an honor student in the front row, had won the prestigious student award and had been selected to author a paper together with Tegel. And Fredrich was probably jealous, but it was more than jealousy, it was anger. All Horbis did was copy, reiterate, and regurgitate the professor's words and theories. Students were discouraged from wildly speculating and instead encouraged to write presentable, coherent papers with no original thought but perfect punctuation to make up for that. And perhaps all this was needed to run a good institution and produce good scholars.

But the hell with that! The hell with scholars and honor students! What if Tegel's progress is a joke, and all of this meant shit?

"The last area we will examine today is Egypt. It is in Egypt where we first have the recognition of reason; but still trapped in instinct. In fact, it is in Egypt's most famous structure, the Sphinx, in which this struggle is most evident."

Fredrich knew he barely gained entrance into the philosophy program here. He was only a lowly gymnasium teacher. But nonetheless, here he sat, struggling.

Tegel looked triumphantly at his audience. It was obvious he was preparing to convey an amazing statement of incomparable wit. "The Sphinx, with its human face, is trying to tear itself loose from its animal body, or more analogously, reason is trapped in the earth, in the animal instinct, and it is in Egypt where this struggle begins."

Triumphantly he glided across the floor. He let the words sink in. And, in Fredrich's opinion, it truly was an amazing statement. He conjured up visions of the Sphinx, of this human-faced animal.

"You see, it is Egypt where thought and logic are given to humans in the form of Gods. These abstract concepts were still tied up in zoolatry and in such ridiculous figures like jackal and hawk headed humans, but nonetheless, it is here that humans first truly deal with these concepts on a daily level. One of their mightiest and most powerful gods was Osirus. He was the god of reason. And so, in a childish, nonsensical way, higher and abstract concepts were being employed on a daily level."

Tegel stopped talking and let the students copy his last thoughts down.

"Okay, I think we will stop here for today. Next lecture we will begin to discuss the Greeks."

Tegel began to pack up his belongings and on cue, the usual students filed down the aisles and made their way to his desk. The usual posse crowded around Tegel. The man truly became a celebrity at this school. Fredrich slowly made his way down the aisle as well, but this time, he actually had something to say to Tegel, who he wasn't even sure knew his name.

Patiently he waited for the throng of students to gradually dissipate. He caught fragments of their conversations:

"Compared to Kant...Descartes said...Plato...Aristotle..."

As usual, Christof Horbis stood in front leading the questioning. From what Fredrich could hear, they weren't even questions; they were more like statements, as if Christof tried so desperately hard to impress everyone. Fredrich wanted to scream in his face, grab him by the shirt collar, drag him up to the wall and tell him, show him, that all his regurgitated knowledge was worthless. But no one would ever listen to Fredrich because he was a nobody.

"Son?" Tegel spoke directly to Fredrich. The throng had dissipated. Fredrich stood alone, feeling almost painfully embarrassed.

"Hello, professor Tegel..." Fredrich extended his hand. Tegel reciprocated the gesture. "I will not be here next class. I have to help care for my wife; she just gave birth. I wanted to let you know," in all honestly Tegel would not have known the difference "and I was wondering if there was any work I would miss."

"Congrats! Well, actually, I was going to hand out an outline I had drawn up. If you have time, you could follow me to my office" Tegel said politely.

"That would be very helpful, thank you." Fredrich waited patiently as Tegel packed up his things. From the corner of his eye, Fredrich saw another student re-enter the hall. Christof.

"Professor," Christof talked slowly and deliberately, accenting every syllable in his words.

"Yes Christof?" Tegel smiled back at his star pupil.

"Sorry to bother you again, but I wanted to settle an argument I was having with another student."

"Well, I am headed to my office if you want to walk."

"Yes, please." Christof gave Fredrich a disinterested nod of hello.

"I had said that Descartes believed that matter and mind came from God. But Fam said no."

Fam, Eric Famulares, was another one of Tegel's star students. Fredrich tagged behind these two giants like a snot-nosed child, desperately in need of some attention.

"Well, you can send him to me and I will tell him that you are right," Tegel smiled at Christof. Tegel loved it, he loved the attention, he loved the applause and praise. And in that instant, Fredrich realized he simply played a game. A game he was destined to lose.

They arrived at Tegel's office. Christof bid farewell to Tegel and left. Fredrich followed Tegel into his office.

"If you give me a moment, I will dig it up for you."

But there was nothing to dig up. The office was immaculate. Every single book had been alphabetized, every paper neatly filed away; there was a small container in the desk for stationery items. The floor gleamed, one could eat off it and the fine oak finish of the bookcase glistened in the candlelight.

There was an awkward silence as Tegel retrieved the paper. And then Fredrich heard a noise outside the window. It sounded as if something was breathing heavily and striking the snow with its feet, almost like a bull. It made Fredrich jump. Tegel looked up at him curiously, and then he smiled.

"Oh, it's just this wild dog outside. The damn thing always comes to my window." Tegel opened the window. "Get! Get out of here mutt!"

Fredrich stared intently out the window and saw a pair of eyes. They were pale, shifty eyes, eyes that looked purely animal, eyes filled with fear and hatred. Then they were gone, followed by heavy steps.

"That damn mutt always bothers me." Tegel smiled, and then he forgot about the dog. "Here it is." He pulled out a freshly printed outline of the next lesson. "You can take a look at this for now. But try to copy someone else's lecture so you don't fall behind. I will see you at the lecture after next? Yes?"

"Yes. I will see you next time."

"Okay, farewell then." Tegel pulled out his chair and began to work. Fredrich left the office and began his walk home.

XV

Fredrich buttoned his jacket against the assault of the wind. He loved and hated the cold at the same time. It stung him, made him feel alive, but it hurt. He walked quickly to get home to Sophie. Beautiful Sophie, fat red cheeks and a baby smell, he loved her so much, but he was scared for her. Truly, what was she to be born into? What was this world? He surveyed his immediate landscape. The street lanterns, the snow, a few horse-drawn carriages, what was all this? He thought of Tegel and Horbis, was she to be born into their world?

"Watch it!" a driver yelled out to Fredrich as he almost stepped in front of a horse-drawn carriage moving speedily.

Sophie was close to being divine, truly, only a few days removed from her blessed state. But she now had to compete with the rest of the hogs. Tegel, Christoff, they were all fat hogs at some cosmic trough, all with their noses stuck into the feed, the shredded skin of the weaker pigs. Is this what he would give to his daughter? She would have to learn the rules of the universe, learn how to fight for the scrapes, learn to be systematically and humbly exploited by the fatter hogs. Is this existence?

It made him want to cry, but he had to be strong, strong for Sophie, strong for Janette and his family. He wanted to give his daughter a new universe, one in which she could write poetry all day and forge her own progress instead of having to read others' philosophy and eat the skin of her weaker cousins.

It was a good thing he only thought these things to himself. It was no wonder he struggled in his studies. Instead of studying, he thought about nonsense that served absolutely no purpose, or at least nothing that could ever be graded.

XVI

The light in Tegel's office flickered. He was there. Sethhauer fingered the oblong heavy stone. He glanced around one more time to make sure no one was looking before he threw it and shattered the window. Before Tegel could scream, Sethhauer had crawled halfway through the window and pounced on him. He threw Tegel through the window. As Tegel's body glided over the broken shards still attached to the frame, tiny skin ribbons curled around the glass. Sethhauer quickly grabbed Tegel's mouth and forced it shut. Tegel dropped out of the window like it had vomited his body. Sethhauer kicked him in the ribs. The crack of bone made him smile and he did it again. And again. Tegel tried to scream again but Sethhauer struck him square in the jaw with the stone, instantly dislocating it. Sethhauer felt the old man's hot tears and it exhilarated him even more. He pulled the old man up by his shirt until their noses almost touched.

"You thought you could embarrass me!" he hissed. "You and your cronies, your little shit posse! Your charlatan theories are a disgrace to western philosophy! Someone should have killed you earlier!"

Sethhauer slammed him face first onto the hard ground. Hot blood oozed everywhere. Sethhauer ran his fingers through it and smeared it across his face.

"I wear this like a badge!" He kicked Tegel in his already dislocated jaw. Tegel whimpered and Sethhauer dragged him face to face again. "You imposter! Your goddam progress has tainted us all! Brainwashed the youths I tried to liberate! Now they are charlatans like you! A generation of brainless fakers who now need a crutch to limp through the rest of their sorrowful existence with!" Bastard!"

Tegel was almost on the point of collapse, but the thing he noticed before he lost consciousness was Sethhauer's eyes. They stared down intently at him, with no remorse, with nothing but animal hatred.

"This is your progress." Sethhauer calmly took a blade from his boot. He slit Tegel's throat and watched him die. The body dropped onto the hard ground. He had suffered and died, but Sethhauer wanted more. Furiously, he began to hack the carcass into pieces. He hacked off fingers and scooped out an eye. He stabbed the fleshy pot belly and tore off an ear. Yet, he remained unsatisfied; he still felt human. Frantically, he searched for a way to disgrace the already dead man even more.

And then his eyes bulged. A sick smile spread across his face. He lunged at Tegel's neck and bit a chunk of already torn skin. He gnashed it in his teeth and savored the blood. Blood oozed into his mouth, hot red sticky blood, and it tasted amazing. He hated this man, this used up worthless excuse for a philosopher.

Was this his vaunted progress? Were all these bloody pieces his divine logic? He spit out the blood and skin chunks. They fluttered onto the snow. Sethhauer dipped his fingers in the still warm blood and began to write a message on the white bricks.

When he had finished, Sethhauer arose. He surveyed the scene. He looked up at the moon and screamed. But it was an inhuman, animalistic caveman scream. Sethhauer had just defended his honor.

XVII

"Hi cutie!" Fredrich squeezed baby Sophie's face. Her fat red cheeks were like putty. She giggled and remained inert. Fredrich fixed the blanket that she lay on.

"Bring her over here," said Janette. "I have to feed her."

"Nice life you have," he kissed her again "All you do is eat, sleep and poop!" Sophie giggled again as he picked her up and handed her to Janette. Her tiny body fit perfectly into the crook of Janette's arm as she began to feed her. Fredrich took the blanket and covered up his wife's exposed breast. Janette smiled and continued to stare down at her daughter.

All was tranquil, all was at peace. The cold seemed to numb everyone. Momma and baby were quietly nestled into each other. Fredrich tended the candle. The soft glow diffused in the room, adding even more tranquility to the scene.

"Bang! Bang! Bang!" Three violent knocks at the door startled Janette and Fredrich. Even baby Sophie jumped. It was a frightening knock: a knock that shattered any peace, a knock that became a transition into a much darker time. Fredrich put the lit candle aside and apprehensively walked to the door. He checked the peephole and hurriedly undid the chains and the locks.

"Who is it?" asked Janette.

Before Fredrich answered her, he opened the door. Three uniformed police officers stood stoically before him. The one nearest to him must have been a captain, because his uniform was decorated slightly differently. Thick grey and white whiskers hung over his pale face. The other two looked considerably younger. One was a man probably Fredrich's age. His husky frame resembled a bull. He had a neatly trimmed goatee and a short, stocky build. The third man appeared to be in his mid-thirties. He had no beard and probably stood over six feet tall.

"Mr. Gingale?" the captain asked.

"Yes," Fredrich answered.

"My name is officer Henrich. These are officers Dallier and Augustus. May we ask you a few questions?"

"Um..." Fredrich was in shock "Sure."

"May we come in?" the captain asked.

"Oh, of course." He sheepishly invited them in. "What's going on?" he tried to sound in control, but his voice cracked.

"Please, have a seat, you too Mrs. Gingale."

Fredrich and Janette sat next to each other on the sofa; Janette cradled the baby tight.

"Let me preface this conversation," The captain looked at Fredrich. "You are not in any trouble; we just want to ask you a few questions." The young burly officer stared softly at Sophie.

"Mr. Gingale, I am just going to come out and say this." Henrich paused. "Last night, Professor Sirus Tegel was murdered."

Fredrich sat astonished.

"We have been told that you were the last person to see him alive. Can you just tell us what happened?"

Fredrich took a moment to collect his thoughts. He took a breath and began.

"Well, I am...ah...was...enrolled in his advanced philosophical theories course. I had class last night at eighteen hundred hours. Since I was going to miss tomorrow's class, I asked him for my make-up work. He told me to follow him to his office, so I did after class. I was in his office for about five minutes, where he gave me the outline. Then I left."

Henrich stroked his thick white beard. "What time did you leave?"

Fredrich thought for a moment. "Well class ended at twenty hundred hours, and it probably took about fifteen minutes to walk to his office and get the outline."

"We have the murder pinned at about twenty-two hundred hours." Henrich said. "Let me make this clear. You are not a suspect, but we did need to obtain your testimony."

"Can I ask...what happened?" Fredrich asked sheepishly.

Henrich took a deep breath. "He was..." there was an awkward pause "he was beaten severely, his throat was slit, then the body was decimated, an eye was popped out, fingers were hacked off..." Henrich lost himself in the gruesome description.

Janette looked appalled, but Fredrich wanted more. He wanted to know what happened.

"And the most disturbing thing of the whole scene was that a chunk of Professor's Tegel's throat was" Henrich paused again, "bitten off." The way Henrich enunciated bitten gave Janette a shiver. Fredrich sat perplexed but not appalled. "On the wall, in Tegel's blood was written the phrase 'is this progress?' continued Henrich.

Fredrich sat in the ocean of carpet. That was a hefty load. How does one respond to that? But Fredrich thought about what was written. Is this progress?

Fredrich held his wife's hand and pondered.

"He and another professor I know had problems."

"Are you referring to Professor Sethhauer?" asked Henrich.

"Yes. I don't really know the details, but I know there was a lot of tension. During my class last week, Sethhauer kicked everyone out because one of the students had mentioned Tegel."

"He forced everyone to leave?"

"Yes." Fredrich confirmed.

"Were you aware Professor Sethhauer was relieved from his teaching position at the university, and has been missing since last night?"

"Ah...no." Was all Fredrich could say. Fredrich knew he probably sounded like an idiot, but he didn't care right now. Sethhauer had been fired? Now he was missing? But really, the central question of the entire matter was... could Sethhauer have murdered Tegel? That day in class when he kicked everyone out, he had seen Sethhauer's anger, but was that enough to kill a man? And not only kill a man, but hack a man to pieces?

The young burly officer pulled out a paper from his pocket. Henrich signed it and he handed it to Fredrich. "Please sign at the bottom." Henrich pointed to the line where Fredrich needed to sign.

"You probably want to check with the university regarding your classes. I am sorry for all this; I know it must be overwhelming." Henrich and the other two officers curtly nodded toward Janette and Fredrich.

"If you hear anything, or want to tell us anything, please contact the police department." The three officers filed out the door and left Fredrich and Janette, alone, stranded in their new-found lament. They waited for the door to close.

"Honey..." Janette didn't know what to say. Fredrich did not need to be consoled, but this was nonetheless a shock. "Are you okay?" was all she could mutter out.

"Yeah...I mean...wow. I really don't know what to say. It's not like he died...he was murdered." The word hung ominously in the air. Fredrich had never known anyone that had been murdered. And not just murdered but hacked and desecrated.

"His eyeball and fingers were cut out." Fredrich said despondently.

"That's sick," Janette hugged Sophie, as if trying to protect her. "Do you really think your other professor would do that?"

"I want to say no, but that day, when he exploded at our class, his anger became palpable. I just don't know. His eyes were..."

Fredrich stopped mid-sentence. Eyes. That day in Tegel's office, when he saw the dog outside, the one Tegel shooed away. Was it Sethhauer?

"Honey, what is it?" Janette asked.

"The day I stopped in his office, I heard an animal outside, I saw these hideous eyes, Tegel said it was a wild dog and just shooed it away, but something seemed out of place. Could that have been Sethhauer outside, waiting for me to leave?"

A chill ran down Fredrich's spine. Janette squeezed his hand.

"Do you think you should say something to the police?" Janette asked.

Fredrich thought for a moment. "I don't know, they might just think I'm nuts."

"Honey, you never know, I think it's something you need to tell them."

"You're probably right," he said.

"Tomorrow is Saturday, I was going to ask you to go to the market and get milk and bread, and maybe you should stop at the police station and just tell them. If you really wanted to, you could chase them down right now."

Fredrich thought about this. The police probably weren't too far. But no, he didn't want to leave his family, not tonight. He looked at the black sky and became afraid. In that black sky, Tegel's progress faltered. Logic became a sick joke.

He pulled Janette and Sophie closer. He wanted to tell them everything would be okay, maybe Aunt Anna watched from somewhere, but a growing fear festered inside him. Sethhauer was out there, murdering any notion of progress or divinity. The snow outside no longer looked like a Christmas card. It became ominous and illogical, it laughed, it shrieked, it exploded. Baby Sophie cooed but her childhood ended right there. There was no childhood, only a black sky.

"Honey…are you okay?" Janette broke his trance. He looked at her and smiled. It was all he could do in the face of the irrational.

"Yeah," he paused for a moment "You're right, Tomorrow I am going to go to the police.

XVIII

Say your prayers dear," Marie said to her daughter.

"Okay mommy." Christiania kneeled over her bed and closed her little hands together. She bowed her head and began to pray.

"Dear God, please protect my family, my mom, my dad, my brother, and Janette. Also, please watch over Aunt Annie in heaven."

Marie watched her daughter pray and it gave her comfort. Christiania was a good girl; she did well in school and said her prayers. There was an unmistakable smile on her face, a smile of content, a smile that assured her mother all was good. Christiana crossed herself in the name of the father and crawled under her warm covers. Marie lit a small candle on Christiana's nightstand.

"Mommy?" her little round face beamed up from under the covers.

"Yes"

"Did you mail the letter I wrote for Fredrich?"

"Yes, I mailed it yesterday."

"Thank you, mommy," she smiled. "I hope he gets it before Christmas."

"I'm sure he will. Good night sweetie."

"Mommy?" she asked one more time.

"Yes sweetie?" she answered her daughter patiently.

"Does Aunt Annie listen to my prayers?"

"Of course, she does sweetie. She's in heaven with God and the angels. Right now, she's looking down at us."

"I wish she could be here with us," Christiana gave a slight frown.

"I know sweetie, but God wanted her in heaven, and we can't question what God wants."

Like seven years old's do, her mind instantly switched to a happier subject. "When can we see little baby Sophie?"

"After Christmas we will go to see her. But right now, you need to go to sleep."

"Maybe Aunt Annie sent baby Sophie as a gift." Said Christiana.

"Maybe. But right now, go to sleep! Or no presents!"

Sophie quickly covered herself with the blanket. "'Night mommy!'" she yelled as Marie walked out the room.

Christiania fell asleep, assured of her existence, assured of both her living and dead family members. But eighty kilometers away, her older half-brother, slept uneasily. His assurances had died with his philosophy professor.

XIX
The Next Morning

Fredrich peeked behind the curtain, and all he saw was white, immense, and overbearing, impenetrable white. The sky, the ground, the falling snow, the buildings, all white, pure, serene but unforgiving. But sadly, Fredrich could no longer enjoy this tranquil scene. Instead, he quickly dropped the curtain. All night and into the morning he had been uneasy. Not afraid, but uneasy. Something did not sit right with him. Obviously, the murder weighed heavily on him, but it was bigger than the murder. Something had been brewing inside of him, something bigger than a murder, than birth or death.

His wife and child slept peacefully, Anna and Tegel were dead, and Sethhauer was out there. Something had gone wrong. But perhaps "wrong" no longer had any meaning because it was a human word, so was progress and logic. They were all human creations only adhered to for the purpose of living peacefully.

Fuck peace! Fuck security! It was all a joke! There was nothing but snow! He sounded like a crazy man. And this is why he only thought these things, as opposed to speaking them.

This is why he struggled in school. Christoff Horbis did not think of these things, he studied instead, he tried to impress his teachers...but now his teacher was dead. Really, how could anyone afford to ignore this, whatever this was? The blood, the murder, the snow.

Once again, Fredrich faltered, even his thoughts. If his thoughts were graded, he would still receive a failing mark.

"Sweetie," Janette walked into the living room.

Fredrich turned around.

"Hey honey, what's up," he tried to sound like nothing was wrong.

"Are you going to go to the police station?" she asked.

Fredrich took a deep breath. "They are going to think I'm crazy," his tone was slightly annoyed, and she picked up on it.

"You need to tell them, what if that's an important part of the case, they need all the help they can get."

He knew his wife was right, she usually was. But his pride didn't let him back down. He truly would feel like an idiot, telling them about a pair of eyes he saw outside. He remained silent for a while.

"Okay, I'm leaving now. I'll go to the police. What do you need from the market?"

"Bread and milk. And why don't you pick up some soup and pork for dinner tonight." Her tone softened.

"Okay, I am going now. I should be back in an hour or so." He walked over to the coat rack and began to bundle up. Scarf, mittens, winter coat and heavy boots, he tied up everything, took some money, kissed his wife, and left.

It truly looked like someone had thrown a white blanket over the earth. All were bundled in their tiny apartments, fireplaces raged, and chimneys pumped black smoke above the white scene. Fredrich felt alone, abandoned to this white world, like the first brush on a fresh canvas, he and the chimney smoke were the first beings in an otherwise blank universe.

The glass milk bottle made his hands freeze. He probably should have gone to the police station first, but he didn't. He went to the market, but the bread and herring offered no comfort. He walked alone, bundled in snow, so desperately wanting to be home in front of his fireplace, with his wife and baby.

Like a gaffed fish he flopped when the fist struck his jawbone. The glass bottle did not break when it hit the pillowed snow. Fredrich scrambled around and tried to regain his footing among his felled groceries, but a heel slammed down hard into the back of his head. The snow tasted cold.

"You bastard!" Sethhauer dragged Fredrich by his collar through the snow. "You pathetic excuse!" He knew the voice instantly. "People like you...it is...people like you!" Sethhauer's words were choppy and almost incoherent, just like the day when he kicked everyone out. "You try to copy everyone else; you spit out whatever a professor tells you!" Fredrich, now finally recovered from the initial shock of the assault, broke free from Sethhauer's grip. He stood face to face with this man, his former professor, now the attacker. Sethhauer's jaw and teeth were stained red with Tegel's dried blood. His eyes were identical to that day outside of Tegel's office.

"You fuck! You pathetic fuck! I saw you that day, kissing his ass! Probably trying to quote him and impress him! Pathetic!" Sethhauer took a wild, haymaker swing at Fredrich, but he ducked out of the way. Fredrich's initial shock was gone, it turned to anger.

"You have no idea why I was in his office!" Fredrich tried to muster up some courage.

But Sethhauer did not exist, there only remained an animal.

"It felt so good to kill him, so satisfying," Sethhauer sneered. I tasted his blood. But I want more! And you, you..." he couldn't finish his sentence.

Fredrich was not an animal. Animals do not feel satisfaction; they do not feel the insatiable bloodlust that Sethhauer felt.

"All my life I have fought against ignorance! I fought against sycophants and apologists like Tegel...like you!"

Sethhauer could not be reasoned with. Fredrich's only salvation would be defense, or death. Sethhauer lunged at him with teeth bared, but they couldn't pierce Fredrich's winter coat. Sethhauer rolled to the ground and snatched a loose stone. Instantly, he bashed Fredrich and broke his nose. Fredrich stumbled backwards and fell against the wall.

"I wanted to kill you when I saw you that day...but I will finish it now." Sethhauer said calmly. Fredrich wished he had screamed it, but he had said it calmly, eerily.

Sethhauer took another lunge at his injured prey, but Fredrich gathered his strength and knocked away the stone from Sethhauer's hand. Weaponless, Sethhauer still attacked. He grabbed hold of Fredrich's coat, but Fredrich wriggled his way out of it. He stood, freed from his coat, panting, bloody, but nonetheless, alive. This time he went on the offensive and lunged at Sethhauer, punching him below the right eye. The blow sent him stumbling back into the wall, but he quickly lunged at Fredrich once again, this time biting his exposed arm. Sethhauer's teeth punctured Fredrich's thin shirt, he felt the teeth protrude and break the skin. Instantly, Fredrich pulled away, and the wound ripped open, blood instantly spilled everywhere.

"You piece of shit! What do you know?" Fredrich knew it was pointless to argue, but he had to say something, anything. But reason failed miserably in the face of this madness.

Sethhauer lunged again but Fredrich defensively put his knee up and caught Sethhauer in the gut, Sethhauer bounced off but quickly regained himself. He stood and faced Fredrich, wildly panting, eyes enraged and bulging.

The snow became relentless. Both men strained to see. They circled each other, like Roman gladiators. But no one watched. And there was no snow in Rome. The two philosophers, turned gladiators, fought to their death for no one to see. The only color, the blood red and black chimney smoke. All were indoors, warming by a fire, saying prayers, eating lunch. No one bothered to lift their curtains and witness the duel. Fredrich stood erect, and stoic, ready to face his enemy. Sethhauer, barely stood, he more crouched. Fresh and crusty blood covered his entire body.

"I will never quit, I will never stop," Sethhauer breathed wild, gaping breaths, "All my life, I have fought against you," he said the word with a sneer. "Apologists, and sycophants false prophets and purveyors of false knowledge. "

Fredrich found it ironic to hear this raging animal beast of man using such intelligent words. He sounded like a deranged Socrates. "I am not your enemy, I actually believed in some of your theories..." Fredrich began a useless defense, but a true one.

"Well believe in this you charlatan! Progress is dead! I murdered it, I hacked its fingers off, I gouged out its eyeballs and I wore its blood! That is what you can believe in!"

"You killed a man!" Fredrich screamed. "You killed one defenseless, helpless individual, an old man twice your age, what did you prove? What did you accomplish? Nothing!" he wanted to add that Tegel's ideas would live on, but he refrained, because he didn't know if he believed in Tegel. He didn't want to align with Sethhauer, but he couldn't bring himself to defend Tegel either.

"I needed to start the revolution!" Sethhauer gulped, Fredrich assumed he swallowed the blood that pooled in his mouth.

"You sick fuck, you haven't started anything, just a manhunt, so they can hang you!" Fredrich said with confidence.

"Bah! What do your laws mean! Fake institutions meant to cage me! Meant to cage the irrational! You can't do it! Hang me! Please! Hang everyone until there is no one left! Then it will be a perfect state!"

His brain devolved; nothing made sense to him anymore. Fredrich debated what to do. Fredrich could not try to bring him into the police. But suddenly, Sethhauer took a running start at his opponent, who had been momentary handicapped with reason, and put a shoulder into him, knocking him to the ground. Sethhauer stood over him, but Fredrich remained ready to parry any blows.

"Know that I will never stop. I will hunt you until we die, and then I will hunt you in hell!" With that, Sethhauer sprinted off into the blizzard, into the snow and endless white. He sprinted into the forest and disappeared.

Fredrich remained inert on the ground and blood crystals froze on his lips. The unbroken milk container laid camouflaged in the snow, the bread had been trampled. Still, no one had ventured outside, they all remained cozy and tucked into their cramped tenements, tending fires and eating soup, trying to stay warm. Janette and Sophie were inside too. Quickly, Fredrich picked himself up. He had to get home, he wanted to get home, he needed to be with his family. Despite the pain in his head and arm, he sprinted the half kilometer back.

XX

He gently opened the door to his apartment. The blood began to dry on his face and his arm, but new blood oozed as well. He locked the door behind him. He couldn't let his wife see him like this, but he obviously couldn't hide it. He at least wanted to clean some of the blood off his face, so as not to look as bad as he must look right now.

"Honey?" she called from the bedroom.

"Yes," he tried to sound fine.

"Come into the bedroom and look at Sophie!"

"I'll be there in a minute." He choked out trying to sound normal.

"Okay." She said,

In the living room stood a bucket of water. He rummaged through the cabinet to find a washcloth. But his broken nose made it hard to concentrate, made it hard to even stand. He felt dizzy and began to stumble backwards. For support, he put his hand on the mantle but instead grabbed Anna's porcelain doll. The room spun and closed in, he stumbled further and dragged the doll off the shelf, accidentally throwing it to the floor. Before he could make any attempt to grab it, the doll shattered on the hardwood, the smile on its face broke into pieces, no longer a smile, just hardened, jagged snowflake like pieces.

"Honey what was that?" his wife asked, alarmed.

"Nothing, I broke a glass..."

"You are worthless!" she yelled playfully. "Let me clean it up."

"No! Stay in there!"

But before he could stop her, she came in with the baby. And when she saw him, she stopped and froze. She tried to talk but couldn't say anything. She only saw her husband covered in blood and torn clothes, with a shattered porcelain doll on the floor.

"Ah...ah..." she tried to say something... anything but could not.

"Sethhauer...found me...attacked me...I fended him off..." that is all he could say to his wife. Truly, what else could he say? That he had been a victim in the battle for existence? He had been bitten and clubbed and the assailant vanished into the white oblivion? Could he tell her that Sethhauer stalked him now? That a savage roamed the streets of

Germany? No. All he could say was...

"I broke...the doll."

Methodically he bent down and began to scoop up the pieces. He couldn't help but feel a connection with the broken thing. Was he no different? Was he not just a glass doll caught in a battle of two bigger forces? In the battle for existence? Smashed to pieces, but glued together and used for another purpose? And always whole before sunrise? Smashed and glued, constantly re-used in someone else's battle? Smashed and glued, smashed and glued, smashed glued, smashed glued, until the pieces got smaller and smaller; smashed and glued until he became fine porcelain snow scattered in the oblivion?

"Sit down, let me clean you up." Janette said despondently. She put the baby in the bassinet, wet the towel, and began to dab her husband's face. The fire raged and all the curtains were pulled. Silently, Janette tended to her husband's wounds. He wanted to say something, something to calm his wife, something intelligent, but all he managed was..."I'll try to glue the doll for Sophie."

Janette nodded and dipped the towel into the water bucket, which stained the water red and made it unfit to drink.

The Inevitable Odd

Part I

I

1985 In a small apartment
25 miles north of New York City

"Fuck you! How dare you talk to me like that!" Nancy walked into the kitchen and wiped her face with a paper towel.

"Whatever. I'm sick of this shit. Every day you have a new complaint. This isn't clean or I forgot to do something," Tommy mimicked his wife.

"I hate you!" she threw a paper cup of coffee in Tommy Senior's direction, aiming to miss. The cup exploded on the white wall and brown veins streaked down onto the carpet.

"Are you serious? You crazy bitch! What the fuck is wrong with you!"

"I hate you! That's what's wrong! I hate you so much! I can't stomach you!" Nancy's reddened puffed up face tightened into a glare.

"Crazy bitch," he shook his head.

Tommy Junior sat quietly in the corner through all of this. He clutched his antique abacus tightly. He had no idea what this thing was, but the barely audible clacking of the beads soothed him for some reason.

"I've had it! I hate you! I hate it here! This shithole of an apartment! I wanted a house!"

Tommy Senior watched his wife-soon to be ex-wife cry in the kitchen. She hated him. Less than five years ago they made supposed lifelong vows, but they broke easily, easier than either of them had thought.

"Clack. Clack." Tommy Junior's abacus filled the intervals of awkward silence.

"I'm leaving," Nancy said calmly, almost indifferently.

"I'm taking the baby and going to my mother's. I can't live like this."

Tommy Senior stood at the other end of the apartment. He wanted so desperately to reconcile this. But his pride swelled.

"Get the fuck out," he walked into the bedroom and slammed the door.

II

As Tommy sat and waited for his mother, a fly buzzed a few feet away from his head.

"Here you go sweetie," Nancy handed her son a chocolate ice cream cone. A faint whiff of garbage wafted over to him from the trucks parked in the gas station next door.

"Is it good?" Nancy tried to force a smile through her still puffy face.

"Yes mommy. Chocolate is my favorite." Tommy Junior licked the ice cream until his mouth and lips were frosted in chocolate.

"Baby, it looks like we're on our own," she twisted his brown locks.

"Where are we going to go now mommy?" he asked innocently.

She began to cry.

"We're going to go to grandma's." She put her arm around him.

"I love you so much."

"I love you too mommy."

Nancy hugged her four-year-old son. She stared at the garbage trucks across the way. What would happen to him? In that instant she felt an unmatched sorrow for her baby boy. He would never know the life a child should. Instead, he would grow up with half a family, a single mother. In that instant she realized she would have to be his father and mother, but she didn't know if she could live up to that awesome responsibility. He nestled into the crook of her arm and finished his ice cream.

"I told you Nancy, I told you this would happen! You should never have married him!"

"I'm sorry mom! I didn't think this would happen!" she began to cry again.

Tommy Junior quietly played with his abacus. Counting the beads, over and over in his own universe of beaded numbers, away from the arguments, away from the thrown coffee cups and accusations.

Bridgette sat next to her daughter and poured a glass of water.

"Well, you are going to have to live here for a while. Until you can get a job and find a place to live."

Nancy wanted to throw up. She felt 18 years old again. She had to move back with her parents. She had to get a real job, support herself and her son. High school all over again but with a kid.

Tommy Junior had an amazing ability to lose himself within some private universe.

"Well, what about the baby?" Bridgette asked.

"He's too young. He doesn't really know what's going on. At least I hope not." Nancy turned her head away.

Bridgette stared at her grandson. "Come here sweetie," Tommy Junior unsteadily walked over to his grandmother, still clutching the abacus.

"What do you have there?"

"It's an abicust" Tommy's pudgy fingers clutched the beads.

"Oh, an abacus," his grandmother enunciated.

"Yeah, I like counting the beads." He didn't look up at his grandmother. Instead, he clacked incessantly.

"Dammit Tommy, stop that noise! Stop clacking that damn thing! Give it a rest!" A vein began to pop out of his mother's temple.

"Nancy, stop it! Leave him alone." She hugged her grandson.

"Why do you yell at him like that! What is the matter with you?" The gold crucifix on her neck dug into his skin as she squeezed him but Tommy kept quiet.

"I'm sorry...I'm sorry," Nancy cried into her hands.

Bridgette lightly squeezed her grandson's cheek.

"Go downstairs and watch T.V. Tommiebutz." Tommy Junior smiled while his grandmother called him that.

As he descended the stairs, his mother's crying faded into the walls. He stood in the ocean of carpet, and it ebbed away. His fingers clenched tight around the abacus as he began to count. The docile pastel colors of his grandparent's outdated den comforted him in a strange way.

He clacked the abacus, clacked its beads, and unknowingly counted his new solitude as a number.

III

"What time is the hearing?" Marion checked the sauce on the stove.

"Three o'clock," Tommy Senior answered her.

"Well, it's one-thirty now. Why don't you eat and then take a nap? I'll wake you up by two-thirty."

"Okay," Tommy Senior said blankly.

His mother waited for the sauce to thicken. His father came into the kitchen and sat in his customary seat at the head of the table.

"Tom, you can take your grandmother's old apartment in the garage until you get back on your feet. Save some money and then you can move out." Larry, his father, poured a glass of wine.

"Yeah, that will probably be the best thing." Tommy paused for a moment. "I feel like I'm starting over again. I wanted it to last. I loved her but," he paused again. "I guess it just wasn't meant to be. The damn

Sorrento curse," he said half-jokingly.

Larry looked at his son. "It's not that we're cursed, we just take a few times to get it right," he smiled.

"I dunno, it just seems that divorce and marriage go hand in hand with our family." Tommy took a fork full of pasta.

"Well, you couldn't have stayed married to her any longer. All those fights and arguments. It just wouldn't have worked out." Marion tried to reassure her son.

"I know that. And I know this is for the better, but I'm worried about the baby." Tom took a sip of wine.

"Well," Larry said, "You just have to be there for him. It will be difficult because you won't be around him, but you must always be there and provide for him. I'm sure the judge will grant you a good visitation schedule."

"I know Pop. I just feel guilty. The poor kid won't have a father around. I feel like I've failed, like I failed him."

"Tom, you didn't fail him. You're human. You just made a mistake and there's nothing wrong with that. Little Tom won't be loved any less. And look at it like this, on holidays he'll get double presents now." Larry smiled, trying to lighten the mood.

"Yeah, that's true." Tommy gave a half grin and finished his pasta.

"Don't worry," Marion said, "We'll get through this."

"I know," Tom began to eat.

The only noise was the buzz of the heating unit inside the closet. Tommy Senior drifted in and out of sleep. His old home would be his new home. He wanted to cry but didn't dare. All he could do was accept the fate assigned to him, accept the Sorrento curse of divorce like a spell. And somehow, he knew it all along. Even on their wedding day, as he said "I do." this moment became inevitable.

"By the power vested in me, I decree that Nancy Sorrento has full custody of the said child Tommy Sorrento Junior. Tommy Sorrento Senior will be given visitation rights on Wednesdays from 7pm to 9pm and every other weekend. Adjourned."

The two former soul mates walked in a silent procession down the new altar. Out the door and alone again. Tommy Junior was not a child. He became Wednesday and every other weekend, 3rd day of the week and 1st and 3rd of the month, like rent that was past due, like a bead on the abacus clacking in the courtroom. Countable and numbered, added, divided, reduced, and forgotten.

IV

The alarm clock buzzed and buzzed. Nancy stirred groggily from her slumber. She walked across the tiny room she and her son shared and gently roused him from his sleep.

"Wake up sweetie. Today's the first day of kindergarten."

He stretched and yawned. Nancy turned on the light and opened the closet.

"You can wear that light blue shirt we bought the other day." She looked over at the clock. "Okay it's 6:30. The bus comes in an hour. Do you want cereal or waffles for breakfast?"

"Um...waffles!"

"Okay, let's get dressed and then I'll make you waffles."

"Okay mommy."

She dressed him in a light blue button-down shirt and blue shorts with a red bow tie. As she prepared him for school the nagging loneliness that threatened her every day resurfaced again. But she fought it the best she could.

"Mommy, can I give daddy a call when I get home?"

"Of course, sweetie. You can call him later and tell him all about your day."

She fixed his waffles and straightened his bow tie. At 7:28, The unmistakable hiss of the school bus pulled up to the house.

Nancy, Bridgette and Paulo, her father, waved goodbye to Tommy. He wasn't nervous or scared. He didn't cry. He simply was ready for school. His family waved goodbye as his tiny frame disappeared into the bus.

"Okay class, everyone is going to have a seat by alphabetical order.

The circle of children stared up at Ms. English. She was an elderly woman, well into her 60's.

"Does anyone know what alphabetical order means?" A little blonde boy raised his hand.

"It means by letters."

"Very good." Ms. English gave him a gold star.

"What is your name sweetie.

"Jonathan," he said.

"Okay Jonathan do you know the first letter?"

He thought for a moment.

"A."

"Very good" she gave him another star.

"Now we are going to sit in our seats and learn the alphabet at the same time."

Ms. English began calling out various names one by one and the children sat accordingly. Tommy waited until she got to the T- he knew what letter his name started with.

"Okay, now that everyone has their seat and a list of the alphabet, we are going to learn another very important thing."

The children gazed up at her.

"We are going to learn our numbers. And for the rest of the year, we are going to study our numbers and letters until we get them right. So now on the back of your alphabet card. I want you to copy what I put on the board."

She began to write 1, 2, 3, 4... and so on. Some of the children already knew some of the numbers but they all copied them down.

Tommy dutifully copied the symbols on his paper even though he knew most of them.

"Now we are going to stop at 10 today. But there are many more numbers."

"Ms. English," A girl with brown hair and fair skin raised her hand.

"Yes Marissa."

"What is the last number?"

Ms. English gave Marissa a bemused smile.

"Well sweetie, the numbers never end."

"But the letters do. They end with Z." her little finger pointed to the Z on her alphabet chart.

"The numbers are different, they go on forever and ever, they go on to what's called infinity."

The children gave her a puzzled look. Their little brains could not comprehend the giant of infinity. None of them dared to-except one, unwillingly. Tommy Sorrento sat at a lone desk, a circumstance of configuration. He sat apart from the rest of the desks by no doing of his own, the harsh alphabetical order of the world isolated him and in his solitude amongst his peers. The word-the essence of those numbers, of infinity took hold of him like a strangler. Desperately he tried to understand it, he wanted so badly to know, like gasping at the strangler's hands, he probed his limited intellect for an understanding, but none came. The only thought was of the abacus, of counting to that magical infinity. But it was arts and crafts time. Infinity would have to wait. He took out his crayons.

V

"Tom!" Nancy walked toward him. She picked him up and kissed him on the cheek.

"How was school!" she kept kissing his ruddy cheeks.

"I had fun," they began to walk into the house.

"Tell me what you did." Nancy started to make him a soft pretzel as he spoke.

"We learned about the letters and the numbers."

"Is your teacher nice?"

"Yeah. Her name is Ms. English. She is really nice, I like her."

His mother took the pretzel out of the toaster oven. "Tell me about the numbers and letters."

"We learned the alphabet and how to count to 10. Ms. English also said that the numbers never end."

"That's right sweetie, they never end, they go on to...."

"Infinity!" he finished her sentence.

"That's right again!" She kissed his cheek. "You're so smart."

She poured him some juice. "I was thinking we will go to the mall later. I'll buy you a toy for your first day of school."

Tom had a smirk on his face. "Mommy how many days of school are there?"

"Um," She thought for a moment. "I think 180, why?"

Because then I'm gonna have a hundred and eighty toys at the end of the year!"

"Don't push it." She kissed him on the cheek.

"Five minutes and then we'll go!" she yelled over the hum of the blow dryer.

"Okay mommy." Little Tom played with his abacus while he waited. Silently he counted each bead as a person.

"Mommy...daddy...me...one...two...three...we can all be numbers," he said to himself. As he repeated the simple chant to himself, he unknowingly made his now non-existent family into an equation.

"Tom let's go." his mother called.

He put the abacus down and walked over to his mother. But unknowingly to them, to anyone in the universe, one bastard bead inaudibly clacked and remained apart from the rest.

"Do you want to take your abacus?" his mother asked.

Tommy pondered it for a minute. "No, I'll leave it here."

"Okay sweetie let's go." He took hold of his mother's hand.

Tommy Senior sat in his empty apartment alone. The January sun had set hours ago, leaving him in a desolate wasteland of ripped furniture and a stained carpet. But this was his palace now. One year ago, he would have been with his wife and son, with his family. But those days were gone. His memory could only harden into a fossil of the better life he once knew.

Part II

I

"Tom, get up!" His mother yelled into the room. He rubbed the sleep from his eyes slowly. The familiar world of his dresser and plaid bed sheets returned to his sight but something plagued him from his sleep. Something awful. A dream? No, something worse than that, something closer to reality.

"Tom, hurry up, get in the shower you're gonna be late." his mother crawled back into bed. Tom walked through the room. She fell back to sleep. George, his stepfather, snored heavily.

The cold water changed to warm and beat on his skin. He began to scrub himself but could not cleanse the awful terror of his nightmare. He remembered it piece by piece. A grey sky, the incessant rain pounding on the asphalt. Grimy dumpsters were perched like coffins in an alleyway.

And then there was him. Alone. Not simply by himself but the only person left in his own wretched hell. No Satan, no fire, or demons. Just him. Solitary and suffering eternally. The violent pounding on the bathroom door startled him.

"Get out of the shower! You've been in there over twenty minutes!"

He turned the water off and dried himself. When he opened the window, a chill of January air hit him. Like a creature of habit, he performed the same routine every morning since freshman year. Every single morning, he walked past his mother and stepfather, every single morning he stayed in the shower too long. And every single morning when he finished, he opened the bathroom window and gazed out into his neighborhood.

It was now junior year. The neighborhood rarely changed. But after two and half years of looking he noticed certain things. The house behind him had eight bushes and two trees in the backyard. The house next to them had two pieces of vinyl siding missing. For some reason, he noticed the trivial worthless things that no one cared about. They made up his life.

Yet, this morning was different. He performed his ritual out of habit but paid little attention. Instead, the dream pre-occupied his mind. As he waited outside for his ride, the day's business ran through his head. What test he had, what homework he had missed and so on. But still, the dream stank like fish in his memory.

II

"What did you get?" Mike looked down at his own test.

"Fucking 60." Tom stuffed the paper in his desk with disgust.

"I got a 77." said Mike with a slight grin.

"And lemme guess," Tom asked rhetorically "you didn't study."

"Course not man."

Tom shook his head. This was an all too familiar scenario. Mike passed with minimal effort. Then anger rose up in his chest. And of course, Mike didn't make it any easier.

"Sorry man, I know it's tough. Shoulda studied."

"Yeah man, I'm sure it's tough being you." Tom took out his notebook.

"Nah, it's easy," Mike opened his notebook too. The teacher methodically began to draw graphs on the chalkboard. The soft scrape on the board almost lulled Tom back to sleep.

"Now a lot of you had problems with quadratic equations. Guys, we went over this. I don't know how so many of you missed this. Well, let's start from the beginning," his tone was slightly annoyed.

He began to write an equation.

"Now, what are the roots of this equation?"

A boy in the front row raised his hand.

"Well, one of the roots is the square root nine of but the other is the square root of negative nine."

"Good Jay, what do we call the negative root?"

"Extraneous."

"Good. What is the problem with the square root of negative nine?"

James didn't answer. The teacher rolled his eyes in frustration at the class.

"It is called an imaginary root. We write it as 3i. Why do we write it as such?"

Another girl raised her hand.

"Because a negative number times a negative number is always positive. And a positive number times a negative number is a negative number but that's not the same number times itself."

"Good," The teacher said. "There is no negative number in the universe that can have a square root. We must write it as an imaginary number."

Tommy doodled in his notebook. But suddenly, something caught his ear. The words rolled around in his head. They repeated themselves.

No negative number in the universe can have a real square root. He hated math. He hated all this useless shit of x's and roots but for some reason that idea stuck to him.

No negative number in the universe could have a real square root. He tried to conceive of that 3i but couldn't. It languished in his head, unable to be held, like a jellyfish. But none of his stupid thoughts mattered. He still failed the test.

Mike scribbled something in his notebook. Tommy zoned out again.

"Excuse me, fellas in the back, pay attention please. Then I wonder why no one does well on tests." he turned around and began writing on the board.

"Not me man, I passed," Mike whispered obnoxiously.

Tommy sighed.

III

What a shitty day he thought to himself. First the damn dream and then the test. He put his math book in his locker. The halls thronged with people like a vein of blood. Girlfriends kissed their boyfriends, some students strolled, leisurely, into their classrooms; and others hurriedly sifted through the crowd. Freshman scurried to and fro, trying to avoid upperclassmen. But he stood apart from them. Right now, at his locker, he was a citizen of a different universe.

"Hey asshole." his friend's voice sounded above the crowded halls. And Tommy knew exactly what he was about to do. But his reflexes were too slow to stop him. He felt his wind pants slide down by his knees. The embarrassment made his stomach clench up. A group of senior girls snickered at the fool in his underwear. Tommy stood in his briefs, pants around his knees. And yet he should have been used to his. Friendly jokes between friends were only for them. They meant to make everyone else laugh. Tommy felt like his own almost bare ass. A butt of all their jokes. A failure standing in his underwear. Then his anger rose again. Just like this morning, it swelled.

He pulled his pants up. All the while Joe laughed incessantly.

"Fucking asshole," he said it almost inaudible.

The push sent Joe flying across the wall. He hit the lockers with a hard thud.

"Don't you ever pants me again." Tommy walked away.

"C'mon man it was just a joke!" Joe called back to him.

"Did you take out the garbage?" she asked with an annoyed pitch, already anticipating his answer.

"Not yet," he said dully.

"Why not dammit!"

"Because I want to do my homework first!"

His mother gazed at him. This was a familiar argument.

"You are lazy. And irresponsible. You have one job to do around this house and you can't even do that! What's the matter with you? I didn't raise you like this!

He tried to block her out, but she was relentless.

"Why didn't you do your homework earlier? It's almost ten o'clock!

Tommy didn't look up. He couldn't understand how he and his mother could love each other so much and then fight like this. But she was right. He should have started his homework earlier.

"That's right! Just sit there! I forgot you have it so bad here! You have such a bad life! One damn chore that's it! Lazy!"

Still, he sat motionless. Not daring to look up.

"Go to your father's, maybe it will be better there!" her comment echoed down the stairs. She loved to punctuate her arguments with that snide comment. Go to your father's. It never failed.

Finally, she left him alone. She left him to be the king of his basement. A faint musty smell rose to his nostrils, but it was heaven. He settled back to his homework. It might as well have been Greek. He read the directions to himself.

"Give the two roots of the quadratic equations listed below."

This shit was worthless. When the hell would he ever need to know the two roots of a quadratic equation? He struggled through the problem and came up with the square root of nine and negative nine.

Square root of negative nine.

No square root of a negative number could exist in the universe.

The thought took hold of him, raping his intellect like a prisoner in the shower.

3i. 3i time's 3i equals -9.

Imaginary numbers didn't exist, yet that was the answer. That would get him two points on the test. But none of his stupid ideas made a difference. But fuck the test! For some reason, they made all the difference. That imaginary number, that imposter 3i mocked him. How could it exist?

The garbage needed to be taken out. He failed, was the butt of jokes, and was alone but real, like that 3i.

His mother screamed at his stepfather. The insults echoed throughout the house as they fought, they made Tommy cringe. It returned like it always did. The coffee, the stench of garbage, counting on the abacus. A repeated divorce.

How the fuck did this relate to -9?

It didn't. But for some reason he couldn't let it go.

"I hate you!" he could hear her screaming upstairs-or was it 10 years ago?

Imaginary numbers can yield a real number, and real numbers have imaginary square roots. But how? For some reason he thought of himself as that 3i, something that exists but shouldn't, yielded by an imaginary family that didn't exist.

"You're fucking crazy Tommy." he thought to himself.

This is why he failed math. This is why he forgot to take out the garbage and this is why he was the butt of jokes. Because he thought about stupid shit like this.

"Fucking loser." he slammed the math book shut. There were no imaginary roots, only real trash that needed to be taken out.

But again, like all the other things he didn't want to think of, this new hideous truth lodged itself in him like a claw.

3i didn't exist but may well have been the only truth he could ever know.

IV

"Hey Dad."

"Tom, what's up?"

"Not much, haven't talked to you in a while."

"Yeah, I know."

"So, what's up?" Tom Senior asked again.

"Not much. Haha Dad, it's boring around here. Failed another math test."

"Shit Tom, how is your grade in that class?"

"Hanging by a thread, I think I got a 70 or something. I talked to the teacher, he said as long as I do my homework, I will pass."

"Okay, just keep on top at that."

"How's your mother?" he asked.

"Pain in the ass as usual."

"Haha, she breaking your balls?" asked his father like he had been there before.

"Always."

"When are you coming down again?"

"I was thinking about next week."

"Okay, just give me a call when you want to come down."

"Sounds good, love you Tom."

"Love you too Dad."

As soon as he hung up the phone, Nancy walked into the kitchen.

"Who was that?" she asked.

"Dad."

"Oh. When are you going down there?"

"Next week."

"Well," he could already hear the annoyed pitch in her voice. This happened whenever he talked about his father. "You can't go next week because we have to go down to Grandma's house. It's her birthday next week."

"Okay, so I'll go another day, her birthday isn't the whole week."

"But we're not sure what day we're having the party!"

"Whatever mom, it's not that big of a deal. I can do both."

"You better be at your grandmother's house." she stormed out of the room. "She comes before him." And she wasn't wrong. While he got along with his father, his father was not around and did not really take an active part in raising him. Tommy knew this in his heart and knew one day he would have to reckon with this fact.

Like an aging horse that begged to be shot, he needed to be put out of his misery. The obsolete bond of his parents lingered like a comatose patient. Alive but not living, simply surviving in Tommy's heart. The scene repeated itself throughout the years. They had been divorced over a decade but still, like a movie reel, it didn't end. Just repeated even after the projector broke.

Part III

I

Luke Moran doused the toilet in bleach. Almost robotically he began to scrub the inside of the white porcelain ring. A familiar odor rose to his nostrils. How many times had he done this before? The shit began to crust over in blue bleach as it washed to the bottom of the bowl. He scrubbed it until the white smiled back at him.

"How many more bathrooms do you have left?"

Mike looked up at his boss.

"Um, this one and the one at the end of the hall."

"Okay finish those and let's get out of here."

"Okay."

He cleaned and cleaned but no one cared. They just drew the graffiti and re-scuffed the floors.

One more bathroom. He methodically rolled his cleaning cart down the hall.

He checked his phone *"You have no messages."*

A warm half eaten hamburger drooped on a plate. He always found it ironic that from 3 in the afternoon to 12 midnight all he did was clean and yet, he always came home to a dirty apartment and talked to himself.

II

"You ready for this!" One of the seniors slapped Tommy's shoulder pads hard, rattling him out of his daydream.

"Of course," he answered mechanically. What else could he say?

"Let's go guys! We're playing Oldburgh! We gotta beat these assholes seventy to nothing! Remember what they did to us last year! Run the ball down their fucking throats!"

Everyone in the locker room began to scream and howl like rabid dogs. Tommy half-heartedly joined in the mindless clatter. Frank Chicano had asked him if he was ready.

Ready to sit on the bench? Ready to watch all his friends play? Ready to be worthless on the sideline? Sometimes he wanted to grab a pair of pom-poms from a cheerleader. Because that's basically what he was on game day. A cheerleader with shoulder pads and a jock strap.

Tommy wandered from the locker room to the weight room. He didn't like to speak to anyone on game day. In fact, he just wanted it to be over. The worst feeling in the world is being useless. Unneeded and unwanted. And that's exactly what he was. This team didn't need him.

Maybe as a practice dummy to beat on. He worked hard, loved football, and then when the season came, no matter what he did, he sat the bench and had to watch kids who didn't work at all, play every fucking down.

"Fuck these boys fellas! That fucking QB ain't shit! I'm gonna tear him a new asshole!" Mike Rosi screamed.

But Tommy quietly slipped away from them. Instead of going over his play book or talking with the guys he sat alone, listening to Pink Floyd on his headphones. The words filled him as nothing else could.

"You are all receding, like a distant ship smoke on the horizon."

How true was that! He wished everyone would disappear, dissolve into one big stain that he could scrub away. He knew he was being over dramatic; they always told him he was. His head was filled with stupid crazy ideas. His life was good. He had a good family, went to a good school, was in great health, but still the words coming through on the headphones rang true.

"I have become comfortably numb."

Numbed out to every joy. His joy was this, this horrible solitude that he loved simply because he was alone.

Seven o'clock. Time to re-join this predictable mundane world for pre-game warmups.

"When all these kids leave after the game we have to clean the locker room."

Mike listened to his boss. He did his job. No one ever complained about him. He was never late and always quiet. All his life he did what was expected.

The sixty football players marched in unison like a Nazi regimen. He watched them descend the hill to the field. He played football once. He was young. But things were the same back then. He was alone. He had no wife and no children to prove it. Instead, he was the old janitor who cleaned the shit out of the toilets.

III

"C'mon! Hit that son of a bitch!" A vein began to pop out of the coach's head. Tommy stared at it. It looked like a snake.

"I think he's gonna have a stroke." Joe whispered.

"I know." Agreed Tom. His worst enemies doubled as his best friends. Just this week that asshole pantsed him.

Like the voice of God, the loudspeaker boomed over the field.

"Sack by number fifty-six Michael Rosi. Turnover on downs!"

On the field, Mike began to prance around. He then began to dig an imaginary hole in the field. It was his favorite celebration. Tom cringed on the sideline.

"Winter!" the coach screamed "You're a tight end!"

As a soldier called to action, Joe buckled his chinstrap and ran into the game, leaving Tommy alone, stranded on those godforsaken sidelines. The only friend was the lyrics stuck in his head. Pink Floyd repeated itself:

"You are receding, like a distant ship smoke on the horizon." *'Please, recede, fade away.'* he thought to himself. Instead, it was a touchdown. Another victory for the team. But not his team, just a team. Another win that Tommy had no part in.

Small sweat stains appeared on Tommy's grey shirt. But other than that, he was clean. No dirt or blood, no scabs or bites, no bruises, or scrapes. Just clean, unused, white skin like hospital linen. Mike took off his shoulder pads, his face barely recognizable from the dirt.

"Two sacks baby! Seven for the season!"

A senior with the locker next to Mike, who was the starting defensive end, playfully jeered him. "You're not beatin' me! I'm gettin' the sack title this year!"

Tommy pretended not to hear. But how could he ignore them? Those two idiots competing, those same two idiots who never lifted in the off season, never ran a sprint, but nonetheless, here they were starting and contributing. Tommy wanted to ignore it, but Mike never shut up.

"Hey Joe," Mike called across the locker room "I saw that block you made on the touchdown, you freakin' killed that d-end!"

"I know, I earholed him! He never saw me coming!"

Tommy hurriedly packed his things. He wanted so desperately to get out of that locker room. He knew it was a matter of time before...

"Hey Tom!" Too late "Nice tackle out there!"

And like a rehearsed play, Joe spoke his lines accordingly.

"Yeah man, Great block out there! You were all over the field! You played awesome!"

Tom seethed. But there was nothing to say. He couldn't fight back, he couldn't say-well I lift more than all of you but what did any of his weightlifting records matter? What did any of his hard work matter? He didn't play.

"Fuck you guys." Tom forced a smile. He did not want to give them satisfaction.

"I can't wait till next year." Mike began again "when most of us will play." He nodded his head toward Tommy.

"Yeah, but some of the scrubs will sit the bench even as senior!" Joe said.

"Well, I guess I just have to hit the weight room harder next year." Tom tried not to get defensive, but he could hear the tone hardening in his voice.

"You did that all last year and haven't played a down yet! Who cares how strong you are! You're still a..."

Tommy waited for Mike to say it. To say that phrase.

"Bad athlete!" It was almost as if it was said in slow motion.

There was no way to smile anymore. That phrase was worse than any plague. It was their phrase for him.

"Fuck you assholes! I'm sorry I can't be gifted like you! I'm sorry but some of us actually have to put forth some effort!"

"Yeah but," Joe grinned "but you still don't play!"

"Fuck it." Tom grabbed his stuff and walked out. He could hear Mike even as he walked away.

"Seven sacks baby! I'm going for 10 this year!"

Nice friends, he thought. And like that bastard square root of negative 9, he didn't belong either. He was an imaginary root, an imaginary soul that somehow was real.

Luke Moran watched silently. Like a video on repeat, in that kid he saw a remnant of himself. The jeered one, the odd man out, the butt of jokes. A life lived in the solitude of three and five, a clown used for entertainment. A trickle of blood ran down his palm, but he took no notice, he gripped the shoddy wooden broom handle so tight the splinters cut him. But they would laugh at that. His blood would be their circus. Just like that poor kid

IV

"Did you bring home the papers for me to sign? "His mother stood over him, like a guillotine.

"Where is it?" she asked.

"In my locker."

"Go get it."

"Now?" he asked. "The school probably isn't open. I'll get it tomorrow.

"You forgot it! I knew you would! I needed to sign that!"

"Mom, it's eleven o'clock. I'm dirty and tired. I'll get it tomorrow."

"I don't care! You needed to bring that home! I want it now so I can sign it! Go back and get it now!"

Tommy didn't object. He didn't argue. She was right. He should have brought it home. Dutifully, he went to his car and drove back to the school.

The school was the last place he wanted to be. He just spent over eleven fucking hours at this school, the last three of which were spent being useless on the bench. Now to add just a little salt to the wound, he had to go back.

The door was unlocked. It creaked open. Instantly the smell of sweat socks hit his nose. The athletic hallway was practically a second home. He entered the locker room. The lights were still on. Without the clatter of 60 football players the locker room was much different. Almost a mausoleum.

He rummaged through his locker and retrieved the papers. A noise behind him made him jump.

"Oh, sorry I startled you." Luke Moran picked up the broom he dropped.

"It's okay." Tommy said, barely noticing him. He turned back to his locker.

Luke Moran remembered him.

"I know it hurts."

"Huh?" Tommy whirled around "What are you talking about?"

"When they jeer you. When they insult you. I know it hurts." Luke Moran stood next to the urinal.

"What the fuck are you talking about?" Tom slammed the locker. "Get away from me!"

"Just listen. I know it hurts. I've been there."

"Listen freak, I think you need to go home!"

"Don't do to me what they do to you! Just listen! I know it hurts when they..."

Tommy stood taut like a steel beam. What was this man saying? How did he know his pain?

"Look pal, I don't know what you saw, but those kids are my friends..."

"Friends don't insult you like that!" Moran took a step toward him. They're not your friends! You are alone!"

The word was cancer. "Shut the fuck up!" Tommy pounded his locker. "Just shut the fuck up! They're my friends! I'm not alone!"

"It cannot go on like that," Moran knew he sounded insane. Truth be told, he probably was. But in Tommy, he saw himself. He saw his own pain of the last years being re-lived all over again, on the face of that kid. He wanted to warn him, tell him what he would become.

"Don't you see! You are me!"

And then the man said something that Tommy would never forget. Later, he would understand its meaning, but now, he just knew it was the truth, somehow even though it didn't make sense, Tommy knew it to be inevitable. He didn't know how the man knew, maybe he and this crusty old janitor were the same.

"It's not your fault!" he hesitated, paused, and closed his eyes. "The parents' sins will be visited on the children!" The janitor almost broke down crying. Tommy could smell the man's body odor, or maybe his own, the stench of his wretched self.

"Fuck off!" he shoved Moran out of the way and walked outside clutching the papers. When he got to his car, he leaned on the hood like it was a cliff; and he wished it was so he could jump. But how could he honestly be depressed? His life was good. Really good. So many people in this world had it so much worse than him. He was bad at being depressed. Even this he did wrong.

"I just wanted to warn him." Luke lit a cigarette and sat on a secluded doorstep at the side of the school.

"I didn't want him to be me..." The smoke rose to heaven.
"But..." he remembered his own lonely past "it's inevitable."

Tommy finished his junior year. Every day he awoke at 5:30 am to perform the same ritual. He attended his classes; he learned his history and physics and negative numbers. Senior year was more of the same crap. He played football and did well, but the scars of junior year were fresh. Friendly enemies constantly re-opened them. He never saw that Janitor again. And when he examined his life, he couldn't help but feel guilty for taking it for granted. But still, the losses piled up as malignant cells, the rejections became mountains. He could not win at anything.

Part IV

I

Four Years Later

College was supposed to be different. The best four years of your life. A time of breaking away from your parents, a time of independence.

"Hey Tara," he said awkwardly into the phone.

"Oh, hey Tom," she said.

"Are we still on for tonight? It's Tuesday."

"Oh," she trailed into the phone. "The Bachelor is on now."

Everybody told him he would meet his future wife in college. Everyone told him college would be so different from high school.

"I thought we were going to Subway tonight. It's two for one."

"Oh well, how 'bout we go after The Bachelor?"

"It will be closed."

"How 'bout tomorrow then. Tonight is the final episode."

"It's not a two-for-one deal tomorrow." There was an uneasy silence on the phone. Tommy decided to save some of his dignity.

"We'll just go another time," he said to end the conversation.

"Okay." He could hear others in the background. "I'll talk to you later." She hung up.

Real different. Another rejection. And him feeling sorry for himself and taking for granted everything he had.

"Whatever," he said to himself.

Sully, his housemate and best friend, walked into his room.

"Pizza?" he asked. "Oh wait, I thought you were going with Tara to Subway tonight?"

"Not anymore. Pizza sounds good."

"That girl is a fucking head case anyway. Man, you don't need that shit."

"I know." Tom said "But she was cool. I just wanted...ah whatever."

"I'll drive," said Sully.

"Okay, I'll be down in a few minutes."

Next to their table, a group of loud boisterous fraternity kids were throwing cheese and bread at each other.

"What the fuck are these assholes doing?" Tom shook his head.

"Those are the alpha omega kids." Sully took a bite of pizza.

The loudest one had a brand-new polo shirt on. His hair was spiked with blond frosted tips. A girl came out of the bathroom. She sat next to the loud one and kissed him on the cheek. Her red lips looked so inviting. Tommy didn't understand how a girl as pretty as that wound up with a guy like that.

"Look at that chick." Tommy said.

Sully turned around. "Yeah, she's pretty hot. She is in my biology class. I think her name is Stephanie." Sully gazed at her boyfriend for a moment. "Actually, I know him too, I think his name is Shawn."

"I dunno," Tom sighed. "I just thought when I went away to college that maybe things would be different but..." he paused for a moment "nothing changes, it's always the same shit. Stood-up dates and sitting on the bench."

"Man, you just gotta relax," Sully said. "Don't take everything so seriously."

"I know man, and I always feel bad cause I know people have it so much worse than me but still..." he looked away "I always feel like a failure. Even if I win, I know I will just lose again somehow."

"But I don't understand what you're losing at?" asked Sully "I mean you play college football, you..."

"No." Tommy's voice rose "I don't play. I sit the bench just like I did in fucking high school. I work my ass off in the weight room and for what?"

"Your time will come man. You're a junior..."

"Fuck that! There are freshmen that start! I'm stronger than everyone but what does it matter?"

"Re-lax," Sully enunciated the word.

"And look at this asshole. Of course, he gets that girl."

"Man, that girl is a slut. She will fuck anybody after a few beers," Sully said trying to reassure him. "Who gives a shit about those frat assholes..."

"Because" Tommy looked right at Sully, "it's assholes just like him who get the girl I want, or who start, or get a better grade than me..."

"Stop being a bitch," Sully said "Look, sometimes no matter how hard you try, you lose. It happens to everybody. Relax man, loosen up."

"Whatever," Tommy finished his pizza. Sully was probably right.

"Hey, did you ever go out with Tara last night?" Dan, one of Tommy's roommates, sat down on the couch.

"Nah. She blew me off. Gave me some excuse, whatever."

"Man, you got no luck with girls. How many girls freakin' reject you?" He asked obnoxiously.

Tommy cringed a bit. Dan looked smugly at him. His beer can

gleamed in the afternoon sun.

"I don't know dick. I don't keep track." The only good thing about Dan was that he paid the rent.

"You got no game man. That's the problem. You get in front of a girl, and you freeze up. You gotta have game man. I got my girlfriend cause I got game."

Tommy walked into his room. He really wanted to say, "Well you cheat on her with any slut who will open her legs." But he didn't say anything. He never did. Instead, he took all his pain with him and closed the door.

"Whatever," he said to himself. The noise soothed him like it always did. Metallica rang true.

"Life it seems will fade away, simply nothing more to give."

He started writing his paper which he would mostly get a C on.

Every morning, he awoke and forced himself out of bed. Like a rusty engine grinding with no oil, his rusty limbs straightened for the thousandth time. Like any dutiful but war-weary soldier, he rose to the battle every day. And the volley of fire never stopped. Insults, slights, and mortar shells rained down. He struggled against the fire bravely, but it was only a matter of time before one of the shells would pierce his heart.

He methodically checked the mailbox. The wood of the steps flaked in certain spots. There were flyers and advertisements; one of his roommates received a birthday card. Tommy hastily thumbed through the mail until he came to an official-looking envelope with his name on it. Rage welled inside him. In the spot for the return address, it had "Mary J. Bjork Law offices." He tore open the envelope in disgust and read the subpoena before going into the house.

"Dammit! I can't believe this shit!" Tom stormed into the house. Sully and Dan sat on the couch.

"What's the matter?" Sully asked.

Tom crumpled the subpoena into a tight ball and flung it across the living room. "Do you remember a couple of months ago I got into that little fender bender at home?"

Sully nodded. "Yeah."

"She's fucking suing me!"

"I thought the woman wasn't hurt?" asked Sully.

"She wasn't! And this happened like 9 months ago! This fucking bitch is suing me for a million! She's claiming back and neck injuries! I can't believe this shit!"

Tommy sat down. He could feel his skin reddening. This bitch was an ambulance chaser. Going after Tommy like a rabid dog. Trying to sue a 22-year-old college kid. Tommy wanted to hit her.

"Sucks to be you man." Dan said.

"Fuck off! Alright man! What is your fucking problem?!"

"I'm just kidding, relax. You are such a bitch! All you fucking do is fucking cry and bitch and whine. Fucking deal with it!" Dan said "Shit happens! Such a baby!"

Tommy didn't say anything. What he wanted to do was hit Dan square in the face. Right on the bridge of the nose. He tried to imagine the nose bone cracking like a dry twig. Instead, he walked into his room, like he always did. Sully followed him in.

"I'm sorry man. This sucks. She won't win. It's a frivolous lawsuit."

"I know," Tom turned on his stereo. "I know I'm probably over-reacting. But just to see 1,000,000 on paper, it was a shock." He put on Metallica on low volume. "I'm just so sick of this shit. Every fucking day is more bullshit. Nothing major. Just little fucking things that add up."

"Ya know," Sully said "we learned in psychology class about this. It's called the small hassles theory. Instead of major things causing depression and anxiety, it's the daily hassles that culminate. I dunno man, maybe something's wrong with you ya know? Maybe you have depression or anxiety."

"I don't know man. I just think sometimes those are excuses."

"People use them as excuses but they are real. Maybe you should get yourself checked out."

"I just feel like I lose at everything. Everything. Like there's no point in trying, in even existing because I will eventually lose. I'm just sick of being a fucking loser."

"No one keeps score, you just got to live." Sully said.

"I keep score." Tommy turned away.

"See that's your problem, you're not competing against other people. You compete against yourself. Against your own twisted visions. You've created something in your mind that is impossible to beat. These unreachable standards of perfection. You want to get ten sacks every game, a hundred on every test, you want every girl to like you, don't you understand, no one can do that."

"No, all I want is a little piece to call my own. I want to make the dean's list, I want to start one game and do well, I just want a small chunk of what everyone else has. I mean, is it too much to ask?"

"You gotta start realizing what you do have." Sully said. "You have a what? 2.8 gpa? That's pretty good. There are kids who bust their asses and never get over a 2.5. You play college football; do you know how many high school kids go to play in college? I think it's like 6 percent. And girls are a crapshoot. You can go years without one and then bam, just like that, you find your wife. Start realizing what you do have."

"Well, maybe I just want a little more."

"We all do," said Sully.

"I want to be noticed. I want to be recognized. I want people to say wow he really helps his team. I want to contribute to our wins; not be a fucking cheerleader on the sidelines just to say I wear a uniform. I don't want to settle. I want to be great."

"Well, sometimes, you have to settle. You have no choice."

"There's always a choice. Always a way to do more."

"I just wish you could see it from my point of view." Sully let out a long sigh. "Let's get dinner man, I'm hungry."

"Okay, I want to shower first."

"Okay, I'm gonna read," Sully said. "Just knock on my door."

"Sounds good."

But something had changed. Every failure, every game on the bench, every stood-up date, every divorce, every bullshit hassle made him sick. But maybe Sully was right. Maybe he had no choice but to settle with his pain.

No. He would have to do more.

II

A million dollars. That lying bitch. He remembered her from the accident. The skin hung off her fat arm like a white plastic bag. She was a vampire, preying off his mistake, trying to drain every bit of life from him. He was at fault, and he should pay some, but nothing like that. Tara's voice on the phone reminded him of a disinterested customer, blowing off an annoying salesclerk.

No matter what happened, he was destined to lose. Some cosmic force defeated him in everything. And he was a complainer, crying, whining like a child. But he did lose everything; he lost his family and his pride. He was losing his sanity, everything he ever had.

Just like the janitor said years ago. A chance encounter. But there were no chance encounters. The janitor was an omen, Tommy's own personal omen of failure. Replaying itself daily. Like the commentator on the sports channel. His entire existence was nothing more than a failure.

Or maybe he was a crybaby. The annoying kid who needs strike 4 because he whines so much. The one nobody wants on their team.

Those goddamn numbers! They stared at him like an anticipating audience, waiting for his next rant. Waiting to laugh at his misery. 1,000,000 dollars, 2.8 GPA, how many rejections? How many games on the bench? His family was a division problem, ripped apart like a piece of thin meat.

And he existed only in the coma of his parent's marriage.

Maybe that's why he failed at everything? Maybe it was time to end it, take out the feeding tube and let the sweet choke of death finally end his failures.

He looked at his two arms, ten fingers, he began counting, it always soothed him, and he made himself a human abacus.

One, two, three,

But he couldn't count himself. Somehow, he felt excluded from the numbers that built the universe, the odd man out, the 3i, the inevitable odd, made from a non-existent foundation.

All of this from that bitch Bascom. The only thing left to do was cry. He was the bead on the abacus, nothing ever changed, nothing ever got better.

Only it did, at least somewhat.

His insurance company settled, and his rates were not seriously impacted. He wound up playing, at least sometimes, but, like all the other failures, the bitter aftertaste remained, he always carried the residue of failure like a ghost even after it had been resolved.

III

One Year Later. Senior Year of College.

The phone vibrated and rattled on the desk, startling Tom out of some daydream. He flipped it over and checked the ID... *Dad*.

Tommy did not take the call. The vibration stopped and the room quieted down again. A passing car's headlights momentarily lit up the room. Tommy sat alone in the darkness, the only light emanating from his computer screen.

"Where is that goddamn textbook..." he muttered to himself as he rifled through a stack of books and papers, until he finally located the book he needed. He closed his laptop, climbed up his loft bed and turned on his small reading lamp and began to read a section.

The phone vibrated again. He checked the ID ... *Mom*.

He did not feel like talking but picked it up.

"Hey." he said.

"Hey Tom," his mother said.

"What's up?" he said unenthusiastically.

"Did you know a guy named Luke Moran?"

"No." Tom said.

"He was a janitor at your high school. I just read his obituary. He just died. I was curious if you knew him."

"No, I don't think so..." but Tom's voice trailed off. "Wait, actually, I think I do remember him."

"He died last week. Apparently, he was sick. The obituary said he worked at the school for over 20 years."

Tom thought for a moment, and in a rush, all the memories came back to him, he remembered Luke Moran.

"Tom, are you there? Can you hear me?" his mother said, slightly annoyed.

"Yeah, sorry. I do remember him. I met him once after a football game."

"It's sad. The obituary said that he had no wife or no kids. And he did not have much family."

"Yeah, that is really sad."

"Have you called your father recently?" His mother asked, changing the subject.

"Ah..." he hesitated. "I haven't really had time."

"Tom, call him. He said you haven't spoken to him in a month."

"I am busy." Tom said irritably.

"He is still your father."

"Yeah. I know. But finals are coming up..."

"Just call him."

"Okay." he lied.

"Are you still coming home next weekend?"

"Yes, I have a math final Tuesday and my philosophy final on Thursday. Then I am coming home."

"Okay, good. I have to go. I will talk to you later," his mother said. "Talk to you soon."

"Bye Mom."

It began to rain outside. Hard. He flipped open his Math textbook. He didn't really understand, but he dutifully took notes, he tried to remember this worthless crap so he could pass his final and hopefully at least pull a C+ in his Math course. He read a little more and closed the book. He could hear the girls downstairs in their apartment as he drifted off to sleep, they must have been having a party.

IV

There was always an excitement to coming home, but then it faded after a few hours. Tommy sat in his parent's basement. The old musty smell strong as ever, the same stupid pictures still on the same stupid wall. His mother had kept all of his trophies, which were not individual trophies but team accolades and participation medals. They all had dust on them.

"Tom! Dinner! We are having ziti." His mother yelled down the stairs. At least the cooking was good.

"What are you doing tonight?" his mother asked when they were all set at the table.

"Not sure." Tom scooped himself some baked ziti. "No one is home yet." But truthfully, he didn't want to see any of his friends.

"How did you do on your finals?"

"Eh. I got the C+ in Algebra. Got a B+ in Philosophy."

"Do you think you will make Dean's list?"

"Probably not." He said as ate his pasta.

"I ran into Joe Winter's mom at Walmart. She said he is the only starting freshman pitcher and he made Dean's list."

"Good for him."

"I am just saying it would be nice if you could make Dean's list at least once in your college career."

"It's not like I don't try. Math killed me this semester, last semester it was Bio. I just can't get some of these subjects. Joe was always so smart, he got straight A's in high school. That is just not me."

His mother, Ann, scooped herself a helping and dropped the subject.

His phone vibrated... *Dad.*

"Who is that?"

"Mike. He is home and wants to go out. I am going to see him after dinner."

"Okay, but be careful, it's raining."

"I will." He finished his ziti and left.

The town looked the same, except for little things. A new McDonalds had been built. The old Deli closed. He liked that Deli, it had great bacon, egg, and cheese sandwiches. There was no plan for tonight. He hadn't talked to Mike in months. He just needed to get out.

He drove by the high school and remembered that the funeral was tonight. That crazy fucking janitor. That crusty old fart who died alone. Luke Morton...no Luke Moran, who tried to tell Tom that he would end up the same way. Why did he even talk to him that night? Tom never forgot that night, how useless he felt, and then that whackjob talking to him. Tom drove past the school and then the church. Something compelled him to see that old janitor.

"This is so stupid he thought to himself." But he had to go, he needed to see him buried in the ground.

As he parked his car and approached the cemetery, it looked like the service had just ended. Literally, no one was there. The obituary had said he had no wife or kids, but Jesus, he had nobody. There was the priest, and two other people who didn't even look sad. Tom thought of the Beatles song *Eleanor Rigby*.

Tom waited a moment as they drifted away and then he approached the grave. A slight rain had picked up and the dimming grey sky seemed fitting.

"You old bastard." That was all Tom could mutter. What did he say again? Tom searched his memory. He thought it was some stupid biblical quote.... *"The parents' sins will be visited on the children."*

Fucking idiot. Who says that? But it did stay with Tom. Maybe the old fart was right in some ways. That week in school he had learned about imaginary numbers. Things that exist somehow but shouldn't. Rain began to pelt his eyes and face, and the ground turned muddy. But Tom did not want to leave, he couldn't leave. He surveyed the entire gravesite. A few flowers wilted on the new mud. There was a temporary headstone.

"Excuse me, did you know Luke?" An elderly woman came up behind Tom.

"I...ah...I was a student at the school he worked at." Tom blurted out, startled.

"It is nice you came to see him." The woman said. "My name is Pam," she extended her hand and Tom shook it.

"I knew Luke a long time ago. We actually went to high school together. After that, we dated some, but we never truly committed to each other."

"Oh," Tom said stupidly. He didn't know what to say or why she was telling him all this.

"I eventually left him and married. I have five children and ten grandchildren." She said proudly.

"Wow." Again, Tom realized he sounded dumb.

"I hadn't talked to Luke in years, and my husband doesn't know I am here. But when I saw he died...I don't know, I needed to be here."

"Same with me." Tom blurted out. "I only talked to him once or twice, but when I saw the obituary, I felt like I needed to see him too."

Pam and Tom stood silently at the grave for a few moments. The rain had turned into a downpour, but neither really seemed to notice.

"He was strange, even when he was happy, there was a sadness in his voice." Pam said more to herself than to Tom.

Obviously, Tom did not know him well enough to make any of those judgements. But he stared at the newly dug grave, little rivers carved new paths in the black dirt. Why did this man warn him? What did he warn him of?

"Well, it was nice talking to you." Pam gently placed her hand on Tom's shoulder. And Tom stood alone in the cemetery. Was this maybe a vision of his own funeral? A lonely man buried alone, a dead man with no connection to the earth except the dirt he rested in? Maybe. But as Tom considered this prospect, he did not fear it anymore. No, in some sense, it liberated him.

"Fuck you. I am no one's sin. I don't need anyone."

His phone vibrated.... *Dad.*

He rejected the call. Tom might be an imaginary number, something that does not exist, should not exist, but somehow exists anyway. If that is the case, then fuck it. He might as well carve a 3i into his chest for the world to see. The rain pounded his face, it made a mist so he could barely see the grave, but he knew what he had to do. He wondered how many other imaginary numbers were out there, like himself, imaginary things that someone had thought of once and then discarded. What a stupid universe! Tom could not get the image out of his head, of these lonely things in some desolate galaxy, pouring coffee or fucking or whatever. Things existing with no more purpose, created and abandoned, like cosmic garbage.

He stood here, at this moment, against the logic of the universe, against the plan, purposeless and alone, but

His existence became the triumph, unlike Luke Moran.

Tommy had finally won, because he learned.

Prelude
(to something different)

I

When the rusty teeth tore the muscle from the bone, I knew I could not die. I would endure the sickness forever. Blood caked in my mouth. The world I knew since childhood stood above me like a broken God. Every store window was smashed. Steel frames of cars smoldered in flames. Corpses were strewn like confetti among the debris.

My brain had done this. My mind clawed at the normal reality, which was in place for centuries. It had tried to return the earth to its state of chaos before God. The sane reality was uprooted. I had exposed its flimsiness. Earth tried to return to its state of chaos; it took cars and coffee mugs with it. Daily life was bled as it returned to nothingness.

I was the path. Chaos formed a beast out of reality and beckoned it to return, and I was its shepherd. This thing formed out of metal and glass. It formed from our blood. It formed in my thoughts. People killed one another and themselves to escape their new evil thoughts that flowed like blood. They wanted to escape the beast that infected them.

II

A man with a burnt face limped toward me. He took a piece of shattered glass and stabbed my forearm. He hated me because he knew I was the cause. That beast had tried to kill me, but I stood up to it. Reality had won. But this man stabbed me again. I had stopped his onslaught, but I had started the entire process. It was my brain that had altered the world. They wanted me dead because the universe was nothing but a vast emptiness, a chaos of endless time. Then God created the world and most importantly our rational human brains. Our brains held the normal reality like a pair of stranger's hands. Then the infected blood of one sick individual, me, tried to crawl backwards, back to that chaos of eons ago.

Another woman threw a piece of broken pavement at my face. My muscles were torn from the beast's teeth. As another man kicked my teeth out, I saw daily life in its pieces. New cars burnt, groceries on the pavement, dead books. shiny jewelry, I saw things that no one noticed.

III

Night approaches fast. Daily life is re-aligning itself. The fires have been put out and the stores are being rebuilt. People recover. And yet now, they look ominously at their cars. The cans of paint forgotten in the garage forebode something evil. That is why they have to kill me. My mind was responsible for this. Now their sane brains wrestled control. They had to manifest their normal daily life again. The rope around my neck was knotted. Soon they would kick out the stool from under me. The veins and neck bones would crack. They would collide and dangle in the wind.

IV

"You wanna go to the movies."
"I need to get my car washed."
"Let's get ice cream."
"I'm on empty; I need some gas."

I heard everything they said. All their inconsequential pieces of conversation passed through me like sunlight. If I had told them they could not kill me, it wouldn't have mattered. As they fastened the rope around my neck I kept still. I was lonely and unkillable; I was to endure the sickness forever. After the rope choked life from me, my soul left the body but remained on the restored earth. I had become the ghost of daily life. I was invisible. I floated from gas stations and highways to pubs and department stores in a constant drift.

"Let's get something to eat."
"My dentist's appointment is on Tuesday at 4 o'clock."

So many voices, so many useless requests. I hear everything. I cannot be killed. I am the ghost in the sunlight and garages, never noticed, living out eternity in a coffee mug.

I was never smart. Just an average man who no one took notice of during life. Until the day the thought of chaos spawned from my skull like a beast. Until the day my thoughts ran like blood. After that I was famous. I almost destroyed the people's reality, so they killed me.

However, God's thought in my skull, the thought of infinitesimal nothing, was too strong to be killed. I was the keeper of his chaos. The thought awakened in my dead skull and the blood rose up to kill the world. After the destruction, I roamed Earth's ruins. After the infectious thought destroyed everything the second time, I was left alone to wander.

Centuries passed and the dead planet rotated in a useless universe. All of the cars and newspapers meant nothing now! During my life I feared those things so much because I knew. I somehow knew that they were useless and unneeded. I felt the chaos of eons ago swirl in my blood; I felt its presence. Meaningless stars no longer wanted to burn. The world was dead; the sun was lonely. I had killed everything so long ago.

And finally, God's thought, the chaos from which he formed the universe came to claim what had replaced it. Stars burnt out and they disappeared into nothing. There were no more planets or galaxies. There was just a void like hundreds of trillions of years ago. A void in which God stood alone among his failed experiment of humanity. My ghost, his thought, finally was free, I became nothing.

A Higher Fate

Many scholars argue that ancient Iceland had a type of proto-democracy. While their democratic structures looked different than modern democracies, ancient Iceland had a governing body called the Althing, where citizens could bring their ideas and grievances and settle disputes. While not perfect, this democratic system lasted for centuries and provided a model of a society which did not rely solely on hierarchy and arbitrary birth status. In fact, today, Iceland is considered to have one of the oldest parliaments. Many times, our pasts hold the key to our future so we would be wise to examine our pasts, understand them and take what we need from them. But we also have to possess the courage to break free from our pasts, when necessary, even if this entails pain. Perhaps this is how progress is made.

Heklya gently placed another necklace with white pearls across her throat. Heklya was tall, beautiful and strong. She had flowing, blond hair and a maroon dress. Importantly, she had an image to convey, because as she learned, image is critical to leadership. Of course, Heklya was not the actual chieftain, her husband Ari was, but he had been rendered incapable by an arrow years ago. Heklya had been the defacto leader the clan for almost 10 years now. A number of battles had been won, peace had been secured, but there were always more threats, always more troublemakers and connivers. There had also been a number of midnight suitors. Heklya was human, and lonely, she desired love, companionship, of which her husband could no longer give her, but she knew once she took a lover, he would try to take the reins of the clan. She would not let that happen.

Her daughter Runa stepped in the room. Runa was fierce but gorgeous. She also had long blond hair, like her mother. Gunnhildar, Runa's sister, also walked in the room. Gunnhildar was tall, but had large shoulders, brown hair and piercing hazel eyes. Her long dress, the same color as her eyes. Heklya had to constantly be on guard. Her leadership was always questioned because she was a woman. But that made her even more fierce. The girls had reached the age where they could assume powerful positions, always in the shadows of course. Each girl was betrothed to a powerful clansman, but Heklya had taught them to use their womanly charms, and their strength and their cleverness to get what they wanted.

"Oh good, you're here. You are needed at the council meeting." Said the queen to her daughters. Heklya twirled her golden amulet, given to her by her husband years before. It was the last thing he had given her before the accident. She missed him, but she had a greater purpose without him, which she always felt was ironic. She had been thrust into this leadership role but embraced it. The amulet had ancient inscriptions on it, and they soothed her. They told of great ancient battles and victories, or chieftains and warriors. Their past was their guide.

"Go find your sister Vigdis and tell her to come to the royal council meeting now. You come too. Tell them to bring their men." Heklya ruled her family, like her kingdom, with an iron fist. Runa was not so sure leaving the chambers with only one guard was wise. While Heklya was strong, there were many who wanted to see her dead, many who did not think she should rule. Runa sprinted off and went anyway.

Runa ran through the main hall where most of the citizens were trading goods and wares. She felt sorry for these people. As she sprinted by, she saw an old haggardly looking man. There were cracks on his weather-beaten face. A slightly younger woman handed him some worn coins in exchange for a trinket. She could not help but feel sorry for this man, not born to any position of status, a poor man who had to peddle to survive. Who listens to this man and those like him? But Runa put the old man out of her mind and ran to the arena.

Runa saw Vigdis practicing fighting in the arena. "Vigdis, you need to get to the royal chamber for the council meeting..." Vigdis swung her sword and stopped it right at Runa's nose. Runa did not flinch, she expected that. Vigdis, her other sister, was shorter than her mother. She had dirty blond hair and wore a dark blue dress which dragged on the floor and matched the color of the ocean. Vigdis and Runa always sparred, and a great rivalry had emerged.

"Oh, it's you, what is it?" Vigdis spun the sword through her fingers as if it was a baton.

"Mother needs us for a council meeting. Bring Ebbi as well." Vigdis sighed. "Alright." They walked down the hall in silence. Vigdis found her fiancée Ebbi, and he came too.

The conference room arched in a circle shaped with strips of gold going horizontal. Runa and Vigdis found the queen, they also found the head of defense, their uncle Armann and brother of the queen, a scouting patrol captain, and commander of the army. Runa, Vigdis and Gunnhildar and their fiancées were there. Armann was angular and skinny but hard. He clashed with Heklya daily, but they managed to at least give the pretense of a civil relationship. But he was the girl's uncle and family, so they loved him.

"Hello everyone." The queen spoke coldly. "My scouting patrol captain has spotted something odd in the outer islands. He spotted a small garrison lurking by the Three Sister mountains, but the garrison cannot get to the palace, at least not yet. We need to secure defense." Queen Heklya said.

"If they have enough people they could devour half of our army, they are a strong tribe. Your majesty, we don't have that advanced security. Anything could happen. That tribe has defeated us in a few small battles pretty decisively." Stated Armann.

"I know they are strong, but we are smarter than any other clan in Iceland." The queen said coolly.

"We need to send out search parties in case they have split up. Their army is overwhelming. Also, how are we going to get all of our army to defend when we only have five waves?" One of the scouting patrol women asked.

"We will send our first wave first followed by the fourth wave." Said the queen. "I have consulted with my husband." This was, of course, a pretext; a lie to comfort everyone. They all knew that Heklya made the decisions.

"Your majesty, if you don't mind me asking, why are we going to put the first wave in and extend all the way to the fourth wave?' We can destroy them faster if we let them destroy a wave and then an ambush." Armann asked, feigning respect.

"My husband wishes it." That was all she said. However, she had a plan. Armann scowled at her but accepted her decision.

"That's handled then." The queen slowly turned her head to the head of defense. "Make sure you send the first wave on duty then. I excuse you all to exit."

Everyone went out the circle door and left their own separate directions. Queen Heklya opened the heavy doors and went to her chambers and said to her three daughters: "Stay here. I'm going to help organize the waves with your uncle." She looked at all three of them and then exited to the downstairs chambers which left the three sisters alone.

"I am going to go back to the arena." said Vigdis. Gunnhildar left unexpectedly.

"Where are you going?" said Runa.

"I am going to go to my chambers to sleep a little."

"But mother didn't want us to go down there..."

"It's fine I'm just going to take a nap." Runa went to her own room which was a big crescent shape with white walls. She laid on her bed reading *Ancient Tales of Iceland*. She read about the *things*, the local councils. Her mother was the chieftain of a local council, well technically her father was but he had not spoken in over 10 years. All the councils did was fight. Runa read about the victories of her clan, and all the other clans but couldn't help but think how stupid it all was. Why fight? Perhaps they could join the clans and create some type of unified council where the chieftains would have some power but would listen to the people. She had read about certain times when the clans had united. She thought of that man in the market. Maybe this council could listen to a person like that. Someone should listen to him...

All of a sudden, she heard the loud screams of a woman. Runa shot up, sprinting toward the sound of the scream. The yell stopped flat. The yell came from her mother's chamber. When Runa arrived, she saw her uncle Armann, she saw the queen, her mother, on the ground with a dagger thrust into her heart. She was not yet dead. Armann clawed away from Vigdis who had arrived and shot him with an arrow. He came to rest in the corner of the room. He breathed heavily, blood dripping from his mouth. He coughed more blood before he spoke.

"No bitch should ever rule this clan," he coughed. "I should be the rightful...ruler...a man..." his breath became labored.

"Fool!" Vigdis shouted. "Our mother was more of a man than you ever were!"

Armann tried to speak but could only cough. He almost passed out but managed to maliciously choke out "You will...never rule...you..."

Vigdis shot him through the eye with an arrow.

Runa was pale. On her left, her sister Vigdis clutched her bow in her hand. She showed no signs of remorse. Vigdis ran toward the queen and dropped down. Runa did the same, she couldn't believe it, neither could Vigdis. The queen lay dead. Gunnhildar came down the stairs and then all three of them were by their mothers' side. Their mother, the queen, the ruler, was dead. They mourned and grieved, but the bigger question now was who would be queen now.

"What happened?" asked Runa frantically.

"Uncle Armann, he killed her with this dagger," she held it up to the light, "because he wanted the throne for himself." She grabbed the dagger from the queen and held it high and examined it.

Runa stood, dumbfounded. Again, another senseless act. Killing your own family so you could rule? Runa could not process that. She did not want to rule, there was too much responsibility, it was too lonely. She saw what it had done to her mother. And it had finally killed her.

Gunnhildar walked over to her dead uncle, ripped the arrow from this eye and mechanically wiped the blood from the arrowhead. It sent a chill down Runa's spine.

Four Weeks Later, After the Funeral

"...this-this is terrible, who will take the throne? The kingdom is in disarray, we need a leader, we need order..." The chatter had become undeniable, there needed to be a leader. The three girls and their fiancées tried to come to some sort of resolution, but this fell through.

All the sisters stared at each other. "Who will rule?" They asked. Gunnhildar had a smug face. "I declare a duel for the throne."

"You can't fight us both. It's against the rules," said Runa as she watched helplessly as her family splintered over this stupid throne. But her family splintered further. Gunnhildar and Aron, her fiancée, whom she eventually married, mobilized their supporters and declared war on her sisters. They set up a camp and tried to win soldiers with liquor and favors and land. They built a formidable army. Vigdis and Ebbi did the same over the course of the next few months.

"We could just leave. We don't need this, we do not need to rule." Bjarki, Runa's husband confided in her. That is what Runa wanted, actually. To leave, to live peacefully in the fields, away from this nonsense. They could raise a family there. But in her heart, she knew this could not happen. She knew that if Gunnhildar or Vigdis assumed power, they would run the clan through their husbands for their own purposes; they would be immoral and selfish leaders. Runa did not want to lead, but she did not see a choice.

Battle after battle, so many dead on all sides. Sister versus sister. Lands and homes destroyed. This war reached every part of the western coast on the island. The sisters tried to kill each other every time they crossed but were always protected by their army.

One day in Runa's stronghold, Runa sat on her gilded throne reading *Ancient Tales of Iceland* like she always had. An advanced messenger came and waited by the massive doors. One of the guards let him in. The messenger had an extremely important letter for Runa and Bjarki. The messenger came into Runa's chamber.

"Your majesties, a message." said the man.

"Who sent it?" Runa demanded.

"Y-your sister- Gunnhildar."

"Gunnhildar, what does she want to know?" Runa mumbled.

"Give me the letter." She demanded.

The man stumbled to give it to her. Runa read the letter aloud.

I know it's been a while since we've seen each other. A little family reunion would help. Come to the original palace so we can sort things out; meet at dusk. No more killing. Just because we are at war doesn't mean I don't love you. I have sent the same message to Vigdis.

Runa loved her sisters but did not think they loved her. And she agreed with Gunnhildar, no more killing. She still did not trust her, but she felt she needed to at least meet with her.

Bjarki shook his head. "I don't believe it."

"I don't either." Runa said.

"Do you think we could ever unite the clans into some type of governing body?" Runa asked, seemingly out of nowhere.

"What?" her husband said. "How? All they do is fight, and now our clan is fighting amongst itself, no I don't think..."

"Our people have been here for generations, and all they have done is fight amongst themselves and with the other clans." Runa said despondently.

"Exactly," Bjarki said. "I don't think that will change, at least not for a long time."

"Maybe it could." She fingered her bracelet. "We could try; we have to try."

"What do you want to do?" he asked.

"You have the power to send an emissary to the chieftains." She squinted her eyes at him. "I have been reading about the history of the clans, and at times they would come together to solve disputes. We could try this, but make it permanent, there is a precedent for it."

"Draw up the plans and I will send the emissary." Bjarki took his wife's hand. "And then send a message to your sisters to meet."

Greiper, her cousin, was now head of defense after their uncle died. The emissary sprinted off to deliver the messages to her sisters. Runa went to her balcony. She gazed at the village for a few seconds. The village had dozens of houses, long grassy fields and three large windmills. The sun began to set and reflected off the ocean.

"It is time this war is finished." She said to Bjarki.

A Few Days Later.

Vigdis, Gunnhildar and Runa were gathered at the courtyard. It has been a year since they have been together. Their men sat inside.

"Been a while," said Vigdis.

"It sure has," said Runa.

"Alright let's get on with it. What are we going to do?" Gunnhildar spoke.

"I think the Sturlungur Clan needs a unified kingdom with a good queen, such as myself. I can survive a fight, and I can lead armies quite well," stated Gunnhildar.

"I can serve the people right and can also survive a battle," argued Vigdis. They both stared at Runa.

"And what's your reason?" Runa was in deep thoughts. She didn't respond. Suddenly she lifted her head up.

"If we can't decide then maybe-maybe the people who need a queen, a leader, a ruler should choose or at least have some say in the matter. There should be a place where the people can come and air their grievances," Runa declared. Vigdis and Gunnhildar stood there looking amazed and puzzled at the same time. "If we let the people decide the queen, we can't do anything about it." they said. "No, Gunnhildar said, "that won't work."

"We can form a democracy," Runa said. "We can unify the clans. It is where the people choose their leader or at least speak to their leader and help to govern themselves. It has worked in the past, in our history, at least temporarily..."

"You are too sentimental. And we knew you would be." Vigdis said as she brandished a knife. She walked over to Runa and held the knife to her throat while Gunnhildar pinned her arms back.

"We made a temporary truce. We killed our mother and uncle, and now we joined so we could kill you." Vigdis pushed the knife harder into Runa's throat. Runa wanted to grieve for her mother, but right now there was no time. Runa did not flinch; she did not show fear. Her face was cold. "How much of this family has to be torn apart for this throne? You both would make terrible leaders anyway."

"Good thing you will not be around to see it." Vigdis said.

"You may want to wait to kill me." Runa suddenly smiled.

Gunnhildar and Vigdis looked out the window.

"The rest of the clans believe that we should unite. They have heeded my call and taken my offer. We will unite and create a giant council, where all can be heard. You will not be some unchecked warlord; your actions will be limited by the people- if you stay."

"Never!" Vigdis scowled and was about to stab her sister in the throat when the door flung open, and Jon, a former rival, and now allied chieftain, speared Vigdis through the heart. Her lifeless and bloody fell limply onto Runa. Gunnhildar, stunned, tried to flee, but another chieftain slit her throat. She fell to the floor, flopped like a fish, and died.

Runa stood over her sister's bodies, covered in their blood. A new order was born, an order where all could be heard. She grieved for her family, for her mother and sisters and uncle, she grieved for the ones she loved and the ones that tried to kill her. But as she came to realize, all new orders, all progress, were born from blood. Everyone bowed to a fate higher than them. The clan had a unified kingdom.

It was not easy, but after a year, a united council finally met. Of course, women were excluded, but this was to be expected. And women had different levers of power and could work through their husbands. Perhaps in time, even this would change, but Runa knew that change would not happen any time soon.

Citizens were called to participate in the new council. While straight equality did not exist, Runa believed she had done the right thing. Her whole life she had read about the warring clans, but now, they had moved away from that and created something better. The yearly council met and all male citizens were invited. The chieftains welcomed the citizens. An old man stepped into the circle. Runa thought she recognized him. The man spoke.

"I come to the chieftains with a request. I am only a poor peddler. I understand the necessity for taxes on wares, but the taxes are killing me and the other small peddlers. Please consider lowering these taxes. Thank you."

The council deliberated. After some time, another chieftain, Baldur spoke: "We agree. The taxes are unsustainable. We will reduce the taxes on peddlers, however, this may mean that we will have less revenue and will have to assess next year."

"Thank you for listening," the old man said. Runa recognized him as the old peddler from the market. She had seen him the day her mother was murdered. The old man did not recognize Runa. The chieftains heard more citizens. They agreed with some and denied other requests. Progress had been made, slowly, and only after much sacrifice. Runa stepped away from the council and sat on a large rock. She looked at the fields and grass blowing in the wind at sunset. She put her hand on her belly and felt the baby kick.

The Fourth Way

I

An old, yellowing map lay on the floor. Matt picked it up, smoothed it out, and fastened it into a frame. He then hung up the frame on the wall adjacent to his desk. Matt took a long drag from a cigarette. He had told his doctor and his girlfriend he would stop smoking, but he lied; he hadn't quit.

"So, explain this to me, one more time. I still am not sure exactly what you are looking for." Matt held the cigarette between his fingers.

Corneria Johnson smirked. Patiently, and without any hint of annoyance in her voice, she began explaining to Matthew Riston what she desired.

"We need a map." She smiled again.

"Right, I got that." Matt smashed out the butt of the cigarette and quickly lit another one. The room had a grey smoky haze, but neither of them seemed to notice or care. "But I still don't understand exactly what this is a map of and how I would create it."

Corneria pushed a piece of soft black hair out of her eyes. "We can help with that."

Matt adjusted the frame on the wall one more time.

"We want you to map human dreams." She spoke softly.

He did not reply right away. Instead, he kept fiddling with the frame, but this was only a distraction.

"Dreams? Map dreams?"

"And thoughts, desires, hope and fear..." Corneria abruptly stopped. "I can see you still need more time to process this. That is okay. This is an odd request, I know."

"Sure as shit is." Matt scrunched his brow and took another drag. "Sorry, didn't mean to cuss." He said sheepishly.

"I will come back in a week. Hopefully then it will make more sense." She smiled and he noticed how white, not pale, but white her skin was and how it contrasted with her black hair.

Corneria gracefully exited Matt's basement. Matt was not sure how Bethany would react if she knew he had been alone with another woman. This is of course, was a business deal, but one look at Corneria and Bethany might get the wrong idea. Either way, Corneria, and her organization, were offering him a shit ton of money, which he and Bethany needed if they wanted to get married, buy a house and have a kid. He finished his cigarette, straightened out the frame and sat down on the old couch in his basement for a while to just think. He watched as the smoke from his cigarette silently rose to the open window.

II

Matt heard something fall from the balcony on the floor overhead. He didn't know what fell, but whatever it was, it gently brushed his arm on the way to the ground. The thud echoed throughout the mall and as he looked down, he saw a broken human form, like a crumpled swastika soaked in blood, blood which oozed over the dirty marble floors. Matt tried to scream but couldn't. He groped for his cell phone to call someone, but he couldn't find it. A teenage kid leisurely strolled up next to him.

"I guess he didn't like it here. Whatever, fuck him." The kid smirked, took a sip of some fruity drink and disappeared into a store.

Matt stood frozen and dumbfounded. The writhing body twitched some, but these seemed to be involuntary convulsions.

"What the fuck!" Matt shot up out of his bed.

"God dammit Matt!" Bethany shot up too. "What happened?"

Matt breathed heavily, trying to catch his breath. His labored breath filled the cold room. Bethany touched his arm.

"Matt! What happened?"

"A nightmare ...it was awful. Fucking awful. I need a cigarette."

"I thought you were going to stop smoking?" She asked, forgetting about the nightmare.

"Lay off."

"What happened?" she asked again, impatiently, ignoring the cigarette he just lit.

He took a drag. "I was standing there, in what seemed like a three- or four-story mall, like the Palisades mall or something, like the one I used to go to when I was a kid. I wasn't quite sure where I was, but then I felt something whoosh by me from the floor above. I looked down and it was a body. Someone committed suicide, threw himself over the goddamn balcony. There was blood all over the marble...and then I woke up. Fuck." He took another drag.

"Jesus that is screwed up. What a horrible nightmare. What the hell would make you dream that?" Bethany asked, half redundantly.

"Fucked if I know. Not sure why anyone would want to map that."

"What?"

He did not want to tell her about the opportunity, at least not yet, at least not until he was sure what the hell it was.

"Nothing, just thinking about work too, that is probably what caused it, at least in part. No way I am going back to sleep for a while. Hey, while we're both up?" He smiled.

"Are you serious?" But she smiled at him. "You probably did this on purpose to get laid."

"I would love to say I am that smart, but no, that nightmare was fucking awful. And now I am up and won't fall back to sleep."

Bethany shook her head. "First you gotta put out that cigarette and use some mouthwash."

"Done, give me a moment." He put on his slippers and went down the hall to the bathroom. He swished some mouth wash. For just a moment, he shut the light and stood in the darkness in front of the open bathroom window and let the cold into his lungs. He could not get that dream out of his head, and the question, why the hell would anyone want to map something like that and how the hell could it even be done?

III

"Do you have the maps yet?" Bill popped into Matt's office.

Matt, without looking up, answered his boss. "Almost," he clicked his keyboard, "I need a few minutes."

"Okay cool. No rush really, I just need it by Friday."

"Is that when the board meeting is?"

"Yeah, I want to show them the entire state. Can I see what you got so I can take all the credit?" Bill smiled.

"Prick." Matt smiled back as he pulled up the maps. "Here is the entire state of Pennsylvania." He then clicked on a different screen. "These are the major cities, Philadelphia, Pittsburgh, and then some smaller ones like Erie and even Hanover."

"Brilliant." Bill said as he checked the maps. "You made the data points nice and visible, transcribed all of the information..." his voice trailed off as he clicked on a few items. "This looks great."

"Thanks."

"Did you have a meeting today? Did you have to come in?"

"Yeah, I had a short meeting early this morning. A meeting which could have been done by zoom or better yet email. I am home the rest of the week though, so that is nice."

"Meetings without food..." Bill began.

"...Should be fucking emails." Matt responded.

"Here, let me put them up here." Matt clacked a key, and a number of maps projected onto the multiple monitors in his office.

"Nice." Bill began to survey all of the images. As Bill looked them over, Matt admired his own work. There was always something comforting about a map, whether it was on paper or digital. The digital maps, while they did not have that faded, antique look of old maps, provided so much information. In a single glance, a trained GIS analyst and cartographer like Matt could discern thousands of data points, the map spoke to him in ways that language could not. This was an easy map to make, for a stupid board meeting, but that didn't matter. Matt stood with his creation lost in the data. And now the digital maps were interactive, Bill kept clicking away on the touch screen. This map, and really any map, gave him a strange sense of intrigue, like something long lost or unknown had finally been revealed, or like some secret thought had been remembered.

"And there it is, finished." Matt said.

"Awesome, send to me."

"Just did." Matt began packing up.

"Go home. Take Bethany out tonight."

"Will do."

IV

"Did you go in today?" Bethany put the chicken in the oven and then washed her hands at the kitchen sink.

"Yeah, it was a stupid waste of time. But I saw Bill and he checked and approved my map. So, I am done with that."

"Is that the one you have been working on?"

"Yeah." Bill began to set the table.

"This month might be a little tight. I didn't get the hours I thought." Bethany frowned.

"It's okay, we are eating in every day, we will save money there at least."

"Honestly, I really do not want to go out again. There is no point going out to eat. It's all loaded with salt and fat and sugar, and it costs a fortune. We can make anything here." Bethany said.

"Except Pizza," Matt said.

"Okay, that is true. Plus, that doesn't really cost more than a meal. So, let's keep this up and not really go out, except for pizza on the weekends."

"Agreed." Matt shook his head. "We need to save up if we want a house..."

"And a baby." Bethany smiled.

"Okay, so," Matt set out utensils. "I did get an interesting job offer."

"Wait, you are going to leave the county office?"

"No, no, nothing like that. It would be a side gig."

"Okay, what is it?" Bethany checked the chicken.

"Ah…it's kind of hard to explain, that is why I haven't told you about it. I am not sure if I want to do it yet."

"What is it?" she asked impatiently.

"A company wants me to map dreams and imagination."

Bethany did not answer right away. She furrowed her brow and stared at Matt, waiting for more information.

"I am not quite sure what they are looking for. I am not even sure if it's possible to do what they are asking. They are some start up AI company but have something like millions from venture capitalists, they are fucking loaded. The company rep said they could work with me, show me how to at least get started. She also said…"

"She?" Bethany raised her eyebrows.

"Yes, and she was here the other day."

"Really? And you didn't say anything?"

"First of all, when I invited her here, I had no idea what she looked like. She might as well have been 60."

"Was she?" Bethany contorted her face.

"No, she is about our age. But stop, this isn't the point of the story. I am trying to talk to you about a job opportunity."

"When was she here?"

"The other day, when you were at work. It was a business proposal."

He could tell Bethany was annoyed.

"They offered me a million dollars."

Her eyes opened wide.

"The company rep said she wanted to visit again. I'll schedule her visit when you are here. It just worked out last time that you weren't. Again, it is business…"

"A million?" she asked.

"Yes."

"What do they want you to do?"

"That is just it, I don't know if I can do what they are asking." The oven beeped and Bethany retrieved a pot. "I think they want me to map dreams and really imagination. I think they want me to do this to make their AI engines more creative and more human."

Bethany looked at him disapprovingly. "Have you not seen like every sci-fi movie where the computers learn and take over humanity? The *Terminator* movies, *I Robot*, *The Matrix*…"

"Stop with the humanities fear-mongering. All you poets and writers and artists are always afraid of technology. That is not going to happen. Go back reading your poetry." He smiled at her.

She shook her head at him as she set the food on the table and poured some drinks.

"Okay, it probably won't be like the movies. But real life never is. The outcome will probably be much subtler and more insidious. You are trying to make machines human. *We* have imagination, not machines."

"Actually, I think it's natural, inevitable." He said as he took a bite of his chicken.

"What?" she asked. "How?"

"Humans imagined machines and then give them capacity for imagination, and then, machines can imagine something even better."

"You sound like you are arguing for a post-human conception."

Matt rolled his eyes. "Please don't give me your grad school philosophy jargon crap. What the hell is post-human?"

Bethany smiled. "All it means is that at some point in the future, humanity may not be totally human, post-human looks at what comes after human being. This will probably pertain to technological enhancements of the human being."

"Thank you, professor."

"At some point, human and machine may become enmeshed and we will not be able to tell the difference." She said ignoring his sarcasm. "And, perhaps more profoundly, a post-human perspective devalues the position and place of the human being in general."

Matt continued to eat. "Well, it's a million dollars. I don't think I will bring about the destruction of the world or a human being just yet."

"I would like to be here when she comes to see you next." Bethany refilled her water.

"I bet you would."

"Not for that reason. I was teasing. But I am really interested in this project. I want to know more."

"Okay. I will set it up with Corneria."

"Corneria? That is her name? Weird." she smiled at him. "Seriously, I can't wait."

They finished their dinner.

V

Grey. A tundra of grey above. The lonely grey sky seemed part of Matt's heart as he stared at it, transfixed. In the distance, he saw a dumpster. Black plastic bags peeked over the edge like eyes. Was he the last person on earth? God, how cliché is that? Aren't there movies about that idea? But no matter the familiarity of this concept, it was a stark thought. Matt walked in this grey world, over rain-soaked streets, next to the dumpsters and graffitied walls. The alleyway did not end; it did not lead to a wider street and there were no people in sight.

The last person on earth. Where was everyone? Dead? Nuclear war? Did everyone just get lonely and die? Did they blast off into space and live somewhere else? Matt couldn't help but feel an odd peace.

"What the fuck!" he whispered to himself. This time Bethany did not wake up. She turned slightly, and the covers came off of her legs. Matt could see the shape of her hips in the moonlight. He gave her butt a light pat and pulled the covers over her again.

The kitchen was cold. He rummaged through the fridge and found some cheese which he scarfed down. He opened the window just to get some air. This made the kitchen even colder. He sat down at the table with cheese and water and just stared at the moon, trying to process that dream.

It wasn't a nightmare, he thought to himself, nothing like the nightmare the other day. It wasn't a pleasant dream, but there was a certain peace to it. A grey sky did comfort him in some way, which he always thought strange. Why? Why did loneliness and an endless grey give him comfort?

He thought about the meeting with Corneria. They wanted him to map *this*, this endless grey sky, the loneliness and the suicides. Right now, the moon did not comfort him.

"Hey, another dream?" Bethany walked down the steps in the moonlight.

"Oh hey. Yeah. Nothing like last time though." Matt ate the last of the cheese. "Did I wake you up again."

"Actually no. I had to pee but realized you weren't there and came downstairs."

"Okay good. I am going to come back to bed."

"Me too." she said.

They walked up the stairs together.

VI

"Every time something is mapped, human ignorance dissipates, just a little. Every map is a tiny flicker of light in the cold dark universe." Corneria gently tapped her fingers on the glass table.

Matt wanted to roll his eyes. It sounded like something Bethany would say. But he had to admit that he felt like this too some days.

"We have seen your work; it is top notch. And let me say, I am glad that you are here as well." Corneria looked over at Bethany. Bethany nodded pleasantly.

"Right, but I still don't know how I am supposed to map a dream?" Matt looked at Corneria impatiently. He was getting tired of this run around. He wanted clear instructions.

"As you know," Corneria proceeded "We are an AI company. But we are not building some ChatGPT type thing to help undergraduates cheat on their college essays. We are trying to do something *bigger*." She gazed out the window when she said this. At first, Matt thought this might be for effect, but he could hear the genuine excitement in her voice. She really believed in this, or she was one hell of a faker. "We believe that AI is the next evolution of humankind and..."

"The post-human," Bethany blurted out, almost unconsciously. Matt shot her a glance for interrupting, but he could tell she was excited. Corneria did not seem offended at all. "Something like that, yes. A new evolution perhaps even the vaunted *ubermensch*."

Matt almost rolled his eyes. For all her techy nonsense, Corneria was also a humanities dork like Bethany. Bethany's eyes lit up.

"And I will just cut to the chase." Corneria said flatly. "AI engines will only be as good as the information they can draw and learn from. We want our AI engine to not only learn from existing human knowledge, but also imagination. We want it to learn from dreams and hopes and fears, from sexual pleasure and deepest pits of human despair, we want it to go beyond knowledge and encompass the whole human being. No one spoke for a few moments.

"You want to make it human." Bethany said.

"No, we want it to make humans better, but in a sense, we see AI as decentering humans."

Bethany looked at her skeptically and waited for an explanation.

"Part of your post-human conception is that human beings have long been considered the jewel of the universe. And that meant that we thought we were free to subjugate the universe for our will and pleasure. But we are only a part of the whole, a cog in this vast chain of being, and what we want is to re-center humanity for multispecies flourishing in this vast cosmos. Perhaps the vaunted *ubermensch* is humanity's realization that we are part of something greater."

Corneria sat down next to Matt, he could smell her perfume. "We want Matt," she gently pointed in his direction "...to literally create a map of human dreams and desires, of despair and hope, of pleasure and wonder. Our AI tools can help him with this, but we need him to curate and organize the final products and most importantly to begin and direct the entire process with these maps we can then feed these back to our AI engines. They will learn to imagine and hope, and then in turn, will allow us humans to create and think better thoughts."

"This sounds great and noble," Bethany said with a hint of sarcasm "But you keep saying 'we,' and I know you are offering us a million," Matt squirmed in his chair, "So really, after all your high and grandiose philosophical talk, this is about money. Someone wants to profit. Most people do not give a shit about these larger philosophical points." Matt had been with Bethany a few years and she was right. She reflected deeply on these types of larger philosophical questions and always tried to engage people in this meaningful talk; but most times people just blew her off as some bleeding heart or out-of-touch space cadet. But for all of that she never relented.

She continued, "I just read that the federal government slashed its funding, again for the National Institute of Humanities but boosted military spending by millions. In the same legislative session, they clawed back millions from Medicaid but gave permanently extended tax breaks for those making over $500,000. What a fucking joke. Our state pulled back funding for art and history classes while prioritizing STEM classes. They want students to be...what did the article say again," she thought to herself. "Oh yeah, 'workforce ready.' I mean that is important but it's not life. But no one cares about the deeper things you are talking about. It is all about power, money and profit and you and your company are no different."

Matt sat uncomfortably. Bethany was opinionated and fierce, he loved her for it, but it didn't always make for the easiest conversation. But he had to agree with her here.

Corneria grimaced. "I agree. Someone always wants to profit. But do you know who Horace Mann is?" Bethany was initially caught off guard by such a seemingly random question.

"Yes, he is considered the founder of the Common School Movement in the US."

"Very good. Do you know how he achieved this?" Corneria pressed.

Bethany fell silent.

"He basically had to sell it to the rich taxpayers of Massachusetts. He had to convince them it was in their best interest. Mann believed in his mission, he was a fervent disciple of public schooling, he believed he was spreading the Enlightenment, but he had to convince the people with money. And do you know where his financial backers are now?"

Bethany and Matt shook their heads.

"Dead, forgotten. But we are sitting here talking about Mann, and more importantly, I bet all three of us were educated in public schools." Both Bethany and Matt nodded in agreement.

"So, those rich and powerful men died with their money, just like all rich and powerful people do, but the dreams, the hopes of the true visionaries live on and change the world."

Matt found it hard not to be impressed.

"But why teach AI about despair and sadness?" Bethany asked.

"Is that not the human condition? Are we happy all of the time?"

"I suppose not. But what did you mean about sexual pleasure?" Bethany asked matter-of-factly.

"During sexual activity, our rational brains are largely overridden by a primal impulse, something that goes beyond any of our supposed logic. We want our AI engines to do the same. Sexual activity, and not just sex but all sexual acts, are one of the most powerful forces in the cosmos..."

Matt squirmed again. Two gorgeous women were talking very nonchalantly about sex right in front of him. But perhaps that was the point. This was a million-dollar business venture, one that could possibly change the world, and would most certainly change his and Bethany's financial situation, but he could not help staring at Corneria's soft and inviting breasts which peeked out of her tight-fitting blouse.

"This is evolution. Plain and simple. My financial backers want to build an AI engine so they can increase their revenue and buy another yacht, I grant you that. But in a sense, I am using them as a means to an end. I want to commence the next stage of human, and really, post-human and multi-species transformation. In the highest sense, I also see what we are doing as creating the *noosphere*."

"The what?" Matt squinted his eyes, slightly annoyed at all the philosophical jargon that Corneria and Bethany threw over his head.

Bethany lit up. "The *noosphere*. It's a higher level of consciousness; it's like a collective mind where the boundaries of individual consciousness are broken or at least permeable. This level of mind would join humanity together."

Matt thought a moment. "We have something like that with social media, don't we?"

"In a sense. But social media is divisive; it limits and blunts people's minds and keeps them ignorant, which is the opposite of what was intended. A true noosphere would be the linking of minds."

"Like a hive?" Matt said with concern.

"No, a hive mind would stamp out individual creativity. That is not what I want. We would be linked at a high level but still retain individual will and initiative. But just think how much richer your decisions would be if you could truly empathize and understand another's point of view, another's frame. Think how much progress could be made if minds could be linked."

"I don't want a chip in my head." Matt said flatly.

"I agree with that." Bethany said. "That is too far."

"Off the record I agree, but that is a direction that many want to go in." Corneria said.

"Like neuro-link?" Matt asked.

"Yes. But I believe AI can still live outside our body but nevertheless give us access to the noosphere. At the end of the day I want to be able to cut off communication with the outside world. I want to be able to turn off. I don't want people in my head while I sleep." Corneria arched her brow.

Matt had to quickly put the thought of Corneria sleeping out of his head.

"This can be evolutionary." Bethany said almost dreamily.

Corneria brought the discussion back down to earth. "So, to recap, we want you to create a map of human dreams and desires and sadness with the help of our AI engines. You will polish the map, make it useable, and then we will feed this map to the AI engines again. We will need to have an answer soon, but I can give you some more time..."

"I think you should do it." Bethany blurted out.

Matt spun around to look at her.

"Wait, you were the one against this whole thing?" he said incredulously.

"I know, and I am still uneasy. But, I don't know. She makes a lot of sense. This whole thing could be transformative, you could be right there, on the cutting edge of it. The money would definitely be nice, but I think it goes beyond that. You..." she paused for a moment, "you have the ability to direct human evolution."

Map gave her a quick frown. "C'mon, that's a bit much isn't it?"

"She is correct." Corneria said without emotion.

Matt sighed. "Okay, but I do not want to quit my job with the town or anything. I know this is a shit ton of money, but I need steady employment."

"Agreed." Corneria said. "You do not have to quit. You can work from home mostly. The first few sessions though I would like you to work from our office so we can help you get started."

All three of them sat there in silence for a moment before

Corneria broke it. "I will send you the contract. Then we will arrange some training sessions for you to familiarize yourself with our AI engines and our exact requirements. I will be in touch." She effortlessly walked over to Bethany and extended her hand. "It was a pleasure to meet you. It is always nice to talk to someone who understands."

Bethany reciprocated and shook her hand. "Likewise, I hope we see you again."

"You will." Corneria smiled and left.

"Wow, she is a force. I think I might be attracted to her." Bethany said jokingly after the door shut.

Matt looked at her. "I knew you were going to make a comment about her looks."

"You don't think she's hot? Be honest." Bethany said with wide eyes.

"Can we talk about this opportunity please? Can we be serious for a moment?" Matt said.

"Okay," Bethany said as she reached for a bag of chips in the pantry.

"I guess I am doing this. Since I work from home most days, I can probably swing it I may just have to work longer hours at night."

"In all seriousness, that women sold me. I thought this was just a money grab. And I think it still is, at least for her investors, but she seems genuine. That is why I think you should do it. "

"Yeah I agree."

"Who is she? The owner? The founder?" Bethany took another chip.

"I think so. I think she is an entrepreneur, but from what I gathered, she majored in English or philosophy or something in the humanities in college. I think she said that once. She may have also had some money from an inheritance or something. She started the company and some of their AI stuff sold really well, and now she has financial backing for this project. Shit goes way over my head. I am just an employee; I do what I am asked."

"Then go get the hot dogs on the grill!" Bethany fake yelled at him.

"Yes ma'am."

VII

"Get out! Get the fuck out!" Matt shooed the mouse away with his foot- the third mouse in what seemed like 30 seconds. He shooed the mouse out the door but slammed his foot into the door frame. The loud clang woke him and Bethany up.

"Goddamit! What the fuck was that? Did you have another nightmare?" Bethany asked as she pulled the covers over her body.

"Not really. It was just a weird stupid dream."

"What happened?"

"I was sitting in the living room and these mice just started appearing out of nowhere. I shooed two of them out the door. On the third mouse, when I shooed it, I kicked the doorframe in my dream, which actually was the edge of our night table."

"And you woke me up. AGAIN." she said and rolled her eyes.

"I am sorry."

Matt adjusted the covers and tried to go back to sleep.

"Are you gonna map that?" Bethany asked sarcastically.

"Yes actually." He reached over and spanked her butt.

"Ow! Dick." You are not getting any, she inched a little further away from him.

"I mean, I guess, yeah, I would map that. It wasn't a bad dream, just weird, sort of mundane."

"Isn't that life though?" Bethany rolled back over to face Matt.

"What do you mean?"

"Every day of our life isn't despair or misery, and it's also not pure bliss. Most days are just...days, mundane, humdrum, boring."

"Yeah, I guess you're right." Matt said. "I guess that is part of it, life is mostly mundane. I guess that needs to be mapped too."

"And think of how much of our life we spend sleeping."

"On that note..." Matt said. "I am going to try to go back to sleep." He rubbed Bethany's back and closed his eyes.

VIII

"Bethany, do you want a beer?" Candice asked.

"Yes, Nati Bo please." Candice handed her a bottle.

"This is nice, we haven't seen each other in a while."

"I know!" Candice said, a little drunk as she hugged Bethany.

"Sorry though, I didn't know he would be here. He is dating Rita. I didn't know, I just found out when they walked in together." Candice gestured over to Paul, a husky guy in the corner, Bethany's ex.

"It's okay. I have seen him a few times since. He is still kind of a dick, but I just expect that. I texted Matt."

"Where is Matt?" Candice asked.

"Working on his side job."

"Nice."
Paul came over to Candice and Bethany.
"Hey," he took a swig of beer.
"Hi Paul." Bethany said politely.
"How is Mark?" he asked.
"Matt, and he is good. Working."
"Yo Paul!" John, another husky guy called from across the room.
Paul spun around. "Bro what up?"
Bethany stared at these two guys, who she knew well. She dated Paul her last two years in college right before she met Matt, and John was his best friend. Matt and Paul were polar opposites.

John took out his phone. "You see this shit? This is awesome."

"Millions lose government sponsored health insurance. Millions to lose SNAP benefits as well," Paul read the headline.

"'Bout fucking time. I am sick of paying for these fucking freeloaders." He finished his beer.

Bethany stewed. This was actually part of the reason they broke up. They started to differ, greatly, on many political questions. But in many ways, she also thought Paul just never grew up. Like he stayed that same obnoxious idiot football player into his 30s. It got old. He was testing Bethany.

"Isn't that awesome?" He said in her direction. She looked at his chest and read his shirt "Bro's landscaping service." She chuckled to herself. He was still very attractive, but what an ass. She glanced over in John's direction and noticed a large, gaudy crucifix dangling from his neck.

"Do you think Jesus would approve of millions losing their healthcare and food? Didn't Jesus try to heal and feed people?" Bethany asked calmly.

John made a face. "Whatever, I just don't want to pay for lazy people." Paul saw another friend of his on the other side of the room. "Max, check this out," he called as he walked over, and John followed.

She and Candice sat alone again.

"What a douchebag," Candice blurted out when they were out of earshot.

"Seriously." Bethany agreed. She thought of Matt and smiled.

IX

And so, Matt began to build a repository of dreams. Over the course of days, he assembled a dream bank, constantly feeding ideas and prompts in their AI engines. It was a laborious, iterative process, but it began to bear fruit.

"This is coming along nicely." Corneria leaned over Matt and he could smell her. It was not a cheap or artificial scent, it was not soapy, it was almost ethereal, sexual but also strangely relaxing at the same time. He quickly took a sip of coffee and inhaled to distract himself.

"Yes, but this is still the prep work. But I think soon we will begin to get at it."

"From these repositories, you can begin to create your maps?"

"Yes, I think so." Matt said. "I actually started some preliminary maps." He clicked on the screen and his maps came up. Corneria began to examine them.

"This..." she gently touched the screen, "is incredible."

"Is it? I am not sure if this is what you want?"

"Yes, we just need to scale this up."

"There is currently something like seven billion people on this planet right now, and something like 117 billion have ever existed. That is a lot of dreams and desires, a lot of misery, and a lot of sex." He didn't really mean to mention sex, but he did. Corneria did not seem uncomfortable.

"Right, we obviously would only have a small fraction of this. But anything is a start. I envision your work laying a foundation for future generations." She stood next to him.

"This is...dream topography, isn't it?" Corneria asked in wonder.

"Ah, yes." Matt said with pride. "I started to chart a topography from the information returned from the AI engines. Also, online, there are some vivid descriptions of dreams. I started to look for some commonalities in dreams but also tried to capture individuality. I even began to add some details from my own dreams to make it more real and personable."

"A dream topography, charted like a real map, with data points and icons." Corneria kept staring at the screen. "You used your own dreams in this?"

"Is that okay?" he asked.

"Yes of course, you are one of those seven billion, and 117 billion." She smiled. "Perhaps I could tell you some of my dreams and you could use that."

"Ah, yes please." Matt said.

"One recurring dream I have..." she furrowed her brow and squinted her eyes "is that I am in a small town. It looks like it stood 50 years ago. There are small houses and rolling farmlands. Maybe somewhere in rural Pennsylvania. I am a little girl. The town is green and hot. There is an ice cream truck. I cannot see the truck but I hear the music. No matter where I run to, I cannot find the damn truck. And it's so hot." She smiled. "Then, then, I am playing with a ball, throwing a softball against an old rickety chain link fence and catching it with my worn-out mitt."

"Did you play softball?" Matt asked.

"Yes, all through high school and college. But the best times I had playing were when I was a kid."

"Tell me more about the dream." Matt said expectantly.

"Then I see some kids my age and we begin having a catch. It's hot, but there is a cold-water fountain. Before I know it, it's dusk, and I am walking home with my new friends. And then...then, it's just black and cold and I am in an alleyway. I'm an adult and I have never felt such fear, like someone is chasing me, but I cannot run. Then I woke up."

"So not really a nightmare..."

"No, just a weird uncomfortable dream, or at least the last part." Corneria said.

"Well, let me see if I can map that." Matt got to work, clacking and clicking. Corneria watched in amazement as the topography of her dream began to materialize.

"Amazing." she said. "Can you connect it to your dream?"

"Yes." Matt joined his dream to hers on the map. "What did you dream?" she asked. He explained his dreams, the alleyway, the suicide and the mice. Corneria snickered at the mice dream. He then joined their dreams with others and the map grew.

"I am going to have what I call 'dream country' here, and then link it to other sites, such as misery and sexual pleasure."

Matt and Corneria stared at the growing map.

"What does your name mean?" Matt blurted out. He did not mean to ask, but it came out and felt like a natural question.

"It has two meanings. It derives from cornea, which is how we see, and corner, which signifies the joining or two entities, so, sight and connection." My parents were a little weird. She smiled.

Matt nodded in agreement. "It's beautiful."

"Thank you," Corneria said.

X

"I want ice cream."

"It's 10 o'clock at night." Matt said with a frown.

"I know, and I want ice cream."

"What are you five? I have some more work to do, then I am probably going to fall asleep." Matt said with fake annoyance.

Bethany began to put her sneakers on. "I am an adult and that is why I can have ice cream at 10 pm."

"Really? You are going now? Do you need ice cream that bad?" He smiled.

"Yes. I got a craving."

"You're not pregnant are you?" Matt joked.

"Definitely not. Just got a sweet tooth." She grabbed her keys and went out the door.

Matt got on his computer and began clacking. Before he got to work he began checking various news sites, it became a distracting habit, but it did keep him in the know about politics and world events. He quickly scanned different stories from different sites.

Bethany came up behind him and he jumped.

"God dammit you scared the shit out of me!" He yelled.

"Yeah, looks like you are working hard." she said as she grabbed her wallet. "I forgot this."

"Did you see this? Matt pointed to the screen. This is fucking horrible."

"Yeah, I read about that at work. The electric company cut off her power when she couldn't pay. She tried to stay in her van overnight with her kids and run the heat, but it got too cold. It was a few weeks ago when the temperature hit 0 degrees. Two of her kids died." Bethany said sadly.

"That is just horrible, I mean, how does that happen in America?"

"It shouldn't happen anywhere, but especially here. Now I feel bad running out to get ice cream." she frowned.

"No, don't. Go get it, you deserve it." Bethany kissed him and left.

Matt stared at the story on the screen for a long time. He could not get that image out of his head. This woman, who lived in some hovel in some Detroit slum, never had a chance and neither did her kids. She froze to death, and all her dreams died in that van, as did the dreams of her kids. She was expendable, disposable, no one gave a shit about this poor black woman. Matt could not wrap his head around this. He thought of her kids, little frozen bodies, all because she could not pay for something as basic as heat. And the electric company, which he read had raised rates by over 55% just prior to this, didn't give shit about her or any of their customers, they just collected a check. And when you can't pay, too bad, fuck you. It was so inhumane, so horribly sickening and stupid, but also, so normal, it was what we all had come to expect. He remembered what Corneria had said, about misery and sadness, about the human condition. Was this it though? Did this woman and her little children have to die?

He set to map this, he had to. It was horrible but Corneria was right, this is life.

XI

"Why are you talking to me? We never really talked in life?" Matt looked at Steve Robin, a former teammate but not really a friend. Robin looked at him dispassionately.

"It's not really me, you know, that right? It's just a projection. For some reason you thought of me."

"But you died, you killed yourself." Matt said. He remembered when his old friend Todd called him and told him the news. Steve threw himself in front of a train on the Long Island Railroad. No real motive was given; life was just hard.

"I know, and you are not really talking to me, you're talking to a projection."

"But why?" Matt asked impatiently.

"I think you know why. Something is going to happen." Steve said. "And I am glad I am not here to see it."

"Fuck." Matt said as he woke up in his chair. "What a fucked-up dream. Bethany?" he called out. No answer. "Bethany." He called out; but still no answer.

He walked over to the empty bed. "What the hell time is it?" He said to himself as he crawled into bed. "Where the hell is she?"

At that moment his phone rang. It was Bethany. His worry dissipated. "Hey, I was starting to worry..."

A man's voice cut him off.

"Mr. Riston I am sorry, this is the General County Hospital. We have Bethany Myers phone and called her last contact. There was...an accident."

Matt dressed quickly and headed to the hospital.

XII

"I am sorry Mr. Riston, but your girlfriend needs a heart transplant."

"What?" Matt paced the hospital floor. "What happened?"

"A fiberglass girder from the car punctured her heart during the crash."

"Okay," Matt collected himself.

"The issue is ... this must be done ASAP, but we are going to have a problem getting a heart. There are insurance regulations..."

Matt's head perked up and he stared intently at the doctor, waiting for the explanation.

"Your girlfriend's insurance doesn't cover this procedure." The doctor said bluntly.

"How much if I pay for it?"

"That is hard to say. We will have to call the insurance company, the donors, the..."

"Just put the fucking heart in! Can't we do this after?" Matt screamed exasperated.

"We will do our best sir. But these are complicated situations."

"She is going to die! Do something!"

But at that moment Matt realized how powerless he was. Like the women who watched her children freeze to death.

"She just wanted some ice cream..." Matt's voice trailed off. He slunk back into his chair and cried but also wanted to laugh. Bethany was right. Life was mundane. Getting ice cream at 10 o'clock on a random Tuesday perhaps was the most mundane thing of all. And it killed her.

XIII
A Few Days Later

"You have been working almost at a non-stop pace." Corneria stood next to Matt while he sat in his chair.

"It keeps me occupied." He said bluntly.

"I know, but you need a break."

"I have nothing else to do." Matt clicked and clacked and brought another map to life. The dream country had grown; he felt like an explorer of sorts, mapping this new territory, but more than an explorer, he was bringing it to life.

He had not yet mapped Bethany's death.

"You can take a break, please, you do not need to be here." He had never really heard emotion in Corneria's voice.

"It's okay, I want to get this done. It gives me purpose."

Corneria stopped arguing and changed the subject.

"My backers want to upgrade the whole system...they want to create a neuro-link."

Matt sat silent.

"I told you before that I was strongly opposed to that. But I have to admit, it would be an incredible step."

Matt did not say anything for a while.

"I think we should do it." he said flatly after a few moments.

"It still makes me uncomfortable," Corneria said. "But I don't want to be a luddite."

"A what?" A hint of his former joviality crept back into this voice. Corneria smirked. "A Luddite is someone who resists progress, they were 19th century craftsman who broke the machines that..."

"Got it. I think I remember Bethany talking about that a long time ago."

There was an awkward silence.

"I will do it. I will get the neuro-link." Matt said coldly.

"No, we will hold an all call, we can recruit..."

"No. I want it. Give it to me or I will quit. I want it."

"I think you are speaking out of anger, out of hurt. You still have your whole life; you can find someone else..."

"So, I can be hurt again? Bethany died because of an insurance regulation. People die horrible deaths every day. Children freeze in their cars. They commit suicide because they feel lonely... Maybe all those dreams, all those nightmares are the real state of affairs, and the little bit of happiness we feel is the anomaly...like your dream about you as a kid playing softball." He stopped short and composed himself.

"You sound like a philosopher." Corneria tried to lighten the mood.

"Sorry," Matt said sheepishly. "Maybe if I get the link, I can do better, I can..."

"Really, it's okay." Corneria tried to soothe him.

"But I do want the neuro-link."

"Okay, I will see what I can do." Corneria said uneasily

XIV

The operation did not take long, and it did not hurt. There was just a little incision made in the back of the head. Matt scratched the small wound which had been perfectly sutured.

"What does it feel like?"

"Strange. I can work faster. I can create better maps. This is better for all of us, better for your vision."

Corneria could not deny that. The maps had become so much richer, so much more complex.

"But they are only maps." Matt said.

"What do you mean?" she asked quickly.

"A map is only a representation of something greater. I am only making a cipher, a representation, a simulacrum." Matt said with little emotion.

"I don't understand." Corneria said.

"The map is a guide. But perhaps, one day, we will be able to see the real thing."

"I still don't understand."

"You will." Matt got up from his chair. "But right now, no matter how much computer hardware I have in me, I still need to eat." He smiled.

"Do you want to go to lunch? My treat?" Corneria said.

"Thanks, but no. I thought I'd get a quick bite and take a walk."

"Okay, see you soon." She said with a hint of sadness in her voice.

"Bye." He said quickly, as he shut the door.

XV

She waited. The hot dust filled her throat, sweat began to glisten on her skin, but she didn't mind. She tossed the softball against the old chain link fence, despite the sign:

/"No tossing softballs against the fence." No one listened to that anyway. Corneria saw her friend and they began to play catch. She loved the smell of the leather mitt; she loved the dust and feel of the softball.

But then...then....

It changed. It became cold, frigid. She could tell it was January, a month she hated, a cold grey month, of black gravel and dirty slush, snow and cold without the warmth of Christmas, no softball...

She was an adult. She watched other adults scurry in the alleyways, moving toward uncertain ends. Her mitt was gone. It began to rain, a cold rain, when the temperature was just above freezing.

Some people started arguing. She didn't know why, but then more people started arguing, screaming in the rain. She didn't know the cause, but she could just feel that it made no sense, what they were arguing over was trivial and stupid. She longed for the softball field, for the hot summer day, but she had to sit here and watch these idiots fight. She hated this cold place. It could have been so much better...

She woke up. Her window was open, and rain had gotten in. She was drenched. She had opened the window a crack to get some fresh air and forgot to close it and now was soaked in cold winter rain.

"That explains the dream," Corneria said to herself. But no, there was still something missing, some piece she did not understand. Maybe Matt could map it.

XVI

Matt took a drag of this cigarette. Bethany was not here to yell at him. He inhaled a long drag and let the warm smoke fill his lungs. The warm smoke which rotted his lungs felt good. Fuck it he did not care.

The map he created glittered on the screen. The dream topography was all there, in its beauty. Dreams, sadness, it was all there, mapped and charted, but there was still so much to do and he could not do it from his screen. Bethany was gone and he hated everything about this world. But he built himself a new world.

Corneria walked in. "I am glad you still come here; you could do some of this from home."

Matt did not say anything. He just kept typing. "Bethany was a little jealous of you." He suddenly said.

"What?" It took Corneria off guard.

"She thought you were beautiful, smart and sexy."

Corneria stared at Matt. She blushed a little.

"I agreed. You are gorgeous. Stunning actually. And smart. A helluva lot smarter than me. You are like Bethany, a thinker."

"I, um, thank you." she said sincerely.

Matt clicked the keyboard and the screen beeped. "Perhaps in another life or another time we could have been together." Matt said. "But right now, I still have more work to do."

Corneria looked at him, a little confused.

"It's time I left. I built the infrastructure like you asked. You can continue to use it, but I have to do the work I need to do from the inside now."

"What are you talking about?"

"Remember I told you that the map is only a representation. And a paltry one at that. But this map I built is special. I mapped a world which did exist, but only in fragments, my map is more. With the help of your AI engines, we joined the fragments, and now, I want to live in that world."

"What?" Corneria asked with a fire in her voice.

"It's like you and Bethany talked about. It is the post-human. I am doing this for her."

"What the hell do you mean?"

"She did not want to make AI more human. She wanted us to become more human, and live in harmony with the planet, live simply.

We can't do that, at least not yet, not as a species. We are too narrow and stupid, but maybe in time we can. I will go first; I can join the ... what did you call it... the noosphere? I can bridge the human machine divide, but I can also incorporate the Earth and the cosmos. I built a world far beyond this small one we live in now; I built a world of dreams and pleasure and sadness. I want to open the gates to that world for everyone, I will go first. I don't want to live here without Bethany. Maybe I can see her again in this new world."

"No, you can't, what will you do?" Corneria asked desperately.

"I can't live here anymore."

Matt clicked a keyboard. "I am going for a walk." he said calmly.

Corneria looked at him waiting for further explanation.

"Ever read the book *Into the Wild*, where the kid just goes off the grid and lives in the wilderness? Ever read *Walden* by Thoreau?" Matt asked.

"Yes, both." Corneria said with a little sense of self-satisfaction.

"Well, that is what I am going to do. I am leaving and going to wander the earth."

"What?" Corneria asked dumbfounded.

"What did you and Bethany call it? Multispecies flourishing? That is it."

"I still do not understand."

"It's simple. I built a map of dreams and pain. I made a world visible that we try to forget about or don't consider real or important or really give a shit about, as Bethany noted we would rather fund the military than the arts, we shit on artists and philosophers and praise billionaires but this world of imagination and terror and nightmares is always there, just beyond the surface of our reason and logic and bank accounts and yachts." Matt suddenly remembered his odd dreams and loved them, he thought of Corneria's dreams of softball, and loved them too. "I am going to take this map, and the AI in my head and put them in conversation with nature. It is a multispecies flourishing."

"How? How will you put all this in conversation with each other?" Corneria was skeptical but also intrigued now.

"That is why I have the chip. I am going to overlay the map onto nature, but I need to communicate with nature, understand it better. I am sure your backers will see this as a waste of money but fuck them. I am a pilgrim of sorts, opening the post-human frontier. I think it is what Bethany would have wanted."

"I do too." Corneria agreed. "Once you put that map in conversation with nature..." she paused "It really could begin a larger movement toward multispecies flourishing- human, machine and nature, in conversation...the post-human."

"And perhaps, once we get far enough, all the money and power and profit will be nothing, a memory, a fossil. We can stick it all in a museum, next to the goddamn spinning wheel and calculator." Matt said Dreamily. "Fuck the insurance companies."

Corneria looked at him and soaked up his words. She began to play out the possibilities in her head. She muttered to herself. "At first there was only nature, and humans had to live in harmony with it. Then we grew proud and strong, too proud and became reckless humanists, then we developed machines and technology which allowed us to exploit it and each other further. Now it's all of these things together, it's the fourth way." She looked back at Matt.

"I want nature to dream through me; I want to feel her sadness. Let nature imagine, through us..." Matt said.

"You sound like Bethany." she said.

"I know," he smiled and lit a cigarette.

AUTHOR PROFILE:

Angelo Letizia is an associate professor of education and department chair of initial licensure programs at Notre Dame of Maryland University in Baltimore, Maryland. Letizia is a prolific writer. He has authored 14 books including nonfiction, fiction and poetry. In addition, he has also written dozens of research articles, essays and book chapters. Some of his most recent work includes the academic monograph: *Poetic Inquiry and arts-based research for the maintenance of the Republic and what comes after: A Vision for Meta-modernity* published by Routledge. '*The Starry Devil and Other Unwanted Poems*' was his debut book of poetry followed by '*Pilgrims of Infinity*'; '*We Are the Winding Down*'; and '*There Is Still Beauty Here*'. Angelo's poetry has also been published in a number of literary outlets. *Temporary Gods and Arbitrary Arrangements* was Angelo's debut full length novel in 2025.

The College of William and Mary School of Education recognized Letizia as an Alumni Leader in 2024. Letizia has also been featured in *Poets and Writers* and the *Chronicle of Higher Education*. His lives in the United States, in Maryland, with his wife and three children.

Angelo's academic credentials include a PhD. in Educational Policy Planning and Leadership from the *College of William and Mary;* an MA. in European History from *Old Dominion University;* and a BA. in Secondary Social Studies from the *State University of New York at Cortland*.

A Single Girl's Guide to... Must-See Movies

Sarah Melland

RMM
RIPE MELLAND MEDIA